# HUNTED IN CONARD COUNTY

## Rachel Lee

---

**HARLEQUIN**

**ROMANTIC SUSPENSE**

**ROMANTIC SUSPENSE**

Recycling programs
for this product may
not exist in your area.

ISBN-13: 978-1-335-62883-1

Hunted in Conard County

Copyright © 2021 by Susan Civil-Brown

All rights reserved. No part of this book may be used or reproduced in any manner whatsoever without written permission except in the case of brief quotations embodied in critical articles and reviews.

This is a work of fiction. Names, characters, places and incidents are either the product of the author's imagination or are used fictitiously. Any resemblance to actual persons, living or dead, businesses, companies, events or locales is entirely coincidental.

This edition published by arrangement with Harlequin Books S.A.

For questions and comments about the quality of this book, please contact us at CustomerService@Harlequin.com.

Harlequin Enterprises ULC
22 Adelaide St. West, 40th Floor
Toronto, Ontario M5H 4E3, Canada
www.Harlequin.com

**Printed in U.S.A.**

**Rachel Lee** was hooked on writing by the age of twelve and practiced her craft as she moved from place to place all over the United States. This *New York Times* bestselling author now resides in Florida and has the joy of writing full-time.

**Books by Rachel Lee**

**Harlequin Romantic Suspense**

*Conard County: The Next Generation*

*Guardian in Disguise*
*The Widow's Protector*
*Rancher's Deadly Risk*
*What She Saw*
*Rocky Mountain Lawman*
*Killer's Prey*
*Deadly Hunter*
*Snowstorm Confessions*
*Undercover Hunter*
*Playing with Fire*
*Conard County Witness*
*A Secret in Conard County*
*A Conard County Spy*
*Conard County Marine*
*Undercover in Conard County*
*Conard County Revenge*
*Conard County Watch*
*Stalked in Conard County*
*Hunted in Conard County*

Visit the Author Profile page at Harlequin.com for more titles.

To all who understand.

# *Prologue*

The house was dark and quiet, the silence punctuated only by the sound of the refrigerator ice maker dropping ice cubes with a clatter. Digital clocks on appliances cast an eerie green glow, but enough to see by.

He knew where her bedroom was. He'd waited patiently, walking along streets and alleys, waiting for the light in that room to go out. When it did, he waited another hour, keeping to the shadows, ducking from the occasional police patrol. Conard City, Wyoming, was soundly asleep, most of its activity now relegated to the truck stop at the western edge of town. Even the state highway stretched in endless silence, offering little traffic.

Inside the house, he no longer cared about such things. A small pocket penlight with a red lens guided his feet.

He was wrapped in long sleeves, long pants and quiet athletic shoes. A knit ski mask covered his entire head. It muffled his breathing even as the moisture from his breath dampened it. These were accelerating breaths, because he was excited. His heart hammered wildly.

Gloved hands gripped a long, sharp hunting knife. The door to the bedroom stood open. The woman in the bed would have seen no need to close it. She was alone in her own house. This was a generally safe town.

Not any longer. Not for her. He crept to her bedside and passed the beam of the small flashlight over her. She didn't stir.

He knew the lay of the land now. In an instant, he ripped the blanket off her and straddled her in the bed, holding the icy blade of the knife to her throat.

"Scream and I'll cut your throat," he half whispered as her eyes opened wide in terror, glistening in the darkness. He waited for the situation to penetrate.

Then the whimpering began. The pleas. How he loved the sound of that. The smell of her terror intoxicated him.

His fun had begun.

# Chapter 1

*Two weeks before...*

Kerri Lynn Addison sat at the desk in her minuscule faculty office, her service dog, Snowy, lying beside her on the floor. On her desk was a volume of *Homicide Detective's Crime Scene Manual*. The written one, not the companion book with all the graphic photos. She didn't want some unprepared student walking in on the visual presentation of ugly crimes. The book was useful to her, however, in prepping lessons for her criminal justice classes.

But she wasn't reading. She was awaiting Sergeant Stuart Canady of the Conard County Sheriff's Office. As a former cop herself, she shouldn't have been nervous about the meeting, but she was.

She was a *former* because she now suffered from a type of epilepsy as a result of being shot in the head. She didn't have convulsions, for which she was grateful, but instead had absence seizures. That meant that for anywhere up to a couple of minutes, she might as well be unconscious. Out of touch, unaware of anything around her. It was not necessarily something anyone else would notice, unless it went on too long, and she couldn't tell when it happened herself, unless something in the world around her had changed.

It was like a movie that skipped. Sometime during her absence, new characters would appear or people walking in front of her would suddenly be way down the street. Or an animal would come out of nowhere. At least that's how it seemed to her. And when things had changed, she felt confused until she sorted those changes out in her mind, which further froze her. It was even possible that the confusion was part of the seizure itself.

That's why she had Snowy. He was trained to tell when a seizure was coming and would persistently poke her with his snout, giving her time to stop whatever she was doing. When it came to crossing streets, for example, that early warning might be a lifesaver. He kept her safe while the confused aftermath stymied her.

Leaning over, she patted his back. He lifted his head briefly, acknowledging the touch, waiting in case she wanted to rise. Nope. She just wanted the comfort.

He was a snow-white dog with a kind of gray mask, like a husky or a malamute, but the trainers had said he was probably mostly German shepherd. He was an unusual mix for a service dog, labs being recognized among the best, but Snowy had an instinct for predicting her seizures. It was a relatively rare ability and, since she didn't need him to do anything else, they were a perfect match.

Right now he was calm, watchful and totally comfortable. The minute she put his vest on him, he became the epitome of a professional. Let loose to run in a safe place, he became all energetic, playful dog.

Since her office door was closed, she spoke to him. Her confidant. His ears pricked as he listened.

"I shouldn't be nervous, Snowy. I used to be a cop, too. But... I don't want to have a seizure while he's here. I'd be embarrassed."

Snowy answered with a quiet, short huff.

Embarrassment was one of the things she still struggled with. It could be awful to drop out in the middle of a conversation and come to, finding others looking at her, wondering why she hadn't responded. One friend had told her that she looked coldly angry at such times, but she didn't know if that was true. Either way, she didn't want her first meeting with Stuart Canady to start like that.

A rap on the door, even though expected, startled her and she straightened in her chair. "Come in," she called.

The man who walked through the door was the stuff of a Western movie hero. Rugged, face aged a bit by sun and wind, but clearly not that old. He filled his khaki uniform with a body that must be trained to a perfect peak. The belt around his waist carried his pistol and all the other accoutrements a police officer needed right at hand from a loop of black plastic handcuffs, like zip ties, to a Taser and auto reload cartridges. So they still used revolvers around here. Or maybe it was a weapon of choice for him.

Her gaze swept upward, taking in the seven-pointed brass star on his chest, the name tag, the rank pinned to his collar, then met eyes the gray-green color of tornadic clouds. They riveted her.

Then he smiled. "Ms. Addison? I'm Sergeant Stuart Canady, Conard County Sheriff's Department."

She rose from her chair, smiling in return, and offered her hand, inviting him farther into the cramped space. She waved him to the chair on the other side of her desk. "I really appreciate you coming and being willing to give your time to my class."

"My pleasure," he said as he sat and crossed his legs loosely. "A change of pace."

She resumed her seat, leaning a bit forward so her forearms rested on her desk. "It's my first semester of teaching, but I believe it would do the students good to hear what the job of police officer is really like."

"You were law enforcement yourself, weren't you?"

She forced a small laugh, uncomfortable though the question made her. "The uniform helps, Sergeant."

His smile widened. "The gun on the hip probably does, too. And Stu will suffice. I'm not used to formality anymore. We have very little of it around here."

She wouldn't know. Since her arrival, she'd been avoiding law enforcement officers because they reminded her of what she'd lost. In fact, except for her classes, she'd been avoiding people in general. Now she had to deal with it.

"Call me Kerri," she answered. Suddenly she was remembering all her fellow officers back in Tampa, and all the support they'd tried to give her. Maybe she'd been nuts to strike out on her own.

Bringing herself back to the present, she added, "The important thing is that the students know what they might be getting into. All of it, including the boredom between bouts of terror."

A snort of laughter escaped him. "Like the way you feel every time you stop a car for speeding?"

She nodded. It was true. Pulling over cars was one of the most dangerous things an officer could do. The reaction was always unpredictable and, statistically, more officers were killed and wounded during traffic stops. "Like that," she agreed. "A window on reality, and maybe some personal experiences if you don't mind. The class isn't huge, just eighteen students, but many of them are talking about becoming officers in larger communities. A taste for excitement, I guess."

He nodded. "I'll make it clear, though, that most of my experience was with the military police. Depending on where you're stationed, life can be too exciting."

"I imagine." Although she supposed she really couldn't. Her war zone, such as it was, had been city streets. As part of the victims unit, she'd been too often embroiled in domestic disputes, which could become very ugly. She had been getting close to making detective, however, and being part of investigative work had been her love. Now here she was, teaching.

"So when do you want me?"

"The class is on Friday for three hours at two in the afternoon. You can pick your day, and you don't have to spend the entire three hours. I'm looking for a window on reality from you, if you don't mind, a window that won't crush their dreams but that might bring them more in line with what it's like. Especially in a larger jurisdiction."

"You'd probably know more about busier jurisdictions, if we're talking civilian only. This one is fairly quiet compared to a big city," he agreed. "Although it seems to be getting less quiet. You should talk to our previous sheriff sometime. I hear that for the last thirty years he's been swearing this county is going to hell in a handbasket."

That drew a laugh from her. "When did he retire?"

"About fifteen years ago. Still likes to stick a finger in the pie from time to time, though. Good man."

"I'd like to meet him." Maybe. She wasn't sure she was ready to get involved in any depth with the whole cop scene again. But that was for later.

He glanced at his watch. "It's five-thirty. I just came off shift. Can I buy you dinner at the diner? We can talk more there without my stomach growling."

She couldn't drive so she'd have to walk. She'd been avoiding public places out of…what? Fear. Fear? She'd never been one to be afraid about much before. She couldn't let it get in her way now. Steeling herself, she nodded. "Sure. I'd like that. I don't drive, though, so I'll walk there."

He arched a brow but didn't ask. "I'll give you a lift. No problem." He nodded to her service dog. "No problem for him, either."

After being nervous about meeting this man, she'd been asked to have dinner with him. Just a cordial, friendly thing. Why did she keep avoiding the contact? Sheesh.

But it wasn't really fear, she admitted. It was something more craven. She didn't want to become embarrassed. Hell, she was going to have to learn to live with that. Absolutely no way around it.

"What's your pal's name?" he asked as they walked out to his official SUV. The parking lot was nearly empty at dinner hour, and evening classes hadn't yet begun.

"Snowy."

"Well, I know from experience that Maude will give him a burger on a paper plate, if that's okay. I don't know the rules with service dogs, just police dogs."

"Pretty much the same. Don't touch."

He laughed. "Makes sense. But can he have a burger?"

"Sure, if I tell him it's okay. And it will be." Because she really wouldn't need him once she was seated, and she knew from experience that Snowy loved burgers. Heck, if they passed a joint cooking them, his head would lift and he'd start sniffing loudly. He didn't break stride, pull on his leash or anything, but it was clear he hoped she would stop and treat him. She did, too often, she supposed.

He opened the door of his police SUV, a tan color not much different from his uniform and probably a color that didn't show dust much. Along its side the name of the department and the smaller words To Protect and Serve had been painted in a dark green. Beside it was blazoned a gold sheriff's star.

Kerri climbed in and Snowy followed, taking the

back seat as he had learned. "Good boy," she praised him. He gave her his version of a smile.

Stuart watched the process play out before he closed the door as Kerri snapped her seat belt into place. Good dog. Apparently pleasant woman. Sure pretty enough. She was dressed, however, in black slacks and a black silky shirt. Not quite a uniform, but suggestive of one. Interesting.

Then he wondered if he should tell her that Snowy's fur was redecorating her a bit. He decided that would be an unmannerly thing to do. She was probably aware of it.

As he climbed in behind the wheel and snapped his own seat belt into place, he glanced at her again. She was staring straight ahead as if a bit uncomfortable. Hell, she was just going to have a meal with another cop. She must have done that frequently.

Her eyes were striking, a brilliant green that he doubted he'd ever seen before, her hair a rusty red that fit her. It was cut short and businesslike but no less pretty. Her face was smooth, youthful, classic in its lines and sprinkled with cute freckles.

He turned his attention to driving because he'd realized at some point in adulthood that women didn't really like being looked over by strange men. It made them uneasy.

*Eyes front*, he warned himself. He'd only just met her and assessing her physical attributes wouldn't help their budding relationship any. But man, did she have some attributes! He smothered the smile that played around his mouth because he didn't want to explain it.

She didn't offer conversation as they drove to Maude's diner and he wondered if being around him made her uncomfortable. Because he was a cop? Well, there was a service dog in the back seat, which meant she'd been through some kind of hell, and maybe it was the reason she was teaching instead of working a desk in her former department. He'd have to wait for her to tell him, if she wanted to. He could research her easily enough, but that would be an intrusion on her privacy. It was all up to her.

How had matters become so complicated so quickly? He'd only just met her, was planning to spend an hour or so with one of her classes, and that would be that, right?

Or maybe not. There had been a tentativeness when she walked with him to his vehicle, not the cop's confident stride that was drilled into them from day one. *Never show weakness. Always take charge.*

Something had been cut out of her.

At the diner, after Stuart edged them into an angled parking spot, Kerri opened her own door and climbed out, reaching for Snowy's leash as he followed her. While Stu helping her get in may have been simple gentlemanliness, she didn't trust it. Damn, she didn't want to be treated like an invalid, not even in small ways. Yeah, she had a problem, but it didn't make it impossible for her to do most things, including climbing in and out of a car. She was jealous of her independence these days.

Stu opened the diner door for her, and they walked in with Snowy. Dinner hour was obviously beginning, but the diner wasn't overly packed. Almost everybody took a look at her dog, though. He was striking, and would always draw attention, but she suspected most of them were interested in the vest he wore.

Service dog. Stamping her immediately with the word *disabled*. Which she was, much as she hated to admit it.

"I'm lucky," she remarked to Stu as they settled at a table near the back. Snowy crawled in underneath, out of the way, but very close to her. On guard for her as always.

"How so?" he asked, passing her a plastic menu that was surprisingly not sticky. Most places like this served grease with the menu.

"Judging by the attention Snowy draws toward me, I'm fortunate I don't have an obvious disability. I'm not in a wheelchair, I'm not missing a limb, my face isn't half-destroyed. I've seen what those people go through."

He nodded. "So have I. Not too long ago I had words with a woman in the market. She was audibly fuming about a young guy in an electric cart who was blocking her access to produce. Poor fellow looked so embarrassed, like he was doing something wrong."

"What did you say?"

"'Ma'am, you're in *his* way, not the other way around.'" He flashed a smile. "Guess who looked embarrassed then?"

She smiled, liking this man. "Way to go, Sergeant Canady."

He shrugged one shoulder. "I prefer my people to be decent. Anyway, I can tell you from personal experience that everything on this menu is delicious, and most of it fattening if you're worried about that. Maude, the owner, believes in down-home cooking. I can almost guarantee you'll wind up with a good amount of take-home, probably enough for dinner tomorrow."

She looked down at the plastic card in her hands. "Hey, there's a chef salad on here."

He laughed. "I said *almost* everything."

She *was* hungry. Having to walk everywhere meant that she could only carry home a bag or two of groceries. She needed to get one of those metal folding carts and maybe she'd be able to carry more.

Lately, however, she delayed making that walk for longer than she should and let her cupboards grow bare. Not because she didn't like to walk but because she honestly worried about what would happen if she dropped a sack of groceries, something like eggs, when she was having a seizure. Heck, just scattering the stuff all over the sidewalk would ensure that at least a few people came running to help her gather it all up.

She was perfectly capable of picking it all up herself when she emerged from oblivion, but by then someone would be doing it for her. While she appreciated the kindness, she also hated the feeling of dependency that came over her. The sense of indebtedness to total strangers.

She obviously had some issues to deal with.

As hungry as she was, she followed his example and chose the steak sandwich. When she'd been on duty as a cop, she'd been like many others, grabbing a burger from anywhere nearby because it was fast and easy and wouldn't prevent her from answering a call quickly. It would have been simple to choose one now, but the steak sandwich sounded good, as did the choice of steamed broccoli or dinner salad. She went with the broccoli.

She also realized she was being too quiet. On the job, conversations with strangers were easy. She had a role and she knew how to fulfill it. There was no role now, not one that fully fit into the current situation.

Eventually, she dared a question, wondering if he was afraid to ask her any. The obvious question would have been about why she had Snowy, but he was probably avoiding that.

"You said you were a military MP," she began. "For how long?"

"Too long," he said lightly, then shook his head with a half smile. "Not really. Twelve years. Four years ago I resigned and came here looking for a little tranquility."

"Did you find it?"

"Mostly."

Food and coffee arrived just then, all delivered with a loud clatter. Then the mountainous woman with a frown asked, "You wanna feed that dog?"

Stu looked at Kerri. "How does he take his burger?"

She had to grin. "Just plain, no bun, medium." The woman stomped away and she looked at Stu. "Is something wrong?"

"Not a thing. Maude is the orneriest woman in this town, I've gathered. Everyone's used to it and it doesn't seem to bother anyone. I've joined the crowd. You'll notice, however, that she asked about feeding Snowy. There's a good woman under that crust."

"That's good to know." She glanced down and re-alized Snowy was facing outward, toward the edge of the table. Probably hoping for crumbs. "He's such a good dog," she remarked, then looked at him across plates holding a huge sandwich, enough home fries to feed a football team and a bowl of steaming broccoli.

"You like it here?" she asked him.

"Very much. Although I guess I should warn you about the grapevine. It works faster than phones and runs everywhere it seems. Great resource for us cops, maybe not so good for people who want privacy. What about you? This place seems out of the way."

"I wanted a smaller college to…test the waters and see whether teaching is my thing. This was the best offer I got that matched what I was looking for, and I grabbed it."

He picked up half his sandwich and held it while he spoke. The juice that dripped from the meat made her mouth water. "I wouldn't have believed this was the best place. Other colleges have missed out."

She felt her cheeks color. "You can't know that."

"I'm good at guessing," he laughed.

"You came here," she pointed out.

"And I have a hankering to own a nice piece of land where I can ride horses and maybe have some other livestock. Not sure yet, but I really like hiking around here in the mountains and I've always liked riding. Time will tell."

"Oh, that sounds so nice," she remarked. It did. Wide-open spaces, mountains, hiking. With Snowy, she *could* hike. Riding, though? Well, maybe. As far as she knew, she didn't fall over or anything. She ought to try it sometime, expand her horizons even more.

She had a weakness when it came to fried potatoes. Not so much the fast-food variety, but real fried potatoes, so she reached for one of the large wedges. It was hot and every bit as savory as she could have hoped for. "I may pig out on the fries and take the rest home."

"They *are* good," he agreed, then took a large bite from his sandwich.

While he chewed and swallowed, she followed his lead, deciding the sandwich was probably better fresh, too, like the fries would have to be. As soon as it hit her palate, she was grateful she hadn't succumbed to the standby burger. A quiet sound of pleasure escaped her.

Stu grinned. "Can't get any better," he told her after wiping his mouth with a paper napkin. "It all heats up well, too, except the fries. The sandwich is great cold, but the fries..." He shrugged one shoulder. "If you don't mind them limp, they're okay, too."

Maude returned with a hamburger patty on a paper plate. Snowy's head was up, his sniffer working overtime. Maude put the plate on the table. "Guess you ought to give it to him, being he's a service dog and all."

Kerri was touched that she cared enough to know. "Thank you so much."

"Just don't tell the health department." She glared at Stu.

"I wouldn't dream of it," he assured her. "It just happened to fall on the floor and there just happened to be a paper plate lying there."

Maude snorted and stomped away. Snowy showed

small signs of struggling to behave himself, so Kerri wasted no time in placing the plate under his nose. "Snowy, okay." That burger would be gone in two or three bites.

Stu was enjoying himself, watching her reactions to everything new, watching her interplay with her dog. He decided he liked her more than a little, and just wished there was some way to get her full story. One or two times he'd seen what he thought was sorrow flit across her face. Leaving her job, he guessed, hadn't been easy for her. Now she was beginning a whole new life in a strange place with a service dog at her side. He gave her points for gumption.

"Whereabouts are you living?" he asked when the meal was nearly done. She was going to be taking home a whole lot of food with her.

"Apartment house on Tech Street."

"Now there's a story. But first, aren't you uneasy? I mean, that place is practically deserted. In good shape, I hear, but not many folks around."

"I'm not worried about it. It was within my budget. But the name *Tech Street* seems out of place in this town."

"Oh, it is. Want the story, condensed version?"

She nodded as Maude brought foam containers to the table.

"A number of years back a semiconductor plant opened up just outside of town. They brought in a lot of new people as well as a lot of jobs for locals. Hence the apartments. Anyway, the plant shuttered after a few years, most of the new people moved on and the college considered buying the apartment building for students. They didn't, but even if they had, an awful lot of the student body are commuters and it probably would have been a loss. Sometimes the building has been nearly full, but lately it's been mostly empty. I don't need to explain to you why that's a concern for law enforcement. Big empty buildings seem to breed trouble."

"I know." She shook her head a little as she moved food from her plate into the boxes. "I didn't think about that when I rented, just that it was what I needed and the price was within my means. *Is* there a lot of trouble over there?"

He shook his head. "Nope." He knew, after what he had said, that she wouldn't be expecting that answer. Maybe his sense of humor needed some modifying.

She looked up sharply and he shrugged. "Look at this place, Kerri. If we have ever had a crack house, no one mentioned it to me. The current owners bought the building thinking to turn it into short-term rentals for skiers, from what I hear. Well, the ski resort hasn't panned out yet."

"That's kind of sad."

"In one way for certain. Younger folks keep moving away. The community college is like a launching pad for careers elsewhere."

They finished filling their boxes with leftovers. Kerri picked up the paper plate that Snowy had nearly licked through and placed it on top of her empty crockery plate. She hoped that wasn't a violation. Stu went to the counter and paid the bill.

She couldn't help but follow him with her eyes.

There might be something to say for coming out of her shell, after all.

"Let me drive you and Snowy home," he said as they exited the diner. "You don't want to walk carrying those containers."

He was right. Maude had given her a plastic bag, but she didn't want to chance losing all that good food, and since she had to hold Snowy's leash, she only had one hand free.

For a fact, she still had no idea what happened during her seizures. She knew she froze and stopped responding, but she didn't know if she'd drop things. It hadn't happened yet, but it wasn't long enough to be sure.

"Thanks," she said, feeling inordinately pleased to have a little more time with him. Man, she had to take care. It was just a desire for a human connection, nothing more. What made her think anyone would want anything else from her, anyway? She was broken, and while her seizures might not be horrendous and scary for others, she still couldn't drive, and that seemed like a serious limitation, absent all the other baggage she carried.

There was plenty of other baggage. Fears she hadn't had before, some emotional trauma and constant uncertainty about herself. She hoped the next months would begin to wash some of that away. Teaching exposed her to a lot of younger people and other faculty members whether she wanted it or not. That *had* to help her confidence grow.

The drive to the apartment was short. The building was situated on the edge of town, as was the college, an area not within the city limits and patrolled by the sheriff's department.

The few other residents were at the far end of the building, or in the facing apartment structure. She was on the very end of a nearly empty building. Short of moving out to a ranch, she couldn't have been more isolated. She was okay with that, just as she was okay with being on the second floor. Snowy would warn her in time for her to sit on a stair if it became necessary, and the isolation…well, she had never been afraid of living alone. She could take care of herself.

Mostly.

She invited Stu in because it seemed the courteous thing to do, although she felt awkward about it since they'd only just met.

Once the door was closed, she let Snowy off his leash and removed his vest. He spent a minute dashing around, checking everything out. Stu set the bag of her leftovers on her kitchen counter, easy enough to find since the bar overlooked the living area.

"Why'd you pick an apartment so far away from other tenants?"

She smiled. "Simple answer to that. I got an extra window in my kitchen. I like the light."

He chuckled. "You may regret that during the depths of winter. Even with the double-paned glass you'll get a draft."

She began pulling containers out of the plastic bag. "Coming from Florida, I'm actually looking forward to what real cold is like. I may regret *that*."

His eyes almost seemed to twinkle. "It's going to be a change for you. I'll be interested to hear what you think." Then he headed for the door. "You must want your evening to yourself, and I need to get home and clean the kitchen. I overslept just long enough I had to leave the breakfast dishes. I'll call as soon as I know when I can come to your class, okay?"

"That would be great." Her smile was warm. "Thanks, Stu."

"My pleasure."

She stood in her small kitchen as the door closed behind him and wished he had stayed for a bit. He was comfortable company. Well, maybe they'd meet again sometime out of class.

Then she continued putting food away. All of a sudden she paused and looked around.

"Damn," she said aloud. "Why did he bring it up?"

Because for the first time since moving into this unit, she felt her isolation in the building.

Snowy commented with a quiet chuff and as she looked at him she tried to laugh at herself. She was probably far safer here than she'd been at her home in Florida. And now she had a dog, as well.

Isolation? She tried to will the uncomfortable awareness away but failed.

Uneasiness clung to her like cold, wet leaves.

# Chapter 2

In an eyeblink, everything changed. Confusion filled Kerri. Snowy was no longer lying beside her. His head rested on her thigh. What the…?

The faces she had been looking at had all changed and moved. Boredom was gone. Some of the students were standing. What was going on? Had something happened?

A voice spoke from beside her. "Ms. Addison? You okay?"

She looked up and saw the young woman standing beside her. Hadn't the student been sitting in a desk directly in front of her, chewing on a stylus? When had she moved?

"What happened?" she asked instinctively.

Then the pieces began to assemble into the new

picture. She'd had a seizure. She was experiencing the confusion that always followed if things had changed. The confusion would pass quickly.

The young woman, Alice, she remembered, answered. "You stopped talking right in the middle of a sentence and you got this funny look. We waited, but then you didn't answer when we called to you…"

Kerri saw Alice gnaw her lower lip uncertainly.

"I'm okay," she replied. "Just give me a moment, then I'll explain."

Alice nodded and returned to her desk. The others resumed sitting.

Their faces had changed, Kerri realized. Where before they'd been engaged or bored, depending, now they were all looking uneasy.

"I should have told you about this on the first day of class," she said slowly, gathering her thoughts, wishing the seizure hadn't scattered them like autumn leaves. She'd be back to normal any second now, but her new normal wasn't exactly comforting to her.

"Told us what?" another student, Jason, asked.

How much to tell them? As little as possible, she decided. She didn't want to become the discussion.

"I have seizures," she answered. "What you just saw…well, that was the kind I have. I lose touch, sometimes for only a few seconds, sometimes for a minute or two, and when I come out of it I feel a bit confused. Especially if things have moved around. Well, y'all did a lot of moving."

That drew forth a bit of laughter and some of the tension seemed to seep from the room. There was new interest in those faces and she wondered how much

she'd have to tell them. She decided to head it off at
the pass.

"That's why I have Snowy with me. He can alert
me right before it happens, so I don't freeze in traffic
or something. It was kind of you all not to ask why I
have a service dog."

"Not our business," one of the other young women
said. "We were just worried about you. Your dog poked
your leg a few times, then suddenly you stopped talking."

"Weird, huh?" she said. "Well, that's as bad as it
gets. It doesn't happen all the time, though. Think you
guys can deal?"

They all agreed they could. No doubt in any of their
voices.

"Then let's continue class. Where was I?"

Alice spoke. "You were telling us about the Su-
preme Court decision that allows cops to be video-
taped while on the job."

"Yes. That's undoubtedly why you see so much foot-
age online now. Better behave yourselves."

Another laugh from the group, this one entirely
comfortable. Okay, then. She was ready to plunge into
the details of what that meant for police.

Better that than let the hovering embarrassment
swallow her.

Class finished shortly after five. The students hurried out, glad to be done for the day and probably heading straight for food in the dining hall. She'd heard
that it was a pretty good one, too, as well as a popular hangout.

Snowy stood up and stretched, back legs reaching nearly straight out. He even yawned. She wondered what kind of patience that dog must exert to steadfastly remain with her for hours when she wasn't doing anything he might enjoy, like taking a walk.

Well, they had a walk ahead of them now. She allowed a fleeting moment to wonder what she was going to do when it got really cold and snowy, and decided she'd deal with that when the time grew closer. Right now a walk in pleasant autumn air was a treat.

Snowy seemed eager to get going—he'd already learned the new schedule—and looked at her with his tail wagging quickly. Okay, then. She put the last of her desk items in her backpack, wondering if she should detour to her tiny office or just head home.

Home, she decided. She still had to cook her dinner. It wasn't a thrilling prospect. Just last month she'd been frying some breaded eggplant when she'd spaced, coming back to find it all blackened and wondering what the hell had happened. Of course she knew, but in the moments immediately following one of her episodes, with absolutely no memory of blinking out, it was always confusing. She'd asked the neurologist if the confusion was part of the seizure or just caused by the changes that occurred during one.

His answer hadn't been exactly reassuring. "I don't know. It could be either."

Oh, yeah, burned eggplant when she *knew* she had these absence episodes and she still got confused. Like today in class.

She could almost have sighed as she walked toward the exterior door at the end of the hallway. Well, that little episode was probably going to develop legs. Her employers knew about it, but she wasn't keen on being a topic on the local grapevine. As if she could have prevented it forever.

Maybe after dinner she'd call one of her former colleagues and friends back in Florida. She missed them, but being with them constantly reminded her of how much she had lost.

Snowy appeared thrilled to be outdoors and moving. He stayed at her side, ignoring distractions, but she couldn't mistake his prancing step and his perked-up ears and tail.

He was feeling good. Well, so was she despite the incident. The air was dry with the slightest nip. Her stride quickened as they strode toward home. God, it was so different from Florida. The dry weather, the lack of palms…it was like another universe.

Just as her apartment house came into sight, a car pulled up beside her, motor humming. She looked over and through the open passenger window saw Stu. He was still in uniform and just as attractive as she recalled.

"Hey, lady, want a ride?"

"Where? In the back seat?"

He flashed a grin. "Only the front seat for you."

She returned his smile but shook her head a bit. "Snowy needs this walk. He's been pinned lying beside me for three hours."

"Then how about I zoom by Maude's and bring some dinner to your place?"

Part of her tried to pull back, fearing where closer contact might lead. Remembering the pitying looks she'd received at the station when she briefly returned to work. Facing again that she was now irrevocably flawed.

But Stu was smiling, her fears seemed a bit much when she hardly knew the man and she didn't at all feel like cooking dinner for one out of nearly empty cupboards. "Sounds great. Thank you."

"Same as last time? Should I add a latte?"

The meal last week had been scrumptious and had lasted through a second dinner. "It's an offer I can't refuse," she admitted. "And a latte, please."

"See you at your place." The patrol SUV slid away and disappeared around the next corner.

Kerri was still smiling when she got back to her building, and since she figured it would take Stu at least a little while to round up dinner, she went into the back courtyard with Snowy. She unhooked his leash and removed his vest, allowing him to dash wildly around for a few minutes before she pulled a bright yellow tennis ball from her backpack.

Playing fetch with that tennis ball was one of Snowy's absolute favorite things. The minute he saw one, he immediately went into the play bow, down on his front legs with his tail wagging frantically. She watched him dash joyously around and bring the ball back to her, looking up hopefully every time he returned it.

No question but that Snowy was the best thing that had happened to her since she was shot.

"Special delivery," called a voice from near the fence. Kerri turned around and saw Stu on the far side of the fence with a couple of bags. "Want me to go up?"

"I'll be right there."

Snowy evidently sensed that playtime was over. He approached and sat, waiting for her to hook his leash to his collar. She carried the vest along with her backpack. He didn't exactly need it here.

There was a back stairway in the middle of the building from the courtyard. It was a duplicate of the front stairway that rose to meet it across a tiny foyer. On either side, the hallway stretched toward other units. Hers was the farthest down the hall to the right from here.

Stu was already waiting for her.

"What did you do?" she asked as she approached. "Run?"

"Running up stairs is great exercise. Besides, you don't need me to tell you how often that might be necessary on the job."

It was true. Most Florida apartment houses had stairways open to the weather, and even hallways on the exterior of the buildings rather than the interior. What was often missing was an elevator, which, when you lived on the fourth floor, could make carrying groceries a pain.

"This is different," she remarked as she unlocked her door. "The stairways are enclosed and there are heavy doors at the bottom. Where I came from, most of this would be open."

"I never thought about that," he said as he followed her inside. "Different weather?"

"That's my guess. It was just so familiar I never thought about it either, until I came here."

Stu put the plastic bags on her counter as he had last week, then said, "I need to run down for the coffee."

"Oh, you should have told me! There's a gate I could have come through to help."

He nodded. "I know. But I need the exercise, right? Hey, I could have said something, so don't feel bad about it."

He hurried out and Snowy surprised her by sitting at the door almost hopefully.

"Traitor," she said cheerfully, wondering how the dog had become attached so fast. It was okay, though. He wasn't wearing his vest so he knew he wasn't working.

However, she'd experienced just how fast he could get on the job when he sensed a seizure coming. An absolutely remarkable animal, and totally lovable as far as she was concerned.

She had just finished pulling plates out of the cupboard, followed by some flatware, when Stu returned without his gun belt, carrying the cardboard tray holding coffee.

At least she hadn't had to leave everything behind when she moved here. Not that she'd really had much to begin with. The basics, mostly, with a little extra so she could entertain a few friends.

That meant she had two stools at the kitchen bar, furniture in her living room and a comfortable bed to sleep on. Kitchen utensils had tagged along. Considering she didn't care much for shopping, and given that she didn't know how much she could easily find here, she was all too glad to have her familiar things around her, worn or not.

Stu took a couple of minutes to introduce himself properly to Snowy, then was allowed to give the dog a good scratch around the neck.

"I think you've made a friend for life," Kerri remarked.

Stu grinned at her from his squatting position. "That's the idea." He straightened. "Okay, let me help put dinner out."

That it was the same meal as last week didn't bother her at all. When she'd been working as a cop, she sometimes ate the same foods for days on end simply because it was easy to get and she often didn't feel like cooking after a long shift, or a troubling day. After she'd moved from patrol into the victims unit, she had too many troubling days.

They sat side by side at the bar, enjoying the steak sandwiches and fries. He'd even remembered her preference for the broccoli. Good man.

"What exactly did you do in your former job?" he asked her while they ate.

She gave him a wry look. "I'm surprised you didn't investigate my entire background. You have the tools."

He returned her look. "Didn't want to invade your privacy, but that doesn't mean I'm not curious. Oh!" he said suddenly.

"What?"

"That foam container over there. Did you look in it?"

She shook her head. "I assumed it was for you once I found the dinners."

"Maude sent it for Snowy. Hamburger patty."

Kerri felt a whisper of warmth slip through her, touching some of her empty places. "That's sweet."

She glanced down and saw Snowy sitting at attention. "I think he smells it."

"Probably," Stu laughed. "Can he eat it out of the container?"

"He has before."

Stu rose immediately, and opened the box, placing it on the kitchen floor.

Snowy strained toward it without leaving his place. Kerri told him it was okay and he wasted no time.

"It amazes me that dogs eat so fast," she remarked. "Hardly time to enjoy it."

"Doesn't seem to bother him." He put his sandwich down and returned his attention to her. "Your job with the force? Patrol?"

She hesitated. "I was on patrol before. Then I moved to the victims unit."

He winced slightly. "Rough."

"Yeah, it could be. Then I was trained to be a negotiator in domestic disputes and to support victims. Especially rape victims."

"Oh, hell," he said sympathetically. "That's the worst. Why you?"

"Because I'm a woman. Studies have shown that women are more likely to deescalate domestics than men. So it fell to me. I had some success, too."

He nodded slowly. "I bet you did."

"Meaning?" For some reason she almost bristled.

"It's your demeanor," he said as he once again lifted his sandwich. "I bet you didn't go in all tough and full of orders."

She relaxed again. "Nope." Then she had to laugh.

"Guys don't usually feel threatened by a woman, even one in uniform."

"They should know better." He winked as he chewed. "Domestics are really dangerous. It took a lot of guts for you to walk in there."

Guts? She wondered if she still had any. Apart from her disability, she couldn't know if she'd ever walk into the middle of a domestic dispute again. Much as she hated the idea, she might now be too afraid to do her old job, even if she hadn't been left with permanent brain damage.

"What happened?" Stu asked quietly.

She looked down at her plate. She'd done a fairly good job on her sandwich, but the fries remained untouched. Her stomach knotted in response to his question, and she knew she was done eating for a while.

"Forget I asked," he said, as if he'd read something on her face. "None of my business."

He'd hear about it. She was certain of that. The question was, did she want someone else to give him a brief version, or did she want to lay it all out for him? He needed to understand the whole thing if they were going to become friends.

If she'd let him come so close. Having a mountain of problems to deal with already, friendship sounded like just something more she'd need to handle.

But she'd never been an isolated person. She'd always had friends and plenty of good people to hang with. It was the best way to relieve the pressures of the job and forget about them for a few hours.

But she didn't have those same pressures here, and it just sounded like another complication amid the already huge mound she had to handle. Or maybe she was afraid of his reaction. She'd already learned that some people didn't react well to the word *epilepsy*.

Stu let the entire subject drop. The tension in her stomach eased a little, and finally she reached for a thick home fry.

After they finished eating, Stu helped with the cleanup, and she fed Snowy his bowl of kibble. Tonight, unlike the last visit, her new friend seemed in no hurry to leave. For the first time she had reason to wonder about his personal life. Yeah, he'd taken her to the diner for dinner and driven her home, but that didn't mean he lacked people who might be waiting for him. He'd kind of suggested he lived alone when he'd mentioned needing to wash his breakfast dishes last week, but she knew almost nothing about him. Of course, she wasn't exactly forthcoming, either.

As they settled in her living room, him on the recliner, her on the battered sofa, she asked, "No family at home?"

He shook his head. "I'm a confirmed bachelor."

She felt the corners of her mouth lift a little and was glad *that* complication didn't seem in the offing. "Any particular reason?"

He shrugged. "Not exactly a conscious decision but I haven't yet met anyone who makes me want to give up my independence."

She laughed. "Neither have I."

"There you go. It's not that I'm opposed, it's that… well, I guess I'm picky."

"Good way to be when deciding the future course of your entire life."

Then he came straight to the point. "Can we discuss the elephant in the room?"

She blinked. "Elephant?"

"Your service dog." He shook his head slightly. "Tell me to get lost if you want to, but you're walking everywhere with a highly trained animal. Say, you need to meet Cadell Marcus."

She blinked once more. Had she missed something or was he hopping like an uncomfortable flea between topics? Had she seized again? "Who?"

"Cadell Marcus. He's the K9 trainer for the department and he's recently started training service dogs. Sometimes he works as a deputy but he's also got a ranch he's taking care of. I think a lot of his effort is devoted to those dogs."

"That's cool. I'm lucky to have Snowy. My fellow cops chipped in to get him for me. A service dog isn't cheap."

"That's what Cadell said when he started the training. He's making it a charity project, which means he can't do many at a time, but at least he's getting a few out to people who'd otherwise have to do without."

"I think that's wonderful," she said sincerely. "I *would* like to meet him."

"I think he'd like to meet you and Snowy, too."

They were edging toward the uncomfortable again. Deciding at last that she'd have to deal with this subject, she took the bull by the horns, as it were. Stu was justifiably curious. Better the answers came from her.

But she still had a lot of emotional difficulty dealing with all of it. *All* of it. She tensed, looked down at Snowy, who'd settled by her feet, and dove into it.

"I have a mild form of epilepsy," she said, her voice sounding almost smothered. "Temporal lobe seizures. Like absence seizures. I simply go away for up to a couple of minutes at a time. I have no memory of it and when I return I feel confused until I get grounded again. Snowy warns me ahead of time so I don't come to a dead halt in the middle of the street, or while doing something dangerous. He senses it far enough in advance that I can usually turn off the stove or whatever. Avoid a dangerous situation."

"Thank God for Snowy," he said.

"I couldn't agree more." Well, that hadn't been so bad, she decided. He might never drop by with an offer of dinner again, but at least he wasn't making an excuse about needing to get somewhere.

He didn't speak for a beat or two, then said, "I gather this wasn't always a problem, or you wouldn't have been a cop."

"No." Her chest started to squeeze because this was a memory she didn't want to relive any more than she wanted this illness. Some things were better left buried.

"Kerri…"

"Okay. Okay." She jumped up from the couch, needing to pace to release some of the surging adrenaline in response to that night. Did she have to recall it all? Couldn't she just escape with a brief outline?

But her mind was having none of it. It had gone into replay mode, had carried her back to that awful night. She was hardly aware of speaking.

She could still remember the warm breeze that stirred the palms, making their fronds clatter. The humidity that made the air almost thick enough to chew. She seldom paid attention to the weather while on a call, so it sometimes surprised her how clearly she remembered it. A typical Florida summer night, nothing unusual.

There wasn't anything unusual about the shouting from the second-floor apartment. A painted steel railing lined the front of the building-length balcony, the local version of a hall. Nearby residents had emerged from their apartments in nightclothes and were being urged away by the cops who'd already arrived.

The call from several neighbors said the man inside that apartment owned a gun. Clear the civilians, first.

She walked up to the scene commander, a lieutenant she knew well. "So what's up, Pete?"

"The guy upstairs is armed."

"For certain?"

Pete faced her. "For certain. The first two responding officers arrived and knocked. He shouted for them to get away or he'd shoot."

"Not so easy to do through a steel door." She knew these places. It could still be done, though, if the guy had enough firepower. Additionally, that door was his only way out.

She could hear the grinding of the engine of the SWAT truck approaching. "What are their orders? Do you need me at all?"

"You wanna try to talk to him? From what I've been hearing, he's so drunk he should be laid out flat. Violent. Aggressive. And he's not answering the phone."

"How many people in there?"

"His wife for sure. Neighbors think they have a

couple of kids. Apparently, he and the rest of the community don't mix well."

"I wonder why."

Pete scanned the scene, making sure that balcony was clear and civilians were being ushered out of range. "I don't think you should go up there."

"Is he more likely to listen to me on a bullhorn?"

Pete gave her a mirthless half smile.

"If he were alone, I'd let SWAT handle it, Pete. But if there's any chance we can get him out of there without his family getting hurt, I'll try it."

"I know you will." He sighed audibly. The screaming from the apartment continued, laced with threats.

"Got a name?"

"The neighbors know him as Faz, we've gathered. Short for Fasio. Apartment management lists the tenants as Fasio and Darlene Maines."

"Faz, it is." She started toward the stairs at the end of the balcony.

Pete grabbed her arm. "You got your vest?"

"I'm wearing it."

"Let me get you a helmet."

She turned to look at him. "Like that helmet would make the guy feel safer? More cooperative? You might as well send SWAT up there."

Pete just shook his head. "Resign yourself. They're not going to be far behind you. If you can get him to step out far enough, they'll swarm him."

Standard with an armed abuser. She wasn't going to argue about that. She mounted the stairs easily. Adrenaline pumped through her, driving all fear away. Talk the man down. Convince him to come out so he couldn't shoot up his family. Behind her she heard the carefully quieted steps of SWAT. They were deploying rapidly.

When she reached the door, she raised a hand to knock. Not the usual loud police hammering, just an ordinary knock.

She snapped back to the present and looked at Stu. He waited patiently. How much had she said aloud? She had no idea.

But she needed to make short work of the ending. "He came out shooting. I got grazed on the side of the head, but the blow was enough to cause a concussion and a brain bleed. I don't remember much after the bullet hit me. A little of the team swarming him, then I was out of it. He's alive, his family's alive, and he's in prison for a long time."

"Shooting a cop is a stupid thing to do."

"He'd been doing stupid things for a while, I heard. Now he can do them in prison." She shook her arms, trying to dispel the adrenaline and cortisol that were rampaging through her, just as on the night when it happened.

"So no helmet, huh?"

She stopped pacing, still shaking her arms. "No. You don't get very far when you arrive looking like a storm trooper."

"Good point. My God, woman, you are incredibly brave. There's a reason I wore a helmet when I was stationed overseas."

"It was my job to calm things down, not ramp them up."

He nodded. "Remembering that night hurt, didn't it?"

"Hell, yeah." She didn't want to admit how much.

"I've got some memories that still hurt, too. Life and death situations tend to do that. But I hope you're proud of yourself for trying. You were absolutely right about his family."

"I know I was," she agreed. "I've seen what happens when a guy tips over the edge and nobody is in time to stop him."

He rose from the couch. "How about you, Snowy and I take a walk? It'll work through the tension that just swamped you."

She looked out the living room window and realized the evening had grown dark. Colder, too, probably. It was a good idea, though. Walking off the aftereffects of the cortisol blast the memory had given her was the healthiest way to handle it. That or going to a gym.

"That sounds good."

"If you've got any, you might want to find some gloves. Or a warm jacket with deep pockets. I'll meet you downstairs in the parking lot. I need my own jacket."

Outside, Stu unlocked his vehicle. From the trunk he pulled out a light but insulated jacket and donned his gun belt again. Long habit. Walking streets in the dark without the tools of his trade always felt uncomfortable. This might be a mostly peaceful town, but Afghanistan had taught him a whole different bunch of lessons.

God, imagine that woman going alone to meet a raging drunk with a gun. Yeah, he knew she had backup, but it remained she was going to be the first face that man saw, and he was out of his mind and waving a weapon.

She knew that and went, anyway. Courage. She'd clearly been focused on the threatened family, wanting to get them out safely. SWAT busting in there might have caused a rain of bullets from the perp, and some of them might have hit his family.

Considering the guy had come out shooting at Kerri, he ought to be damn grateful he was in a cell instead of a coffin.

The night was chilly, but not enough to make him zip up his jacket. He could taste winter on the air, though. It was coming, even if it might take another month or so before the first flurries arrived to announce it.

He slammed that tailgate shut, pressed the lock button on his key tab and turned just in time to see Kerri emerge from the stairs with Snowy.

Cute dog, he thought. Cute woman. A pair that would catch eyes wherever they went.

But he still had some questions. Like had her injury cost her her job? Were there things she couldn't do? How circumscribed had her life become? How circumscribed did she want it to be?

He'd gotten the sense that she hadn't been comfortable telling him about her epilepsy to begin with. He sure as hell didn't see any reason why she should feel that way. Why it should embarrass her.

But maybe it did. It had certainly caused her some serious life changes or she wouldn't be here teaching at a community college. If she was still having seizures—and that was evidenced by her service dog—

then she probably couldn't drive. How many other things were there? Then he remembered her saying she'd walk to Maude's. No, no driving for her. Hard thing to live with.

But driving…oh, that brought on a whole new set of problems around here. There were simply times when walking anywhere wouldn't be smart or safe. One of them was going to have to look into rides for her in bad weather.

She came up to him with a smile, Snowy clearly back on duty and walking sedately beside her. "Thanks for the idea," she said.

"If you had any idea how many hours I spend on my butt in this car…oh, wait. You do."

At last she laughed, an easy sound that suggested she'd left her nightmare behind. He wished he thought it wouldn't return but he knew better. Memories like that had a way of creeping up on you just as you were falling asleep. At least his did. He'd long since lost count of the nights he'd climbed out of bed to do push-ups and squats in order to shove his memories back into the box.

"Let's walk toward town," he suggested. "Maybe we could stop for a piece of pie or some cocoa."

"Sounds good to me."

On the east end of town, in an older neighborhood of smaller houses, a predator hunted.

Ivan Rampin eyed every house he passed. Plotting his move would take a week or two, but he had to know which women lived alone, or spent a lot of time at night alone. Flying off half-cocked would only get him into trouble.

He had other standards, of course. He preferred women who were in their twenties or early thirties. Reasonably good-looking would be nice but it wasn't a requirement. After all, he enjoyed himself in the dark.

He also had to find a house he could get into without risk of being seen. Or even find a late-night jogger who would pass near the park. But it was getting chillier at night, and he'd prefer to be indoors when he had his fun.

Last spring he'd taken two college women. He savored the memories the way he would have savored a good piece of chocolate cake. Their fear had filled his nostrils with a special scent, one he couldn't get elsewhere. He loved their initial struggles, and their final acquiescence to his knife. He conquered them, and it made him feel powerful and strong.

He'd escaped detection those times and felt emboldened by success. But he wasn't stupid enough to think he could keep taking coeds. Besides, he wanted women with more experience. He was sure they'd be a bigger challenge.

Smiling in anticipation, he kept walking and scanning, sometimes taking to the alleys behind the houses. Watching, waiting.

It was hard to wait. Very hard. But he held himself back because a single mistake could end his fun forever.

Patience, he reminded himself, was a virtue. Hadn't his mother always said so?

# Chapter 3

It was shortly after eight when they walked through the door of the diner. The place had started quieting for the night and few tables and booths were occupied.

Kerri blew on her cold fingers. She was going to need a better pair of gloves. As they slid into a booth near the window from where they could watch the last evening stragglers pass by, she said to Stu, "I think I'm going to have to consider winter clothing."

That caused him to grin. "Not prepared, I take it."

"It's not like it's easy to find suitable clothes in Florida. Oh, sure, I could get jackets and gloves, but I never needed to. My uniform came with a reasonable jacket, but I doubt it would work here."

"I doubt it, too. I'm off tomorrow. If you like, I'll introduce you to a local landmark, Freitag's Mercantile. You can find everything you might want there."

She nodded. "But you have to promise me to help me choose. I have no idea how cold it can get here and what would be the best items to own, especially since I walk everywhere."

"I thought that might be the case."

A younger woman who looked strikingly like Maude approached their booth. "What'll it be?" she asked without any friendly preamble.

"Cocoa?" Stu questioned Kerri.

"Sounds good."

Then he looked up at the woman. "What kind of pie do you still have today, Mavis?"

"Slim pickin's," came the answer. "Most of it disappears at lunch and dinner. I have a couple of wedges of blueberry, and a few of apple. That's it." No apology, not in word or voice.

"I'd like apple," Stu said. "Kerri?"

"Apple for me, too. Thank you."

"Warmed up?" Mavis asked.

They both answered in the affirmative.

Mavis started to turn away, then paused. "You come by early enough tomorrow and I should have blueberry buckle. If you want something different." Then she stomped away.

"Just like her mother," Stu remarked. "Peas in a pod. Her mom had a heart attack recently, but you'd never guess by the way Maude plunged back into work. Except she usually lets Mavis take over after dinner. Must be hard for Maude to do. She's been running this place since the age of the dinosaurs, from what I hear."

"An icon."

"Exactly. This town will never be the same if she retires."

"Mavis is a pretty good stand-in."

Stu laughed. "For certain."

Kerri's spirits began to lift. She was starting to like this town. It felt like a true community, where everyone knew everyone else, and could share their stories. Well, with the possible exception that she didn't want her story shared. She was still too uncomfortable with that. From the sound of it, she couldn't prevent it, though.

Pie plates landed with a clatter on the table. The cocoa was hardly placed more gently and sloshed slightly into the saucers. Forks and spoons, wrapped in paper napkins, followed.

"Thanks," they both said like a chorus.

Like everything else she'd tasted from this diner, the pie was exquisite. A little extra cinnamon, which she loved.

"Oh, yum," she said after a few mouthfuls.

"You can always get the best pies here, whole or half if you want. The bakery one street over doesn't even try to compete."

"I hadn't even realized there was a bakery."

"Apparently, it was Melinda's dream, and she got started a few years back. Absolutely the place for turnovers, muffins, cakes, fresh bread. We'll go scope it tomorrow if you have the time after Freitag's."

The sad thing, she guessed, was that she *would* have the time. In coming here, leaving her old life behind, she hadn't thought about the days when she'd have little to do except walk and play with Snowy, who once again was lying quietly beneath the table. No hamburgers, no interest.

She'd led a really busy life before. Now…well, she guessed she'd better take up reading and maybe knitting or some other hobby.

"I guess I'm going to need to build a whole new life for myself," she remarked. "Too much time on my hands right now and I'm not used to that."

He tilted his head. "Before too long there will be snow on the ground. If you can walk, you can ski cross-country. One of my favorite winter activities. If you're willing, we'll try it."

"I'm willing." Very much so. It sounded like a great way to enjoy winter and get some exercise at the same time.

The smile he gave her across the table warmed her. "We'll look at skis tomorrow, too, if you want. You can think about it because outfitting is fairly expensive. Or we can rent until you're sure you like it."

She didn't say so, but she had plenty of money. A pension, her job and a lump sum from her retirement account. She almost sighed. There were some things she hadn't been thinking about at all, she realized. Like someone to advise her retirement. The college offered options and she still had time to transfer those savings into another retirement plan.

She'd been letting things slide. Time to get going again. This really wasn't like her.

"I think I need to get a handle on my life," she said wryly.

"I suspect the past year or so has been full of shocks and changes for you."

She nodded, but it still didn't feel good. "I've been lax."

"Give yourself some space. You'll get up to speed again."

She hoped so. Thinking about it now, facing how little she'd really been coping, she wondered if there had been other brain damage, as well, yet to be recognized.

"Being shot in the head is the pits," she announced.

Stu looked up from the last of his pie. "What do you mean, apart from the obvious?"

"I can't be sure I've discovered all the damage yet. I seem to be letting too much slide, important things. I've been in a kind of suspended animation in some ways."

He finished his pie, evidently ruminating about what she'd said. "It takes time to heal," he said as he pushed his plate away. "Be kind to yourself. There wasn't just the shooting, but a lot of aftermath, from your epilepsy to a huge change in your life. You have a right to be stunned."

That brought a faint smile to her face. "Yeah, like fish hit with dynamite."

He smiled broadly. "Good analogy. But you'll pick up all the threads again. I'm sure of it."

She wished she could be that sure. Oh, hell, now she had something else to wonder about? She gave herself an inward shake. No point in it, except to worry, perhaps needlessly. Waste of time. If something else was wrong with her, she'd find out soon enough.

The cocoa was rich, rich enough to be a meal in itself. When she finished hers, she felt like smacking her lips. "I need to work out after this dessert."

Stu chuckled. "I feel you. Let's take the long way back."

He insisted on picking up the tab, so she left the tip. The money rested on the table. There was an old-timey feel to that, just leaving the money and not having to wait for it to be picked up, or to go to the register. Mavis was busy with another lone customer and didn't seem to notice when they left. The bell over the door probably told her all she needed to know.

Outside, the temperature had dropped further. Earlier the air had been fairly still, but now a breeze was blowing. Even with her jacket zipped and her hands stuffed into her pockets, Kerri soon began to feel cold. She definitely needed to get better winter clothing tomorrow. It couldn't wait.

But she didn't want to cut the walk short. It felt good to be striding along beside Stu, a quick walk now. Snowy, stuck to her side like the pro he was, pranced as if he was loving it.

Given his thick coat, he was probably better suited to this weather than to Florida. She hoped she'd adapt soon.

Stu took them for a spin around the courthouse square.

"What are those tables and benches for? Picnics?"

"They could be," he answered. "If you can get one. We've got a lot of the older men out here playing chess and checkers as the weather allows. And recently we started seeing a group of women playing backgammon." He pointed to the corner. "That's the sheriff's office. And up here," he added as he pointed again, "is Melinda's bakery. She generally closes around one in the afternoon, but given how early she starts baking, I'm surprised she can make it that long."

"No police cars?"

"Not usually. We get to drive them home. Never know when we might be needed. In fact, around the end of the month we'll be putting snowplows on the front of our SUVs."

That was new. "Really?"

"Really. We've got to be able to get all over this county in an emergency. Yeah, we've got regular plows, but if someone on an outlying ranch gets in trouble before the plow finds them, we have to get through, anyway."

"I never would have thought of that."

"I probably never would think of the stuff you had to deal with in severe storms or hurricanes."

There was culture shock going on here, too, she realized. Just a little. Plows on the front of the sheriffs' vehicles. She could hardly wait to tell her friends back home.

"Things are so different here."

"Well, that ought to entertain you for a while at least."

They came to the back side of the square and started walking again in the general direction of her apartment.

"I shouldn't have suggested a longer walk," he said a block later. "You're starting to look too cold."

"I'll make it," she said stoutly, burying her hands deeper into her pockets. "Better clothes tomorrow, though."

He paused and shrugged off his jacket. "Here," he said, draping it over her shoulders.

"But, Stu! You'll freeze."

"I've got a warm shirt on. Besides, this weather probably feels a lot warmer to me than it does to you. You need time to adapt."

"I don't feel right about this," she remarked as they resumed their walk. But her shoulders were already enjoying the added warmth.

"Don't worry. I'll beg if I need it back. My uniform shirt is chamois, anyway. Get one for yourself tomorrow. Meantime, let's take a shortcut back."

The shortcut soon took them down an alley. Alleys had nearly gone the way of dodos back in Florida, existing only in older neighborhoods. Real estate was too expensive to devote any of it to purposes like this. Yet they had them, and she'd been down quite a few while chasing someone. Bad types seemed to gravitate toward them.

Another walker came toward them. Bundled in a hooded jacket, he walked briskly and muttered a *howdy* as he passed them.

Oddly, Kerri felt the back of her neck prickle as he walked by. Old instincts awakening because this was an alley? The man had done nothing untoward except walk by and mumble a greeting. Maybe she'd been troubled only because seeing someone buttoned up and concealed like that in Florida might have meant trouble.

She glanced up at Stu, wondering if she should mention her nutty reaction. To her surprise he had craned his head around and was looking after the man who had passed them.

She waited until he faced front again, then asked quietly, "Something wrong?"

"Nope," he answered. "I was just trying to remember if I knew him."

"Don't tell me you know *everyone*."

He laughed quietly. "No, I don't. But I'm getting there."

And he wasn't telling her the truth. She would have bet something about the guy had set off his cop senses. Maybe, like her, it was the location.

She turned to her mind's eye, recalling the man, and realized she'd seen almost nothing of him. If she'd needed to describe his face, she couldn't have. It was the way he was wearing his hood, shadowing his face.

Well, it *was* cold out here. Stu seemed to have let it go, so she did, as well. "Need your jacket? I swear it's getting colder."

"It's the way this alley funnels the breeze. I'm fine and we'll reach the end of it shortly."

"Chamois shirts do that much?"

He laughed again. "So does getting used to the cold. Next winter you'll be running around in a sweater and vest when it's around zero. Just like the rest of us."

She couldn't imagine it but was willing to take him at his word.

At the end of the alley, they turned down another decently lighted street. The breeze gentled here, and she no longer felt its bite so acutely. "It can't be *that* cold," she remarked.

"It's not. Lower fifties, maybe."

A sudden memory clicked in her head. "I was in a doctor's office one afternoon with sinusitis. One of those walk-in clinics. Anyway, there was a group of people sitting at the other end of the waiting room. Mind you, this was February."

"Okay."

"So one of them said, 'The receptionist told us they wouldn't be busy this morning because it was too cold. Fifty-five and it's too cold.' And the group all laughed."

"Tourists?" Stu asked.

"Must have been. But I was thinking, you try living down here for a few years, and you won't have clothing for the chilly days, and fifty will be too cold to be comfortable. But you just sit there laughing and jawing and offending everyone in the front office, why don't you."

Stu snorted. "You gotta wonder about people."

"All the time." She shook her head a little. "In all fairness, I was probably a bit cranky because my head felt like a bowling ball and it hurt."

"How bad is the tourist invasion?"

"Depends on where you live. In some areas it can be overwhelming. I have a friend who lives one county over and by midseason she'd be complaining that a fifteen-minute trip to the store for a loaf of bread was taking an hour because of traffic, long checkout lines… yeah, the locals can get annoyed by things like that." That and some of the attitudes people brought with them, but she let that pass.

They turned another corner, and she saw her apartment house ahead. "You weren't kidding about a shortcut!"

"I wouldn't tease about that, not when you're in danger of turning blue."

"Hey, thanks to your jacket, I'm surviving."

Once they got to her apartment, she invited him in, suggesting that after that walk he might need a warm drink.

"Unless you have an early morning or something," she added, recalling the last time. This man was so easy to be around that she was forgetting her own reluctance to create new relationships until she was more certain of herself.

Except, even as she hesitated, she realized she was getting awfully tired of being alone most of the time when she wasn't in class or meeting with students. Maybe she needed to get over some of her hang-ups.

He answered, "Nothing on my schedule tomorrow except introducing you to Freitag's, remember? Warm clothing and all that."

"Are you really sure you have time?" She passed his jacket back to him. Comfortable though it had kept her, it was part of his uniform.

"Of course I do. I wouldn't have offered otherwise."

She smiled and moved to the kitchen. "What would you like to drink?"

Ivan scurried out of that alley as fast as he dared. Imagine running into a cop in that place. Even one who seemed to be out walking his girl. And what a place to walk her, anyway.

He feared he'd looked as out of place as they had. People around here used alleys for necessary things, like putting out the trash, or parking a car to one side, half up on the grass. Most houses were fenced with a back gate, and it sure as hell wasn't a place to take a casual stroll.

Yet there that cop had been, along with a woman and a dog. He distrusted dogs and had watched that one while keeping his head down. He'd been bitten by a mutt when he was eight, and he'd never forgotten the feeling of those jaws on his arms.

All these years later, he wasn't exactly scared of them. More like respectful. And distrustful. But the dog had been well-behaved, hadn't appeared disturbed by him, and so he'd gotten by.

Then there was the cop. He was left to simply shake his head. A strange place to walk, yes, but it had been equally strange for him to be there. Hell.

Well, enough scoping of houses for one night. Maybe he'd walk over to the park and see how many female joggers came running by. Despite things that happened in this town from time to time, most people felt pretty safe. Maybe too safe, but that made it easier on him.

On the residential streets, people still occasionally walked by, but the cooling temperatures had put a stop to the front porch confabs that went on most summer evenings. It was getting to the time of year when most people hopped in a car instead of walking. Oh, there were some hardy souls. There always were.

What he needed were the lonely, alone, or maybe too fearless. He'd find one soon.

He was sure of it.

"Are you meeting people outside the school?" Stu asked as they sat in her living room. She'd ceded the couch to him and he'd settled quite comfortably. He hadn't wanted anything to drink, however, so she nursed her green tea alone.

"Not yet." Maybe never. She'd never been solitary in her life but that had changed. She had too much to cope with right now, and not knowing when she might *blink out*, as she thought of it, kept her at home as much as possible. She put her cup on its saucer on the end table beside her.

"I could introduce you around. There are a lot of great people."

"I'm sure there are. Are you the Welcome Wagon?"

He flashed a smile. "When was the last time you heard of them? I think their name outlived them in most places. Maybe people got too busy."

"We all seem to be busy now." She leaned forward a little, tensing, wondering if she should even bring this up. "Sometimes I think that gunshot took an awful lot more from me than can show up on tests and X-rays. I'll get over it as I adjust. What about you? You said you used to be in the military police. What's that involve? I know so little about it."

He waved his hand slightly, but she was sure he tensed a bit. Just a bit. He was good at hiding whatever bugged him, she thought, but she saw him with a cop's eyes. She decided she was not the only troubled person in this room.

"A whole bunch of stuff," he said after a few moments. "Regular police duties, of course. Just like any police force you see around."

"But it went beyond that?"

"Site security, for one thing. You'd find our people

on the perimeter of most bases or posts. We protect the site, the people inside. And we do that on the battle-field, too, if that's where we are. Posts in hostile areas. We're in charge of internment, as well. You break a law, we've got the jail. You're a prisoner of war, we take care of you, too."

She nodded. "So it's a broader scope."

"Much. We also do reconnaissance and transport support—that can get kind of hairy. We don't get sent out to fight, like a field unit, but our job is always to support and protect. Except, obviously, when we're policing."

"Well, part of policing is supposed to be protection." Then she smiled faintly. "Not usually as dangerous as what you were doing, I suspect."

"It all depended on where I was stationed. I had one or two postings that were yawners. At one I was bus-ier trying to keep my own guys from smoking weed on duty than anything else." He shook his head. "You take a bunch of young people, mostly men from what I've seen, and they're always up to something unless they're too busy to get into trouble."

He tilted his head to one side, his gaze growing dis-tant. "I walked into one posting stateside and knew immediately that something wasn't right. About three months later I busted thirty of my cops. Marijuana use on duty. I might have gotten them sooner, but I wanted to squash the whole thing, not just part of it. And I had to figure out how the stuff was getting on the post. That was interesting, too, because we weren't talking small amounts for personal use. Somebody was selling larger quantities. He was the one I wanted the most, although all of them were risking the post's security."

She drew a deep breath. "That was one heckuva drug bust."

"Didn't make anyone feel proud, I can tell you."

"No? I knew some cops back in Florida who would beat their chests over a bust that big."

"It shamed the uniform," he answered simply.

She understood that as soon as he said it. It was the equivalent of a large city police force taking down that many of its own officers. Yeah, there'd be shame. But plenty of anger, too, at the people who'd brought them down. Blue was thicker than blood.

"Did people get angry with you?"

"Sure." He said it offhandedly, then rose. "Time for me to split. I didn't intend to take up your whole evening. What time tomorrow should I pick you up?"

"What's good for you?"

"Say ten?"

She rose and walked him to the door, aware that Snowy was staring intently at her. Another episode? God, she hoped not. But she sure as heck didn't want Stu to see it.

He pulled on his jacket, said good night, then closed the door behind him. She would have locked it out of habit, except she felt the insistent poke against her thigh.

"Yes, Snowy," she said wearily. "Here we go again."

She sat down in the recliner knowing she was about to lose time again. Chunks of her life, small chunks, going into oblivion as if they'd never happened.

She resented that.

## Chapter 4

Kerri was up at dawn. Not because she was a natural early bird, but because her internal clock still hadn't quite adjusted to the two-hour time change from the East Coast.

That had its benefits, of course. She was able to view the sunrise from the tiny balcony off her living room. It faced east, and somehow she'd lucked out because the only thing across the street was a huge vacant lot. She'd been told that land had been bought and razed by the development company that had built these apartments in anticipation of growth that never came. Now it was covered in tall grasses and weeds.

When she'd first arrived here, she watched kids playing on a rough baseball diamond that had probably been created by several years of running feet. Now it was nearly obscured.

When packing for this move, she'd had to squarely face her own limitations with regard to driving. She had to bring anything she wouldn't find it easy to replace on foot. That meant she'd bought a couple of molded plastic chairs with her and could now sit on that balcony with a matching small table. Nothing else could fit out there, but it allowed her to bring out her insulated mug of coffee and enjoy the pinkening eastern sky.

But it was cold. To her, anyway. She pulled on her jacket and grabbed a blanket from her bed to wrap around her. Her hands quickly grew chilly, but she ignored it.

Lifting her feet, she pressed them against the railing. Snowy settled beside her, content that he'd gotten a quick trip outside and a bowl of kibble while she made coffee. Now he was happy to soak up the morning scents.

The coffee was hot and delicious, its aroma sneaking its way out through the drinking hole in the lid and filling her own nostrils with its rich, roasted scent.

It was beautiful here, she decided as the sky slowly brightened, bringing to her view some distant mountain peaks. Truly beautiful. She really needed to lift her head from pushing at her own problems and just take the good things life was offering her.

The air smelled so clean here, and she could see the leaves starting to change color on some of the trees. For the first time she was going to enjoy a real autumn and she anticipated it with pleasure.

She recalled the story Stu had told her last night, about arresting all those people for drug use on the job.

And about his other duties as a military policeman. Stuff she'd never associated with a police organization.

Reconnaissance? Protection for transports? Perimeter protection against hostiles? Added to regular policing duties?

He must have had his hands full. She also tried to imagine policing a base full of battle-hardened soldiers, all of whom were seriously armed. She suspected that could have been dangerous at times.

She already respected him, but that tidbit last night had swelled her respect a whole lot. It also made her wonder what had brought him here. Much as she didn't like to admit it, she knew she was hiding. She was living in a crouch, persistently expecting the next blow.

She sighed and sipped more coffee, wondering how to emerge from this tunnel she had walked into. She could still work, and she was. While she was not the cop she had always wanted to be, she was on the fringes teaching criminal justice. Teaching young people who wanted to be cops in the future.

She might not be able to be trusted to answer a phone at the desk in her old station, but that didn't mean she couldn't still be useful in other ways. She really hadn't needed to run away from her former life and friends simply because she found it too painful and had come to hate the pitying looks.

Not to mention the people who felt uneasy around her because she was a reminder of the danger they all faced. She couldn't blame any of them for that. In fact, she understood it perfectly. There was a huge leap from theory to fact. Every cop knew he or she was taking risks, that they could be hurt. Until someone was, they managed to mostly ignore that part or they'd never be able to walk out onto the streets.

Then you had someone in the office who was living proof that the danger could become personal. Very personal. And all the while she received sympathy and kindness and respect—and even a medal—she knew there was hardly a cop in her station who didn't think about walking in her shoes, or worse.

She sipped more coffee, sighed and closed her eyes for a moment. All this thinking was going to cost her the sunrise. The sky flamed now, sunlight catching streamers of cloud and tinting them red and orange. In a little while she'd be seeing the incredible blue that still amazed her. There was a brightness to the color, a clarity especially in the morning before dust began to rise, that was stunning.

Something to smile about. God, she needed to come out of this shell and start meeting more people. Give herself something to think about beyond her own problems and adjustments.

Very soon she was going to have to find a way to get around here. No taxi service. Unthinkable. Did everyone here have a friend or neighbor to drive them if they couldn't do it themselves?

Still, as small as the population here was, she guessed a taxi business might not survive. Why pay money for a ride if Bob or Judith next door offered to take you where you needed to go?

She needed to make a lot of adjustments and they didn't all involve her illness.

"We've been dallying," she remarked to Snowy. He lifted his head and looked at her. "Procrastinating," she clarified as if that would help him understand. He tilted his head quizzically. She loved that look. He often seemed to understand more than she would have expected, then other times she was sure she just confused him.

The colors in the sky began to fade, and finally she rose. "Time for my breakfast, Snowy." As the blanket fell from her, the cold crept in. Yeah, she was going to spend a whole lot of money today. Clothes and more clothes.

Stu's idea about cross-country skiing had appealed to her, too. It wasn't like zipping down a slope at sixty miles an hour. If she blinked out on a fairly level surface, she doubted she could get terribly hurt. She'd give that some more thought. Plus, Snowy would warn her. He always did. Inside, the apartment was toasty and she was glad of it. She tossed the blanket over the arm of the couch, leaving her jacket on for the moment, and headed into the kitchen.

She didn't usually bring eggs home from the market. They'd be too easy to drop and break if she had a seizure. But this week she had risked it. The eggs had arrived in one piece, and the idea of a veggie-and-ham omelet appealed to her.

"Ready to cook, Snowy?"

He wagged his tail.

"I thought so." Maybe on her next grocery trip she'd get him some chicken livers. He apparently thought they were a taste of heaven.

And that was another thing. Feeding the dog. Carrying home five-pound bags of dog food might help keep her arms toned, but it interfered with other items and she had to do it too often.

Heck, she thought. Just heck. She really had to spend some time thinking about the logistics of her current situation. Being independent had once been easy. Now it required planning.

It might be early Saturday morning, but a sheriff's office never slept. Stu dropped in, risked a cup of coffee and hoped it wouldn't eat a hole in his stomach. Maude's diner, just down the street, did quite a big business selling coffee to cops. Maybe she should put that on a sign, he thought with a wry smile.

As he entered, the relief dispatcher, a middle-aged woman named Joyce, gave him a wave from her desk where she sat with a headset on and several microphones in front of her. They'd been talking about setting up a separate dispatch office, but so far they'd never been able to fund it. So the dispatcher sat to one side in the bullpen and during a busy time she could get swamped. When she did, a deputy or two would help her out.

Five other uniformed officers sat at desks, but most of them were paying attention to a prerecorded football game. When he came in, however, they soon looked toward him.

"Hey, guys," he said.

"Hey," came the chorus of replies.

He sat in one of the swivel chairs. "Got a minute?"

It sometimes amazed him how many vets filled positions in this department. The previous sheriff, Nate Tate, had started it all back after Vietnam, and as vets came home they often filled vacancies here. It made the place chummy.

Sarah Ironheart walked in, uniformed and ready to go. "Regular patrol?" she asked Joyce.

"It's been as quiet as a cemetery since I got in this morning," Joyce answered. "Regular everything, I guess."

"What's going on?" Sarah asked, joining Stu and the other guys. She'd already gotten her coffee from Maude's. Smart woman. Nearing retirement, he guessed.

"I was just going to ask a favor," Stu said. "You all hear about the new criminal justice instructor at the junior college?"

Guy Redwing nodded. "I have. Wasn't she a cop?"

"Yeah. Shot in the head when she was trying to de-escalate a domestic."

Silence filled the room, except for a creak as one of the guys leaned over to grab the remote and turn the volume off on the game.

"Bad?" Beau Beauregard asked. He was one of the older cops, too.

"Bad enough. She has some kind of epilepsy now. Apparently, no convulsions but she loses contact with the world. Enough that she can't drive. So I was wondering if we could start some kind of car pool for her before it gets much colder."

"That's a great idea," Sarah remarked. "Only problem is I live too far out to be much help without some early warning."

"I don't think we need everyone on the force," Stu answered. "Just a handful who can work in getting her to and from the college, to the grocery, stuff like that. Right now she's walking everywhere with her service dog, but you know how cold it's going to get. Just not safe." Unnecessary addendum, but he wanted to emphasize the point.

"Sure," said Guy. "There's enough of us that we can set up regular rides. Wanna pass the word along?" He looked around and everyone nodded. "I think that's a great idea, Stu. I'll be the first to volunteer. Helping anyone is good, but it's a special duty to a disabled cop."

"Let's make a list on the bulletin board," Beau suggested. "People can sign up to be available according to their duty schedules. We can keep updating as schedules change."

"Thanks." Stu drained the last of his mug, feeling the coffee hit his stomach like battery acid. He rose, preparing to take the mug to the break room and wash it. "I'm picking her up in ten minutes for a trip to Freitag's. Florida clothing isn't going to work much longer here."

"What's her name?" Guy asked.

"Kerri Addison. Nice woman."

"Remind her to get some long johns," Sarah remarked. "Somehow I think that'll be the last thing she'll think of."

Stu had to laugh. "Already on my mind."

Satisfied with the response, he washed his mug, then headed out the door. He just hoped Kerri wouldn't be annoyed that he'd taken the initiative. She struck him as a woman who wanted to be totally independent. Unfortunately, that was never going to be the case for her.

*Never* was a horrible word.

Snowy had enjoyed a share of Kerri's scrambled eggs, including some of the ham and veggies she'd thrown into it. He sat licking his chops looking mightily pleased with life.

That dog could make her grin despite almost everything. She took a quick shower, made up her bed and wondered if she should get a washer and dryer delivered. There was a small laundry room off the hallway and having to carry a basket of clothes to the coin laundry three blocks over was a nuisance. It would only become more so.

Well, one thing she could say for this: she was getting far more exercise than she ever had in a patrol car.

Stu's knock on the door came shortly after ten. When she opened it, she found him standing there with two tall foam cups.

"Hot coffee," he said, holding one of them out to her. "Hey, Snowy, how ya doing?"

Snowy gave a quiet woof. He wasn't yet wearing his vest, so he was quasi off duty and that allowed him to go to Stu as Kerri closed the door behind him. His tail wagged happily as Stu scratched around his neck.

Stu looked up. "I hope I didn't just break a rule."

"Rules are lax at home. Poor boy can't be on duty every waking moment, although so far he still pays attention to his main job no matter what."

Stu gave the dog a last pat and straightened. "How do they think he does it?"

"Detect my seizures before they happen?" She shrugged. "No one's certain. They suggested that there's some minor change in my body scents or maybe I do something minor without realizing it just before a seizure hits. One doc just shook his head and said he thought Snowy could detect a change in my brain waves." She smiled. "Kinda spooky, huh?"

"Well, if someone's going to read my mind, I'd rather it be a dog."

Her smile widened. "You have a point. Thanks for the coffee."

"You're welcome. Have you made a shopping list?" He settled on the edge of the couch.

"I was going to count on you for direction."

He nodded. "Maybe a good idea. I have some experience of winter. Do you need to go anywhere in addition to the general store?"

She hesitated, uncertain how much she wanted to impose.

"Grocery," he suggested before she could speak. "You've probably been lugging everything the hard way. Want to stock up?"

"I'd love to. Especially the dog food."

That drew a laugh out of him. "As in a forty-pound bag?"

"I could lift it, but it's unwieldy to carry, you know?"

"If that's all you had and you flung it over your shoulder, you look like you could do it. But then how do you bring anything else home?" He shook his head slightly. "How have you been doing all this?"

"The hard way. Or maybe I should say the necessary

way." She popped the tab on her coffee and sniffed the wonderful aroma. "This is a treat. I made some this morning, but this smells even better."

"Maude grinds her own beans. Of course. No half-way with her."

Then she watched him hesitate. Finally, she asked, "Something wrong?"

"Not really. In fact, not at all unless you want to get mad at me."

She tensed. She existed in a state of alert these days, as if she lived in constant anticipation of another bad event. Maybe that was normal. How would she know? But she knew what she feared, that her seizures would get worse or more frequent. Or that she'd find out the hard way that she could fall down and get hurt. Or that Snowy might miss one and fail to give her warning.

"I kinda stuck my nose in your business," Stu said. "I think you're going to discover that a whole lot of cops would be happy to provide rides whenever you might need them. Grocery, doctor, work, whatever."

Her jaw nearly dropped open. Part of her wanted to be angry that he'd advertised her problem and asked for help on her behalf, but a more sensible part recognized he might have just solved a huge problem for her. Even in a small town, life could be difficult without local buses or taxis. She'd been learning just how hard since she'd arrived here.

"You really ought to come down to the office with me," he continued. "Meet the crew. You might feel more comfortable about what I did."

Flummoxed, she didn't know how to respond.

"You don't have to if you don't want to," he said

quickly. "I just hope you're not angry with me. There's a problem that needs solving and I've never been one to sit on my hands. I can't just whistle up a taxi for you."

She regarded him wryly. "Still the military man at heart?"

"Well, yeah. I guess. You can take the bars off the shoulders but you can't take the bars out of the man, to paraphrase." Nor could you take the ugliness out of memory. Ugliness that just kept rearing its head in civilian law enforcement. Just like the feeling that something terrible lurked around the next corner.

She let go of it. "It was kind of you, Stu."

"And interfering. Don't forget that part. But I couldn't imagine how you could take care of this yourself. You haven't been here long enough to just call on a friend or neighbor. I also suspect you wouldn't feel good about it if you had to do it very often. So you'll have a whole fleet of volunteer drivers, most likely, and it's pretty hard to impose on one of many. Relax about it. Nobody has to volunteer if they don't want to."

He was right about that.

Ten minutes later they headed out, Snowy at her side. The morning had warmed some from when she had watched the sunrise, and her light jacket felt almost perfect. Cool. That was going to make selecting warm winter clothing a whole lot easier. She hoped Stu was in a mood to offer advice.

Freitag's Mercantile was on the main street, a building that reached back to early in the last century. Painted in dark green and dull red that highlighted its facade beautifully, it beckoned her to come inside.

A handful of people walked in and out, but the street was not yet busy.

Inside, the old wood flooring creaked, and the place smelled just a bit musty with age. Older women walked around, ready to help, and Kerri felt as if she'd stepped back in time.

"The charm is enough to win me over," she remarked to Stu.

"I agree. I've loved this place since I arrived. And guess what?"

"What?"

"They have an old-fashioned feature called a stockroom. If what you want isn't available out front, they'll probably be able to find it in the back. Failing that, they'll order. They don't make them like this anymore."

She had to agree with that. Snowy at her side, she followed Stu's directions toward the back.

"You'll want a windproof parka, preferably with a snorkel hood. Those hoods are great when the wind's blowing and they'll keep your face from freezing. It works by directing the heated air from your breath upward across your face. Get some good snow pants, too. And while you're at it, take a look at thermal underwear."

She looked at him. "Seriously?"

"The weather's serious. And the material these days is thin and silky to wear. It won't drive you nuts."

That was good to know. The whole idea of a union suit, as her grandfather had referred to it, had always made her want to itch.

She hadn't gone on a shopping spree in ages, and this time she had a good excuse to do it. She enjoyed herself despite the constant uneasiness about whether she might seize again. But maybe the most amazing thing of all was that Stu didn't grow impatient. For a guy, that must make him one in a million.

They returned home midafternoon with a huge quantity of clothing, a whole bunch of groceries and stomachs full with hamburgers from the diner. All in all, Kerri seemed to be in a pretty good mood. Some of the tension Stu always felt in her had fled, and she laughed easily. Good.

He insisted on bringing everything up to her apartment, except the few bags she initially carried up with Snowy at her side. "My pleasure," he said when she insisted she should help more. "Look, you want the truth?"

She hesitated, appearing to expect something bad. Well, he didn't have anything bad to say.

"It's simple," he told her. "I can run up and down those stairs faster than you can with Snowy. And I can carry a whole lot more because I don't have one hand occupied with a leash. So get upstairs and start unpacking. The exercise will do me good."

A smile appeared and she grabbed the handles of three large clothing bags before heading up the stairs.

Damn, he thought as he continued to unload the back of his truck. The temperature was dropping again. Maybe he'd gotten her to Freitag's just in time. Early winter? Who knew these days? Most people kept commenting on how the weather in these parts had changed. More snow, more rain, more cold and more heat.

Kerri was unpacking when he got upstairs with the

first load of groceries. Judging by her purchases, she'd been doing without a lot since she got here. She soon had her freezer packed full, a gallon of milk on the top shelf of the fridge and a whole bunch of cheeses and fresh veggies. Her counter now boasted two loaves of rye bread.

Snowy was interested in the forty-pound bag of dog kibble, but he didn't notice the container of frozen chicken livers. Kerri had told him what she did with them and he figured Snowy must be living in dog heaven.

She disappeared into her bedroom to start putting away clothes, and when she reemerged, she was wearing a new hunter green chamois shirt, casually untucked over her jeans. Thick socks covered her feet.

"Just in time," she said, echoing his thought. "Maybe this evening I won't need to sit under a blanket to watch television or read."

"You'll definitely be more comfortable," he agreed.

Then he saw it happen. Snowy approached her and prodded her leg with his snout. Attention getting. She looked down, sighing. "Not again," she muttered. "It's too soon."

But he noticed she headed for the recliner. "Leave any time you want," she mumbled. "I'm about to take a brief vacation. Thanks for everything, Stu."

She turned as if to back into the chair, then froze, upright.

She was gone. He could see it in the emptiness of her gaze as she stared blankly. Her left hand seemed to have a mind of its own, tapping lightly at her thigh. Other than that she didn't move an inch.

Her face hadn't gone slack but reflected something he might have identified as anger under other circumstances. Not knowing if he could do anything, he simply waited and observed in case she appeared to need help.

Snowy remained glued to her side, watchful, looking up at her. A minute passed. Then another. Just as he started to worry, she blinked.

Snowy gave a little huff and went to lie down. Kerri remained standing, but the tapping of her hand had stopped. Her eyes darted around and he got the feeling she was trying to put pieces together. After another minute or so, she sagged a bit and dropped into the chair.

"I'm sorry you had to see that," she mumbled. "I *did* go away, didn't I?"

"Not for long," he reassured her.

"How long?"

He decided he had to be truthful. "About two minutes."

"Damn. It's getting worse." She put her head down in her hand, covering her eyes. "Thanks for everything. You don't have to hang around."

He refused to be dismissed. "I don't want to be anywhere else. Want something to drink?"

"Water, please."

He rose and started toward the kitchen, but her voice stopped him. "I'm sorry, Stu."

"Sorry for what?"

She stopped hiding behind her hand and gave a little wave. "Just sorry that you had to see that."

"Sorry?" he repeated, his chest squeezing with pain

for her. "For God's sake, Kerri. You were an officer, honorably wounded in the line of duty. From where I sit you never have to apologize for your injury or the fallout from it."

"But I took up your whole day!"

"Which I enjoyed, thank you very much."

"I'm so freaking useless!" The words burst out of her, and he gathered from an earlier remark that she meant it, however unfairly.

"Stay there," he said. Yeah, like she was going to run out of her own home. "When I get the water, we'll talk a little."

She looked like that was the last thing on earth she wanted to do, but she merely nodded.

He found a glass in a cupboard, filled it halfway with water and carried it out to her. She accepted it and drank most of it.

"Thanks."

She didn't need to thank him for every little thing, but he wasn't going to get into that now. He sat across from her, propping his elbows on his knees and clasping his hands loosely.

"I'm sorry," she said again. "Overreacting."

"Frustrated," he corrected. "I know a lot of people who went from sixty to zero overnight because of a wound. They defined frustration. Quit apologizing. You haven't had much time to get used to all these changes, and you strike me as someone who doesn't like being dependent. Oh, yeah. You had a partner on the job but that's a different kind of dependence. Now you need a ride to get most places. A service dog. And you're afraid your seizures are getting worse. Are you sure of that?"

"I can't be," she said quietly. "Usually they're further apart. I had one after you left last night. Now another one, and both of them, near as I can tell, weren't brief. Is that scary? Hell, yeah."

"Do you think you need a doctor?"

"Not yet." Sighing, she leaned back and made eye contact with him for the first time since the onset of her episode. "Two instances don't make a trend."

"No," he agreed. "Maybe all the running around today made you a little more susceptible."

She nodded slowly. "It's possible, I guess. I'll just have to wait and see. I don't think there's much more they can do for me, anyway."

He had no doubt that she was going to rebuild her life to fit her new limitations because she'd been a cop. Cops didn't quit easily. But that didn't mean it wouldn't be difficult and rocky at times.

"How long have you been dealing with this?"

"A little over a year."

"Then you picked up stakes, left everything familiar behind, to start a new life? Dang, Kerri, that's brave. Tough, too. It was bad enough when you were trying to fit back into your own skin, but to change your entire life? That takes guts. Most people would be hanging on to everything familiar."

She averted her face. "Sometimes I don't feel very tough."

"I'd be surprised if you did." Time to change the subject, he decided. Give her a break from the turmoil for a bit. But he sure wanted to know more about this woman. "So, did I hear you say something about a washer and dryer when we were at lunch?"

That got her attention back, and some animation returned to her face. "Carrying bags of dirty clothes to the coin laundry isn't my favorite thing."

"I doubt it's anybody's," he said with a chuckle, hoping to leaven the moment. "Shopped around any? If you don't mind a few dents or scratches, I know just the place. Brand-new equipment but some folks want the shiny. You skip perfection and you can save a wad."

By the time Stu took his departure, Kerri had agreed to join him on an appliance hunt the next day. Before long, a washer and dryer wouldn't be an option. He suspected she wasn't the type who'd want to call someone to carry her to the coin laundry and then pick her up after a couple of hours. No, she'd try to tough it out.

Which brought him back around to all the changes she was facing and dealing with. She might have been better living in a big enough city to have public transportation, but she'd chosen this place. Maybe because of the job. Maybe because it wasn't as busy and if she stopped dead on a street here she wasn't likely to come back to an utterly changed world. Or to find herself lying on the ground because some idiot couldn't wait to get past her.

Damn, he couldn't begin to imagine all the things she had to worry about now. Then there was probably a heap of things she was worrying about that she didn't need to.

Remembering her heartfelt exclamation that she was useless now, he felt awful for her. He firmly believed that nobody was useless. Nobody. Not even that kid two streets over from his house who had muscular dystrophy so severe that he couldn't hold his head up and had be spoon-fed. Even had trouble breathing at times. But the people who took a chance on knowing him got a quick lesson in love and indomitability. As his mother said, he was always a bright star on a dark horizon.

He arrived home and pulled a frozen dinner out of his fridge. A bachelor his age really ought to get into cooking, but he hated it. After that lunch he and Kerri had shared, he wasn't feeling very hungry, anyway. The only thing he added to the meal was a big serving of broccoli. His nod to health.

The evening passed with a book and some background music, a great way to unwind. He even dozed off in his favorite chair, letting the world slip away.

Then, at five in the morning, his work cell rang. Struggling up from a dream that somehow involved Kerri, he reached for it.

"We need you," came the voice of the sheriff, Gage Dalton. "We had a brutal rape over on Conyers. All hands on deck."

## Chapter 5

Stu arrived at the scene, emotionally loaded for bear. He'd seen too much violence against women, both during his military tour and otherwise. Some of it had been cultural, but that didn't excuse it and never would. To his way of thinking, the bigger the animal, the more it had a duty to protect the smaller ones. In almost every case, the guy was bigger.

Cars with flashing lights lined the streets. An ambulance was taking off in the direction of the hospital with lights but no siren. A positive sign, he hoped.

He made his way to the edge of the cordon that closed the street and surrounded a ramshackle house. When he reached the sheriff, who swam in a sea of deputies getting their orders, he asked the inevitable question.

"How bad?"

"She's alive," Gage answered. "Apparently, she put up a struggle. Medics tell me she was beaten and cut more than once, but nothing life-threatening."

"No, just scarring and trauma."

Gage looked at him from dark eyes. "Yeah. Maybe worst of all, she's not conscious." He turned his head back to the streets. "You have logistical experience from being an MP, right?"

"In what sense?"

"I need someone to organize a sweep of this entire town. We can't risk missing anything, certainly not some guy hiding up a tree or in a bush, or any potential evidence. Details. No bare spots."

"I can do that." He knew he could. He'd had to do it before…in war zones.

"Then have at it. I'll tell Jake Madison." The chief of the city police. "You get full control while we clean this up."

Some cops were already out there, many on foot, searching the surrounding area. That would have been the first move. Dalton wanted something bigger and more careful.

Stu fully agreed. He sped back to the office, using his lights, to get a detailed map of the area. Nothing left to chance. Yeah, he'd had to do that before. And right now there wasn't a whole lot of time.

The office was already turning into a command center. The regular dispatcher, a crusty older woman named Velma, was puffing on a cigarette, despite the no-smoking sign above her head, and talking into a microphone. The younger woman next to her was also engaged, speaking through her headset. They were rallying everyone. A couple of deputies squeezed in beside them, adding to the cacophony.

Stu found the map he wanted and spread it out on a table in the conference room. His orders were going to have to be as clear and concise as possible, because they were going to be passed through the four people at the dispatch desk.

God, that had been harder than he'd expected, Ivan thought as he slipped down alleys as silently as he could and hid in the darkest of shadows until he was far enough away that even the arrival of the swirling lights of cop cars became nearly invisible.

He hadn't expected the woman to fight after she'd felt the prick of his knife. It hadn't happened the last two times. Terror had held his victims as still as mice.

Not this time.

He'd tried a few slashes of the knife to convince her he was serious, but that hadn't worked. The knife cuts, which must have been painful, only seemed to ratchet her up. He'd wound up having to punch her in the gut to shut her up, then hammer her in the head until she was dazed. Only then could he have his fun. To be honest, he'd had a lot of fun when she blacked out. Nothing to stop his wildest dreams.

Not as much fun as when they didn't resist, but what the hell. He'd gotten what he wanted and then some. Mostly. He needed to be more careful about his selection next time, but how the hell was he supposed to know when someone would resist?

Although he hadn't minded cutting her all that

much. Not at all actually. And when that hadn't shut her down, the punches had satisfied his anger.

So okay. He could deal with whatever kind of woman he came across.

He pulled the ski mask from his head and stuffed it into his jacket pocket. With both hands he smoothed down his hair. His knife had already gone into the holster that he wore inside his pants. Now all he had to do was bury his hands in his pockets to conceal any blood until he was safely home.

He'd done well, he thought. Long sleeves and thin gloves so he'd leave nothing behind, and if she scratched at him there'd be a few fibers but no skin. He didn't think she'd scratched him, but regardless, both the ski mask and the shirt were going to wind up in his backyard smithy to burn over hot coal. He had plenty of others to replace them and they were all generic, anyway.

That's what came from taking that class last year on crime and evidence. He'd learned a lot.

Aware that if anyone saw him walking around at this hour of the morning he'd be remembered, he was cautious, staying away from any lighted places, hugging the shadows, ducking beneath windows. Amazing how much darkness you could still find in a town. He made it to the outskirts without any trouble.

When at last he slipped in his own back door surrounded by a privacy fence into a house that was probably within a couple of years of being condemned, he relaxed and smiled.

He'd had a great night. An absolutely wonderful one. As he threw the knife into a bucket of bleach, he thought about the next knife he might make in his forge. It had been a while since last he'd spent any time out there making anything. The knife that sat in the bleach to cleanse it of any blood or DNA residue had been his last project. He could use it again, of course.

But maybe it would be fun to make a special knife for his next experience.

Smiling, he sat at his table and opened a quart of orange juice that was still room temperature. Yeah, he had some good plans.

As the day started to brighten, before the Sunday church crowds really got on the move, Stu had every able-bodied cop not on regular patrol assigned a search area. The town was now blanketed with officers on foot looking for any sign that might be useful, from footprints on dew-damp grass to discarded weapons or clothing. Even for freshly broken twigs in shrubs.

It was probably too much to hope the guy had left an easy-to-follow trail, but any clues would be useful. A lot of violent criminals, for example, tried to ditch their weapons rather than carry them in case they got stopped.

Eventually, one by one, the various zones began reporting in. The news was nothing.

By early afternoon, he'd ordered the search teams to switch to different portions of the grid and sent them all around again. Fresh eyes often caught things that weary eyes had missed.

By midafternoon, he was certain the perp had left nothing useful behind. With the sheriff's blessing, he began to wind it down. These people needed sleep, needed time to get ready for their next shifts, time to spend with families. They couldn't search forever.

From now on, the hunt for this rapist was going to have to rely on brainpower, instinct and experience. God, he hated it when they didn't have useful evidence, and he was as conscious as anyone that the first forty-eight hours counted, not just in murders and abductions, but in any crime.

So far, according to Gage, all they had was a jimmied back door lock.

"The day of unlocked doors in this town is going by the wayside," Gage remarked. "When I started working here, almost no one locked up unless they were going to be away for more than a couple of hours. It's not like we didn't have the usual kind of crime, burglaries and so on, but not much of it. Now major crimes are becoming more common, although most of them seem to be directed at a single individual, which leaves many folks feeling safe. Apparently not so much anymore."

"Rapes happen, unfortunately. I've never seen this large a police response to one."

Gage winced as he sat across the table from Stu. The car bomb that had killed his first family decades ago had left indelible marks on the man, from his burned cheek to his perennially aching back and a permanent limp. "I doubt you've ever worked in such a small town. We had to try. Now we're going to have to move to a task force. Ever run a task force before?"

Stu heard it coming. He didn't want the job but he couldn't turn it down, either. "Yeah. In the Army. That's a bit different, I suspect."

Gage shook his head a little. "I've got lots of vets

on this force as you know. What I haven't got is a former MP officer. I need whatever expertise you've got."

"Then you have it," Stu answered. Not that he wanted to provide it. He'd seen lots of crimes, lots of terrorism, lots of victims both military and civilian. He couldn't have begun to say why rape bothered him so much. Just the mere idea of it set his hackles up and filled him with a deep disgust. Maybe because it was such an uneven battlefield? Or because it was so personal? He didn't know.

"How's the victim doing?"

"Still concussed and in and out of consciousness. The doc says she can't be questioned yet and given the concussion she might not remember much, anyway. We'll see. I've got Connie Parish camped out at the hospital."

Good idea to have a woman there to talk to her when she could. Stu nodded approval.

Gage sighed. "Anyway, we both got dragged out of bed on a few hours of sleep and we've been at it ever since. I suggest we both head home for some sleep. We'll have to wait on the victim and on the doctor's reports and I'm sure neither of us is going to be sharp for much longer. I'll put you at the top of the call list with dispatch so neither of us has to worry about missing anything urgent."

That was the first time in a long time that Stu looked at the clock. It hit him with a jolt. He'd promised to meet Kerri at her place to go hunting for laundry appliances this afternoon and he was almost three hours late.

"Damn," he said.

Gage cocked a brow at him. "What?"

"I stood someone up and didn't even make a phone call."

"Then boost your afterburners and get out of here."

As he was half out the door, Gage called after him. "Good idea about the car pool."

Yeah, and a lot of good it would have done Kerri today.

Kerri had taken Snowy out for a long walk when she realized Stu wasn't going to show. She had no doubt that work had kept him away. Being a cop had given her a perspective on that. She knew how stuff could come up, even when you were theoretically off duty.

She had to admit, though, that she'd really been looking forward to seeing him again. Oh, well. There was Snowy to keep her company, and a brilliantly beautiful day with dry crisp air, with surprisingly warm sun to counter the chill in the gentle breeze. Perfection.

Until she realized that almost no one was out and about. She hadn't lived here that long, but she knew Sundays were usually busy at this hour with people coming from and going to church. She even walked past Maude's and the place looked emptier than usual.

It didn't require her cop sense to know that something major had happened. Before she completed her walk, she found out what it was.

And older man, leaning on a cane, was walking toward her, and said, "Good morning."

"Good morning," she answered.

"You might want to get along home," he said, stopping.

"What's wrong? And where is everyone?"

"Most are at the church. There'll be a lot of praying today. Sandra Carney, one of the teachers from the high school, got raped last night. I hear it was bad. Cops been out searching since she managed to dial 911 early this morning, and they're still at it."

"Nasty," she said. Her response was the calm, controlled one of a police officer, but inside she began to churn. She'd seen too many rapes and she'd never become deadened. Even toward the end of her police career she sometimes wept when she was alone.

"That's what I'm hearing. I got nothing to fear out here, but you're young and pretty. Most folks are holding their kids close and finding comfort in the Lord. Praying for Sandra, too. Anyway, who knows what kind of monster is running around out there. You get home and look after yourself, okay?"

"I'll do that. Thank you."

"We gotta look after each other, missy. Otherwise, what's the point of being here?"

She liked his attitude and took his advice. Not because she was frightened, but because his concern deserved her attention. That didn't keep her from going on high alert, however. She scanned every yard she passed, and for the first time began to notice there was a larger number of cops out than usual. Massive sweep, she decided. Probably looking for any kind of potential evidence anywhere. She wondered how many people had been questioned in the vicinity of the rape.

She shook her head, reminding herself she was no longer in law enforcement. Not her place to intrude.

But she felt a sudden burst of rage that she couldn't

help. Damn, that jackass with a gun had stolen everything that mattered from her.

As soon as she realized she was in danger of a self-pity party, she forced the rage down. She could still walk, she could still talk, she could still have most of a life. Too many people could no longer say that.

She'd been lucky. She needed to keep reminding herself of that. Damn lucky.

*Get out of the pit*, she warned herself, unaware that she was no longer walking, but marching back toward the apartment house. Shoulders squared, back stiffened, her strides a steady cadence.

God, she thought, the rape must have been horrific to have people flocking to church and staying off the streets. Her heart went out to the victim.

That had been a freaking mistake, Ivan thought as he attended church that morning, following his normal routine. He'd picked the wrong victim.

He didn't know this town well enough yet. He'd come here two years ago to attend the community college because the heat had started to move a little too close to home in Gillette. It hadn't reached him, but his one rape there had begun to draw attention in his general vicinity. So he'd gone off to college, promising himself he'd never do that again.

He hadn't counted on compulsion. He'd had some control of it when he first arrived here, and not until his fourth semester had it gained control of him.

But no one had even looked his direction. He'd learned how to cover himself, he decided. What's more, rape on a college campus, even a small one, didn't seem to be as big a deal. Why, he couldn't have said. The two women had simply gone home. Their stories had passed by word of mouth, but no official complaint had been made.

Of course, he hadn't hurt them. They'd probably felt it was just better to get away. This one was different.

And this time he'd been an idiot because he'd picked a well-loved teacher. How was he supposed to know that? He had a certain physical type in mind and didn't care who or what they were.

This one, however...

The church service went on a whole lot longer than usual, and Ivan had to stifle a strong urge to get away. Other than the routine readings and prayers, the homily had been all about Sandra Carney, painting a picture of a dedicated teacher who was loved by her students and everyone else who knew her.

And then the damn praying for her recovery had begun. Ivan mouthed the appropriate responses but didn't feel them at all. He'd never felt anything in church, but he went every Sunday, anyway. It always helped to be known as a God-fearing man who took his faith seriously.

In truth, he had none. The fires of hell had never worried him, and he didn't believe in heaven, either. He believed in luck and believed a person made the most of their own. What he couldn't accept was a deity reaching down into personal lives.

But he stood there, anyway, making a show of giving a damn, all the while telling himself that if this teacher had just stayed out of his way, she'd have been fine.

How she was supposed to stay out of his way, he

didn't bother to consider. She'd been like a plum ripe for plucking.

Not his fault.

Finally the endless service terminated, followed by the part he enjoyed best: coffee, doughnuts and cakes. There was usually more cheer, and Ivan liked to socialize, but this morning the conversation and voices were subdued. Eventually he couldn't stand that anymore, either. He bought a pie from the bake sale and headed back to his own hidey-hole. At least away from all those mealymouthed people so he could savor last night's victory.

It would be especially sweet with a piece of mincemeat pie.

Stu called and began to apologize but Kerri cut him off. "I heard what happened. Listen, I'm in a cooking mood so why don't you just come over for dinner? Unless you're still busy."

"I've kind of been ordered to rest up. We've been going since around 5:00 a.m. But I'd like dinner if it won't put you out."

He was on his way over, after a shower and change, and her heart lifted a little. Meeting that nice gentleman on the street had reminded her of how much she enjoyed running into people and having casual conversations. When she hadn't been riding patrol, but had walked the streets in her uniform, she'd met some great people.

She often thought cops spent too much time in their cars and not enough getting to know people by spending time in their neighborhoods. She understood that the cars were more efficient in terms of time, especially response time, but she didn't like being the "stranger in blue."

Community policing had her hearty approval.

Glancing at the time on the DVR beneath her small TV, she decided she had better get started. She couldn't invite someone to dinner and then offer them nothing.

At least she didn't have to thaw anything. Earlier she'd made eggplant parmesan, a favorite of hers, planning to cut it up into several portions for the week. Now, instead of doing that, she'd pop the entire baking dish into the oven to heat up and melt the cheese.

Stu showed up about an hour later smelling of soap and shampoo. He wore a navy blue long-sleeved shirt, jeans and cowboy boots and looked so tired that she didn't even ask, she just went to make coffee.

"How bad was it?" she asked over her shoulder as she started scooping coffee.

"I didn't have to see it, thank God, but Gage said it was brutal."

"The sheriff?"

"The same." He slid onto a bar stool facing her and rubbed his eyes. "Thanks so much for dinner. Going to the diner would have been an invitation for an inquisition, and I'm in no mood to cook tonight."

"It's not my favorite thing, but necessity and all that. I hope you like eggplant parmesan."

"Very much." He smiled slightly. "That's ambitious."

"That's easier. One more step than making a lasagna, but easier, anyway." She reached for two mugs and placed them beside the coffee maker as it dripped its way to completion. "I ran into a nice old man when I was out walking who wanted me to get home and be safe. Is that the feeling that's running around? I didn't see many people on the street but he said they were all in church."

"Pretty much everyone," he agreed. "The victim was a popular schoolteacher. People who didn't know her as that probably remember her from when she was a child here. Born and bred as they say."

"It's such a damn shame." She stood staring at the coffee as it dripped, trying to squash memories of similar cases when she was a cop. Apparently, some memories would keep regurgitating for the rest of her life. "Rape is an awful thing."

She looked over her shoulder at him. "If you'd rather go crash on the couch, the coffee will wait."

"A decent cup of coffee is what I need right now. Crashing can come later. I'm really sorry we didn't make it to the appliance place like I promised."

"If *I* don't understand, who would? No apologies. So what did you do all day?" She watched him rub his eyes, clearly weary.

"Command and control."

"What?" She wasn't sure what he meant.

"Gage wanted me to use my experience to organize the search for the perp or some evidence. We'd have been happy with either one. We didn't find anything."

"And the victim?"

"At last word she isn't able to talk very much. Serious concussion."

"God!" She closed her eyes a moment, then started

pouring coffee. She carried a mug to the bar for him. "Black?"

"Black. Thanks." He lifted it and drank as if it weren't scalding hot.

She leaned against the counter, thinking of that poor woman, hoping she'd have no aftereffects from the concussion. The rape was horrible enough and would resound through the rest of her life, but a concussion, as well?

Unconsciously, her hand strayed to the groove in the side of her head where the bullet had left its mark. She'd been trying to break herself of that gesture for months now, but still sometimes slipped and touched her scar.

Then, catching herself, she turned to the oven to preheat it. "Really, Stu, you should try to crash out."

"And leave my hostess listening to me snore? I don't think so."

He said it humorously and drew a laugh from her. "Okay, okay, suffer however you choose."

"I'm not suffering. I'm enjoying a great view through bleary eyes."

"They'd have to be bleary to think this is a great view. Guess what I enjoyed yesterday morning? I never even thought to mention it while we were out."

"What's that?" He sipped more coffee, then no doubt finding it cool enough, he drained the mug.

"More?" She grabbed the coffeepot and poured him a refill. "What I discovered was dawn on my balcony. It's a tiny balcony, but I couldn't have asked for a better view. I sat out there for the longest time wrapped in my blanket and soaked it in. I gotta say, for some reason the sky seems bigger here."

"That's Montana's turf. You must have heard of Big Sky Country."

She grinned. "I certainly have. But it seems to apply here, too. I wonder why. I mean, I used to go out and look over the Gulf of Mexico. That's a pretty big expanse. Something is different here."

"I noticed when I first arrived here, but I couldn't guess why it is."

She came around the bar and took the stool beside him. "I wish there was something I could do, Stu. I hate sitting on my hands."

He twisted his head to look at her. "You have a job."

"You know that's not what I mean."

He shook his head slowly and looked down into his mug. "I know."

But what else could he say? She hoped she hadn't made him feel pressed but it was true. She wished she could do anything to help catch the perp. She'd dealt with these crimes as a cop, and they awoke strong instincts in her. But the case, like all cases under investigation, had to be kept close to the vest. Like it or not, leaking information could give warning to the criminal.

She turned her cup slowly in her hands, not especially interested in the coffee, thinking about her situation. The need to be useful was strong in her. It always had been. But in this case there seemed to be nothing she could do.

Unless, perhaps, she wanted to get out more and start making acquaintances among the local people.

Really work at it, something she'd been avoiding because of her seizures.

She honestly didn't want to have to tell everyone she met to ignore it when she blinked out. Or explain it all. That was one of the reasons she hadn't troubled to try to build a social circle.

But if she had one, she might hear things. Things people weren't always willing to share with the police because they were unsure, or worried about revealing something that might make someone else angry with them. Just routine, everyday stuff that could sometimes wind up being useful. Cops rarely had casual conversations while in uniform, or with people who didn't know them well.

Maybe she could do that. But the thought of putting herself out there made her nervous and caused her heart to race a bit. Man, was she becoming agoraphobic because of this?

This had to stop. Now. Before she grew a new disability.

Stu had fallen silent, either because he was exhausted or because he couldn't discuss the topic she'd brought up. He didn't seem like the kind of man who'd have a problem being blunt, however.

So she decided to save him by changing the subject. "What would you suggest is the best way to start making myself a social circle? I'm apt to become an agoraphobe at this rate."

She saw his lips curve upward.

"What about your colleagues?"

With a start, she realized he was right. She'd been avoiding most contact with them, hadn't given a single one of them a chance to get to know her, or her them for that matter.

"Man, do I feel stupid," she said.

"You're not stupid. Don't say things like that."

"But you're so right. I've been avoiding that, and as soon as you said it I realized how I'd made all my friends back in Florida. At work, or in my immediate neighborhood where I ran into people at the time."

He swiveled his stool until he faced her. "I've been enjoying getting to know you, and I'm sure a lot of other people would, as well."

She hesitated, unlike her because she always used to just say things straight out, but she had changed since her shooting. Maybe that was another problem from it? But this wasn't the time to ponder that. "I just don't want to have to keep explaining my epilepsy."

"Then don't. If it happens with them, explain afterward. Word'll get around and you won't have to explain to very many. No one is perfect in this world. Why should you have to be?"

Good question. Developing an interest in her coffee at last, she began to drink it.

"Listen," he said. "I'm really sorry about shopping for the washer and dryer. I figured we could find something today and have it delivered tomorrow. But now I don't know how tied up I'll be for a few days."

"I understand, Stu. I walked in your shoes not so long ago. It's hell on the social life."

He laughed at that. "Yeah, it can be." Then he shook his head. "You know what's killing me?"

"What?" She leaned a bit toward him, listening intently.

"That some creep is out there right now probably savoring the memory of what he did last night."

That jolted her. She knew exactly what he meant and had been trying not to think about it. Her insistent need to do something to help arose partly from that, not just the damage done to a woman last night. "I've talked with them. Rapists, I mean. They're beyond disgusting. One big power trip. They don't give a damn about the damage they've caused, only that they can find a way to blame her. Or wiggle out from under. So many of them get away with it, too, because too many women don't want to testify."

He put his mug down and propped his hand on his thigh, almost as he might have if placing it on his hip. "I get that they don't want to face the guy again."

"I think it's a lot more than that. Unless a department has a very sympathetic victims unit, they're often scared off before they get anywhere near court. Questions get asked that should never get asked, questions that insinuate bad things about the victim. Guess who too often winds up feeling as if they're on trial? It's gotten better, I understand, but it's often still not great."

His frown had deepened, but he nodded as he continued to listen to her.

"You know," she went on, "I understand why you can't bring a defendant's prior bad acts into a trial. Just because he has an arrest record for a small amount of marijuana doesn't mean he was selling the stuff on the street corner. Only the facts in evidence. Don't allow the jury to think he's just a bad actor unless you can prove it."

"Right."

"So why don't they give the victim of a rape the same deference? Why should it matter if she hasn't been living like a nun for twenty years?"

He shook his head. "I know what you mean. It's gotten better, though, hasn't it? I know I never let the police under my command question a victim that way. I can't speak for what might have happened if there was a trial."

"It can be awful. I've had to testify. I was supposed to go right back on duty, but occasionally I hung around. Not pretty. Anyway, most of the cases get dismissed because the woman's frightened, or doesn't want to be publicly dragged through a gutter, or simply can't bear to face the creep again. Then there are the plea bargains because the evidence isn't quite strong enough."

She looked up abruptly. "I'm getting wound up. Sorry."

He half smiled. "I like it. You're passionate, and you worked in a victims unit. You know what you're talking about."

"Wanna hear about a truly infuriating case?"

"Sure." His gaze encouraged her.

"Eleven-year-old girl. Stepfather molesting her. She finally has enough and calls her birth father. He called us. I was sent over there on my white steed to pick the child up. Totally believable. Child services believes her and puts her in her real dad's custody. Then a couple of weeks later it comes before the DA. Down there we call them state's attorneys."

"Okay. I get the feeling this is not good."

Kerri shook her head and closed her eyes. "My blood

still boils. I believed the child. She was a wreck. The child welfare officer believed the child. The state attorney believed the child. No question. But no charge."

"Why the hell not?" he demanded.

"No physical evidence—the man hadn't gotten that far yet—and the SA believed a defense attorney could claim that it wasn't unusual for a kid to hate her stepfather and make up stories."

For the first time she heard him seriously swear.

"I know the attorney was right. How many of these cases had she handled? But that child got no justice and the man who had molested her walked away."

"Oh for the love of God." His fatigue seemed to have burned away as he pushed off the stool and started pacing her small living area. "And how many times did that little girl have to tell her story to strangers? It must have been as bad as what was actually happening."

"I don't doubt it." The story still made her heart squeeze for that child. Worse, the girl hadn't been the only one. She'd only been a cop for ten years, but she'd heard enough, seen enough, to have nightmares for many more years.

After a few minutes, Stu settled down and rejoined her at the bar.

"More coffee?" Kerri asked.

"I can get it, thanks." He rounded the end of the bar and strode into her tiny kitchen. After he'd refilled his mug he came to stand facing her across the counter.

"I understand what the prosecutor was thinking," he said. "I fully comprehend. Why put the child through more testimony, especially for a courtroom? Especially without physical evidence? He said, she said. The worst of situations. But I have to admit it infuriates me that anyone can get away with molesting a child. If I were the other parent, I'd be considering murder."

She could see it in his eyes. He was capable of killing. But of course. He'd been a soldier. As for her, she'd never had to shoot her service pistol once on duty. "As is too often the case, the girl's mother didn't believe her. Not one bit."

"Ah, hell." He banged the side of his fist on the counter, but not very hard. "The people you need most, and one of them betrays you. I've heard about it. Especially about moms."

"I suspect it's awfully hard to believe that someone you've loved and trusted has betrayed you and your child that way."

"No other reason for it." He sighed, shaking his head as if driving back ugly thoughts. "I guess the same situation just extends for women right on up. Family don't want to believe a kid about a father, stepfather, pastor, scout leader, whatever. Then when they get older, they're scared into silence. Pretty bad."

"I won't deny that."

He frowned again, the edges of his mouth tight. "But it makes me fume to think of these monsters getting away with it. Or that the guy who hurt the schoolteacher is sitting at home right now reliving his crime with pleasure. Enjoying every bit of the harm he inflicted."

Kerri had worked with a bunch of men who didn't understand the way Stu seemed to. They treated it as a crime, but too often as if it were all about sex, and as if it was no worse than a mugging. Not all men, of course, but too many, to her way of thinking. Not even sensitivity classes really helped. The many layers of rape continued to escape them.

He stared off into space for a while, then returned and came to sit beside her once again. The oven timer beeped and she went to pull out the eggplant.

"I have to let it stand for a bit before I cut it," she said. "You big hungry or little hungry?"

That returned the smile to his face. "I seem to remember a doughnut or two sometime during the morning."

"Then big hungry," she decided, glad she had an ample quantity.

He opted for a beer instead of wine to accompany the meal. "If you go to Mahoney's too often to play darts, you drink beer," he remarked. "Imagine ordering a glass of wine in that place."

She laughed quietly. "I can just see it."

"I can just hear it. There's a lot of that punch-a-shoulder kind of camaraderie."

She'd been in enough cop bars to know what he was talking about. Put a bunch of guys together... "I guess you missed your darts last night," she said. "I'm sorry. Did I keep you away from it?"

"If you did, all for the best. The way those nights go I stay up too late for the gab. Getting to bed early, considering the early wake-up call, was a good thing. Anyway, we all miss them at times because we're on duty."

There was that, she thought as she brought out her blue willow plates and served him a large portion of the eggplant. "More if you want it."

He pointed to the plate. "I always loved this pattern. My grandmother had a set but left it to my aunt. I haven't seen it since."

"Where are you from?" she asked as she put out paper napkins and silverware.

"Upstate New York. I got used to winter early in life."

That made her laugh. "Then I'm a hothouse flower?"

"I didn't say that." But he flashed a smile.

"Did something happen to your aunt? I ask because you said you haven't seen the dishes."

"I went into the Army, and when I came home I visited my mother but my aunt had moved away. She and my mother had some kind of troubles between them, but I don't know what. Mom never talked about it. And my aunt never tried to get in touch with me. Which is all right, because I never saw her much when I was a kid."

"But she got the china."

He chuckled. "She got the blue willow. My mother got the Noritake. Make of it what you will. Anyway, Mom died four years ago from cancer and *I* have the Noritake. It's in storage. What's a bachelor going to do with all that fancy and expensive china? Beats me."

"You'll have someone to share it with someday," she assured him. "Life tends to follow that path."

"And you?" he asked.

"The usual number of parents. One difference, though. Both of mine were police officers."

"Were?"

She nodded. "Grief never goes away, does it. It comes less often, but it never completely goes. They loved sailing. They set out one day for Bermuda and were never seen again. Not even any wreckage. Pirates? Maybe. Bad weather? Most likely."

"That's tough."

"For me, yeah. For them?" She shrugged one shoulder. "Mom always said it was the best way to cut free and forget everything. Especially the job. That always sounded good to me, once I started working. To be so far away it couldn't touch you anymore. I choose to think they were happy right till the end."

"That's a good way to think about it."

They continued to eat in silence. Kerri felt she might have gone too far to make him comfortable, although he *had* mentioned his mother's cancer. And glaringly unmentioned was a father. She decided she shouldn't go there.

They finished eating and Stu helped her clean up and put away the leftovers.

But at last he said, "I really need to hit the sack. It's been a long day."

"Of course you do. I was wondering how long you were going to make it."

"Lucky I didn't fall face-first into dinner. Depending on how things go, I'll try to take you out to look at the appliances some evening this week."

Then he was gone and she was alone with Snowy again. She turned on the TV for the sound more than anything and sat with Snowy beside her on the battered brown couch. He rested his head on her lap.

She couldn't stop thinking about the teacher who'd been raped, though. She wanted to be out there, helping with the investigation, trying to bring that poor woman some justice. Even if the teacher fully recovered, how was she going to be able to go home until the man was caught? Fear would dog her steps until he was behind bars.

Some fear would follow her for years if not the rest of her life, but it would be close to terror until they put hands on the guy.

And she couldn't help. Not in any way.

"It stinks, Snowy. It really stinks."

He lifted his head to look at her before returning to his comfortable position.

Yeah, it stank all right. Her every instinct was crying out to get to work, to track this bastard. To do anything useful.

But here she sat, all because of a drunken jerk with a gun. She'd been telling herself for months that she was lucky he had a lousy aim, but sometimes it didn't feel like it.

This was one of those times.

# Chapter 6

The class Kerri taught encompassed one afternoon a week. Next semester, the dean had told her, she'd have a second one. It would certainly help keep her busier.

In the meantime, come Monday morning, she was at loose ends, having prepared her lesson well in advance. Taking herself in hand, she told Snowy they were going for a long walk.

He was with her to protect her from her illness, after all, and the urge to keep hiding except when she *had* to go out had reached borderline ridiculous. People were going to see her have seizures. Staying at home so much could cause a lot of problems.

Not to mention drive her crazy. She did *not* owe the rest of her life to a drunk with a gun. He'd taken his pound of flesh from her and was entitled to no more. She was just going to have to learn to live with it.

She had thought she was doing well when she took the job here. She thought she'd mastered herself when she walked out for groceries.

Hah! She was beginning to realize she was still at the baby steps stage. She'd been fiercely independent her entire life, sometimes to the point of frustrating her mother into fury. And, being a cop, her mother didn't become infuriated easily.

She could still clearly picture her mom standing in front of her, wagging a finger and growling, "I'm not going to let you do that. It's my job to see that you make it to eighteen alive!"

Well, she'd made it. So far. She wondered what her parents would think of her withdrawal now. She was sure they'd be concerned for her, but they'd also probably push her harder than she was pushing herself.

Oh, well. She looked at the temperature on the TV and went to get one of the winter shirts she'd bought to wear over her blouse. It would probably be sufficient. If the green chamois failed to keep her warm enough, she could always turn around.

Downstairs, outside, the breeze nipped at her cheeks. It smelled so different here. Was this the scent of the coming winter or was she just missing the distant smell of salt water and the ever-present humidity? No way to tell.

Despite it being a workday, more people were out and about. She met a lot of friendly smiles and greetings, and wished she could remember how to start a conversation without saying, "I'm Officer Addison and I wonder if I could have a word with you?"

Eventually, one woman of about forty stopped. "You're the new teacher at the college, aren't you?"

Kerri smiled and nodded. "Kerri Addison."

"My son is in your criminal justice class. Or as he calls it, Crim Jus."

Kerri tensed, wondering if her seizure would come up. But the woman was still smiling warmly. "I'm Jane Jessup. Scott loves your class. He says it's great to have a teacher who's actually done the job."

"Oh! Scott. He's a great student. Nice guy, too." And he'd probably told his mother about Kerri's in-class seizure. That gave her a twinge of discomfort she refused to give in to.

"I should hope so. I'd like to think we raised him right." Jane Jessup laughed. "You never know for sure until they fly the nest."

"Well, judging by the young man I see in class, I don't think you need to worry about that. He seems to be serious about joining the police force."

"So it appears." Jane's smile faded a bit. "I worry about that. It seems so dangerous."

Kerri resisted the urge to touch the bullet scar on the side of her head. How was she supposed to answer that? "It's not the most dangerous job in the world. Be glad he doesn't want to be a lumberjack. Anyway, I can't guarantee he'll never face real danger, but if it's any consolation I never had to draw my service weapon in my whole ten years on the force. If he gets good training, he can talk a lot of people down."

Jane nodded. "You hear so much these days about SWAT being called, about officers being shot at a traffic stop."

Kerri told the truth. "Honestly, traffic stops may be the most dangerous part of the job. Personally, I think we overuse SWAT, and there's rarely an OK Corral situation. I'm not going to say it never happens because it can. But most cops make it to retirement in one piece."

Jane's smile broadened again. "That's good to hear." Then her smiled vanished and her expression grew grave. "Oh, say, you heard about what happened Saturday night?"

"The schoolteacher. Yes, I have. Do you have any idea how she's getting on?"

Jane shook her head. "No word yet. It's especially sad because she was one of Scott's favorites in high school. In my book, anyone who could make Scott look forward to a math class has to be stellar."

Kerri forced a laugh, wanting to lighten the moment. "Nobody's favorite subject."

"Not many of us, anyway." Jane grimaced. "I hated it. Probably the only reason I'm not an astronaut."

Kerri grinned again, enjoying Jane's sense of humor.

Jane pulled out her cell phone. "Let me have your number. I'll give you a call sometime and we can meet for coffee. I have a couple of other friends I think you'd like, too. I'm warning you, you can't hang around this town without making friends."

As Jane walked away, Kerri looked down at Snowy. "Maybe we should keep our eyes open. I doubt we'll see anything the sheriff's people overlooked but you never know."

At least it gave her a small sense of purpose.

In his ramshackle house not too far from the college campus, but far enough away to be private, Ivan began to plot his next attack.

It almost shocked Ivan how fast the urge was com-

ing over him again. It hadn't been this way last year.
Something had changed. One of the things that was
different was the whispers he sometimes heard inside
his head, pushing him. He dismissed them.

But the compulsion was there, and he reminded
himself that it would take time to uncover his next target. He was also nervously aware that if he acted again
any time soon, the police were bound to investigate
more intensively. They wouldn't be able to brush off
two rapes as independent.

He cussed himself out, but the recent encounter had
simply whetted his appetite for more. He could skip
town any time he wanted to, clearing out before he
could be discovered.

In the meantime, he broke one of his own rules
about keeping a low profile. Maybe it was time to break
out his bike and be seen riding around town. Become
familiar.

Maybe a higher profile wouldn't be so bad. It might
even provide cover.

And maybe riding his bike would calm his urge a
bit. It was too soon to act again. Too damn soon.


Stu didn't quite catch up on his sleep, but close
enough. The department had wound down a bit, mostly
to regular duties with some extra help to continue pur-
suing evidence of the crime.

So far the techs, of which they had a few, had little to offer. The guy obviously had some sense. They
couldn't find any fresh prints that didn't belong to the
teacher. At least so far. They found a few fibers they
were having checked out, especially ones that had been

on her and on the bed. The blood, it appeared, was all hers. No hair that wasn't bleached blond with dark roots, but they were checking it, anyway.

In short, a scene that was probably too clean to offer much. Now they awaited word about her wounds from the hospital and waited for her to fully awaken from her concussion. The doctors said she was borderline comatose, but when she woke she was extremely confused about everything. They waited in hope that she might remember something useful, although with that concussion she might not remember much at all. Which might be a blessing for her, but not helpful to them.

Sighing, he rubbed his eyes and looked at the clock. Time to call it quits. He hated it when investigations seemed to have no leads, and so far this one had none.

Then he remembered his promise to Kerri. Leaning forward, he reached for the landline and punched in a number.

He made a call to the lumberyard, which had followed the national trend and added home improvement to its line of products. Les even had a separate section for the dinged and scratched appliances. It annoyed Les no end when merchandise had been roughly handled. He might have been able to make a claim for it, but with time he'd found a market that amply covered costs. All he had to do was check every piece out to make sure it operated properly. He even included a warranty.

He'd do well by Kerri. He also said he'd be there until after eight if they wanted to come by. That was one of the nice things about a small town with a tight customer base. Cheating would put you out of business. Adding an extra bit of service only bought you loyalty.

"Yeah, I've got a couple of sets of washers and dryers," Les assured him. "At least a couple, all good brands. They'll fit in those apartments. I've delivered them before."

When he called Kerri, she was grateful and eager. Now he had plans for the evening, which meant he could get out of the mire of thinking about this rape. He'd even told her he'd buy her dinner after she had a look.

"I'm not going to be picky," she'd promised him.

"With Les you don't have to be."

Relieved, he went by his house to change into civvies, noting the changing weather yet again. Too cold too soon. He wondered if that was an omen for the coming winter.

Oh, well. He wondered how many times he'd have to clear the same few inches of snow. A lot or little didn't seem to matter much. When it was dry enough, even a few inches of snow kept blowing around making daily shoveling necessary.

Because of a back injury he'd suffered in Afghanistan, shoveling was out for him. So he had a nice little snowblower, and he often helped his neighbors out, too. Although one crotchety guy kept insisting it was good exercise. Yeah, unless the seventy-year-old dropped with a heart attack. The guy's wife kept nagging him to either let Stu help or get his own snowblower, but Haney was truly set in his ways. Or implacably stubborn.

Kerri seemed happy to see him when she opened her

door, and even Snowy offered a tail wag and a doggy grin, although he remained close to Kerri.

"This'll be fun," she said, looking honestly happy about it. "I took a walk earlier and kept thinking about how nice it would be not to have to walk to the laundry."

"Well, grab your jacket and let's go. It's getting colder out there. I'm wondering if we're heading into a really bad winter."

"Of course we are," she answered pertly. "I'm here. It's going to teach me a lesson."

Man, when she let go, she had a good sense of humor. Snowy was certainly ready to go. He took a minute out front to attend to his business, and Kerri quickly cleaned up after him, tossing it in the nearby trash bin.

"Did you have a nice walk?" he asked as they drove across town to the lumberyard.

"Very nice. I met Jane Jessup. You know her?"

"Kinda."

"She was nice. Her son, Scott, is in my class and she's nervous about him wanting to go into law enforcement. I assured her most of us make it to retirement in one piece."

"True." He glanced at her as they stopped at the town's one traffic light. "Must have been difficult for you to say."

She shrugged with a small shake of her head. "No reason worrying about it if that's what he wants to do. You get into a tense situation or standoff and you deal with it. Part of the job. What happened to me doesn't happen to many despite public perceptions."

Still levelheaded about the job even after what she had suffered. He was impressed.

She spoke again. "What you did, however, must have been a whole lot more dangerous."

"As an MP? Yeah, at times. Try dealing with a bunch of heavily armed people who have become tightly bonded in the face of death and danger. They'll protect each other no matter what."

"Sounds familiar," she replied.

"I'm sure it does."

Les was waiting for them in the front of the store. Being a Monday night, things were quieting down. Come Friday evening, this place would start buzzing with people who had home projects.

Les, a lean man with a lovingly tended gray mustache, shook hands with Kerri as Stu introduced them. "Have I got some deals for you," he said with a wink. "Okay, I've got deals but I'm no used car salesman. Come on to the back."

Beneath a sign announcing Dings, Dents and 30% Off there was an array of appliances, from refrigerators to stoves and even microwaves.

"I've always loved the smell of lumber," Kerri confided to the two men. "When I was growing up, it permeated the house because my dad always had a project in the works."

Les flashed her a smile. "It's like perfume. Wonderful. Except the years have kind of stifled my nose. I notice a whiff when I first arrive in the morning, then nothing. When I was younger, a deep sniff would do it."

The purchase didn't take long. There were three sets to choose from, all recognized brand names. Les asked a few questions, then suggested the model with the biggest capacity. "You don't have to, of course, but when it comes to washing heavy winter gear or a good-size comforter, the larger capacity will do it. Smaller models not so much. Plus, you can adjust the water level to the load size." Then he shrugged. "Of course, that's a feature on all these models. And you're just one person, right? For regular laundry you might want something smaller."

At home—well, back in Florida—she'd had a smaller capacity machine, which was just fine for most things. Her uniforms, her shorts and tees. But then there were jeans and she'd probably wear a lot of them in a colder climate. And she hadn't really thought there'd be much of a decision? Hah! A washer was a washer, right? Last time she'd shopped, she'd gone by price and nothing else except that she recognized the brand name.

Les clearly sensed her hesitation. "How about I leave you alone for ten or fifteen minutes? You can look through the manuals and see what you think."

He wandered off and she was left staring at a bank of white machines. "I said this wouldn't take long," she remarked. "That I wouldn't be picky."

"It takes as long as it takes," Stu answered. "Just keep in mind that you don't have to buy a matched set. If you don't want the large capacity, there's always the coin laundry for the biggest things."

She shook her head. "You just persuaded me. If I never have to go to the coin laundry again, I'll be happy. Sitting there for a couple of hours, even with a good book or my laptop, isn't my idea of fun. And the place is usually deserted." She looked at him. "Isn't that odd?"

"Depends on when you go, I suppose."

"Yeah." She *did* have more free time than most people.

An hour later, having agreed to take delivery of the set the next morning around nine, Stu and Kerri sat once again in Maude's diner. That, too, was awfully quiet. Just one man sitting in the farthest corner, nursing a hot drink. Maude stomped over to them, slamming down two coffee cups, and eyed Kerri. "We *do* have salads. Good ones."

Kerri blinked, astonished by this. "I saw them on the menu."

Maude nodded. "These men will eat fried food every day of the week, but most women like to be more careful some of the time. Just wanted you to know I can serve a Cobb salad or some pretty good cod. Gotta get the fish frozen, sadly, but I have it."

"Oh, I love cod," Kerri said, smiling at the gorgon.

"I can make it poached or fried."

"Dang," said Stu. "Where have you been hiding these talents?"

Maude scowled. "On the back side of the menu. I got a bunch of them. Not my fault nobody turns the damn thing over." She eyed Kerri again. "If you're in the mood, let me have some fun."

At that Kerri laughed. "Cod, it is. Fried, please. And is there any way I could have a small Cobb salad?"

"Take a big one," Maude advised. "It'll make a good lunch tomorrow."

"Make that two," Stu said.

Maude's scowl deepened. "Men. Think they'll live on that."

Kerri had to cover her mouth to keep from laughing again. Who ordered all the fried steak and burgers here?

"Whatever you think I need, Maude. Never ate a thing from your menu and regretted it."

Maude nodded. "As it should be."

"Oh my God," Kerri said, her quiet voice trembling with laughter after Maude disappeared into the kitchen.

"She's something else. I'll grant you that. Folks say she's mellowed a lot. Maybe so. After only four years, I couldn't judge, but she's tough."

"Maybe that's necessary running a small operation like this."

"I don't know, but I've heard people got used to having their meals served with a slam and a glare. Then she had a heart attack. Maybe that changes you."

Lots of things could change you forever, Kerri thought, lifting her coffee cup.

"You met Jane Jessup today, right? Anyone else?"

"A few people, briefly. Everyone's talking about what happened. I started to feel warned. I can't explain it better than that."

He nodded slowly. "Making sure you didn't miss it, maybe? Hinting that you might need to take precautions? That sounds like a lot of people around here."

"The hardest part for me was not being able to question anyone." She pursed her lips and for just an instant allowed the pain of losing her career to pinch her.

"Imagine how those people would have reacted to that. They don't even know me."

A badge would have helped, she thought. At least she wouldn't have sounded like a ghoul.

Dinner arrived, including a burger patty for Snowy. The Cobb salad was huge, more than a lunch for tomorrow, and the fish had been fried in a light, fluffy batter. It nearly melted in her mouth. Despite her comments, Maude had brought Stu the same.

"This is fantastic," Stu remarked. Then he looked across the table at Kerri. "You're having a hard time not being able to help out, aren't you?"

"Well, yeah. Hardly surprising." She stabbed her fork into the salad and came up with lettuce, turkey and a bit of bacon. "I suppose I should stir the dressing around."

"I think I see guacamole, too. I never connected Maude with that. Speaking of which, I heard today that we might have a Tex-Mex restaurant opening soon. Brave people in a town like this."

"Why?"

"Because we're so small. Maude is an institution. That's how she makes it. The truck stop caters mostly to out-of-towners who find it an easy place to park their rigs. But another restaurant? Even the pizza place at the edge of town is hanging by a thread, I hear."

He was trying to distract her, she realized. She appreciated it. She just wished the distraction would continue when she got home alone.

"Well, I love Tex-Mex," she said. "It wasn't always easy to find the good stuff, not when I was a kid, but these days we have lots of good Tex-Mex places. Then there's Cuban. If you ever get to Florida, remind me to tell you where to buy the best Cuban sandwiches. They don't taste the same anywhere else, from what I've heard. Partly because they don't make real Cuban bread, and partly because it requires mojo marinated pork. Anyway, every so often you stumble on the real thing. I'm going to miss those."

"I can't believe I'm eating and you're making my mouth water."

She was grateful for the laughter that bubbled up inside her. "They are to die for." Then she hesitated. "Is there anything at all I can do to help with the case?"

He paused with a piece of fish on his fork. "This is flaky fish. Kerri, I don't know. You were a cop. You know how close to the vest we have to play it." He shook his head. "Listen. Just listen to what people say to you. Maybe because you're *not* a cop, someone will reveal something that doesn't seem important enough to mention to us, but it could be useful."

"I can do that." Well, that made her feel a bit better.

"You could just relax, though."

Her headshake was a definite *no*. "It's not in my DNA."

"Somehow I was afraid you'd say that."

On his way home, Stu pondered both the rape case and Kerri's reaction. Both had him on edge now. The rape case for obvious reasons, but Kerri for another.

Maybe she'd lost her cop face since she'd been shot, but he suspected she had no idea how much her expression gave away. She might have been calm and considered in her responses but her face was telling a different story. She was desperate to be involved again. She wanted a pathway back to the work she had loved.

Impossible, though. Even he could figure out that a cop who became essentially unconscious for a minute or two at a time couldn't be on the streets, couldn't interview witnesses, hell, couldn't even take phone calls. It was a tragedy for her, but she'd never forgive herself if she messed up.

But the push was there, and he had the strongest feeling she was going to try to get involved somehow.

And that really disturbed him. She had no backup, no official support, and if she did something to draw this creep's attention, she might get seriously hurt.

He had to find a way to prevent that. Either that or hope the guy had left town and was hunting elsewhere.

Because if there was one thing true about people who raped strangers, it was that they'd do it again.

He had to figure out something. He didn't want her to be miserable or feeling useless. He wanted her to feel good about herself again.

Because if there was one thing he'd picked up about her between the lines, it was that she didn't feel very good about Kerri Addison. She was coping but she'd lost a spark, a part of herself. Hadn't she said one night when they were together that she felt useless?

He wouldn't have described her that way at all, but how he described her and how she felt were two very different things.

As it turned out, the rapist hadn't left town. Two nights later, while Sandra Carney still hadn't recovered enough to be released from the hospital, another rape occurred.

May Broadwyn had been restless and unable to see sleep. After several hours of struggling with a mattress that felt like it was full of gravel rather than padding, and a pillow that had grown some hard lumps, she decided to go for a run.

She'd loved running since early childhood, and during high school and college she'd joined the track teams. There was nothing like a good run to make her feel better about almost anything, and she had no doubt running would tire her out enough to fall asleep.

Despite it being the wee hours of the morning, she pulled on her running clothes, topped her head with a knit cap against the night's chill and set out to run across town.

Accompanied by only the slap-slap of her feet on pavement, she drank in the town's silence. People slept all around her and she wished she could join them in slumber. She *did* have to go to work in the morning, like every other weekday morning, and she'd like to be able to do it with her eyes open. Working as a clerk at the courthouse required a lot of attention to detail and a foggy mind wouldn't help her.

Only one car passed her on the street, a city police car. The cop waved and she waved back. She couldn't see him in the darkness, but she was sure it was someone she knew. One of the perks of her job.

After reaching the far side of town, she paused to bend and stretch a little, taking a brief breather but not one long enough to allow any muscle to stiffen in the deepening cold.

Then she set out again, deciding to take a detour through the city park on the way home. It wouldn't be much out of her way, but the dappled shadows and the fresh scents of loam and changing leaves always pleased her.

That decision would change her forever.

There was little moon to guide her, just a sliver to drip silver light through the trees. The paths were lit by small solar lamps at ankle level and their glow hardly disturbed the experience.

If she hadn't been so absorbed by the rhythm of her run and the familiar sound of her feet pounding it out, she might have heard something else. She didn't until it was too late.

Ivan was out prowling for his next target, more interested in the backyards of houses than anything else…until he caught sight of the woman jogging. She couldn't have made him any happier when she turned into the park.

Out by herself in the middle of the night. Heading into the deserted park with no one else apt to come upon her. It wasn't the largest park, but big enough for his needs.

She must be strong and healthy to judge by the way she was running. That meant she'd probably fight, too, and the idea only whetted his appetite.

Feeling the leg of his pants, he found the knife in its sheath. Yeah, he could do this now and take home another delicious memory.

He spared a moment's thought for how to come at her. There weren't a lot of choices, but he could run, too. She wasn't pushing it so he wouldn't be caught up in a race. He adjusted his ski mask and made sure the Velcro around his gloves was tight. He left his jacket in a tree so it wouldn't get in his way. The cold air that wiped out the jacket's warmth only excited him more. She'd feel so warm around him.

Swing around to the left, he decided. Because the pathways were limited, he'd have no trouble circling her because she wouldn't go some other direction. Then he'd come after her from the side, his footsteps silenced by the soft earth and the breeze that was beginning to rustle the drying leaves overhead.

Liking his plan, he put it into action.

Edith Jasper found her around five-thirty in the morning. Edith was out walking her harlequin Great Dane, Bailey, as she did every morning. Edith liked to say that Bailey was going to keep her alive forever because he loved his long walks. That meant Edith did a lot of walks, as well, leaving her in pretty good shape for seventysomething. She'd never tell anyone what that something was. Heck, she rarely admitted to the seventy, either. She got a kick out of it when people pegged her in her sixties.

It was still dark out, a good time for Bailey to nose around and get whatever news he could from the markings of other dogs. No running, yelling, laughing little kids to keep distracting him. No, this was Bailey's time.

Except this morning he started getting restless soon after they entered the park. Instead of nosing around bushes and the legs of benches, he wanted to hurry. He raised his head high and she watched him draw in scents, huffing occasionally to clear his sensitive nose only to sniff again.

Then he became agitated. Bailey never pulled on his

leash. Well trained and, Edith suspected, aware that she was getting up there in years, he always remained happily at her side.

But this morning he was clearly not happy and tugged on the leash. Hard. She was afraid he might pull free.

"Bailey!"

For a second, just a second, he gave her a hangdog look almost as if to say, "I'm sorry. I'm being bad. But…"

She caught the "but" when he started tugging her again.

"Dang it, dog!" Impatience was clear in her words, but he didn't pay attention. It was unusual for him not to listen to her. At times she thought he was more sensitive to the tone of her voice than any human would be.

Realizing she was going to lose this battle, and scolding Bailey wasn't going to do a bit of good, she quickened her pace as much as she dared. The ankle-high lighting along the path gave her some confidence but she was unfortunately at a stage of life when she feared falling more than almost anything. Yeah, she'd had tests for osteoporosis that said she was okay, but she also remembered her mother breaking her hip and winding up in a wheelchair.

On the pathway, though, with good walking shoes, she should be fine. She hoped.

But then Bailey whimpered, the saddest sound she had ever heard him make. Her heart quickened as she wondered if her beloved dog was getting sick. She couldn't bear the thought.

He soon disabused her of the notion. He pulled away from the path into the thin woods to the side.

"Bailey, no!"

But Bailey had more than a few pounds on her and much more strength. Whatever he was after, he wasn't going to stop.

Feeling as if her arm might pop out of the socket, she followed. What the hell else could she do?

They hadn't gone more than a hundred feet from the path, into a small copse of trees, when she saw the pile of rags. She also heard a moan.

Suddenly very glad that there wasn't more light, she approached cautiously, noting the way Bailey suddenly seemed to be standing guard over the rags. Dark stains, wet stains, clothes in disarray, the pale, almost invisible face of a woman. She stirred and moaned again.

Edith reached for the phone in her pocket, nearly dropping it as her hand shook wildly—911 was on her speed dial, and she pressed the button.

"What is your emergency?"

Words began to tumble out of Edith.

# Chapter 7

Stu's phone rang just as he was stepping out of the shower. He wrapped a towel around his waist and went to grab it from the bedside dresser. "Canady."

"Have you heard?" Kerri asked him. "There's been another rape, this one at the city park."

What the...? "Kerri, where are you? How'd you hear?" He was already pulling a fresh uniform out of his closet, tearing away the dry cleaner's bag with his free hand.

"City park. I was out walking Snowy. Right now I'm sitting with a witness, Edith Jasper. She found the woman."

Sitting with a witness? Stu's heart slammed. Who was letting Kerri into this? And why? The mere fact that she was talking to a witness might get her into trouble with the department or prosecutor.

"I'll be right there," he said, tucking the phone against his shoulder.

"No rush. Edith just didn't want to sit alone until they're ready to take her statement. That's all I'm doing, Stu. Anyway, I have a class today. You said you'd stop by, and I just wanted you to know it isn't necessary, before I forget and tell you too late. You're going to be too busy."

Yeah, he was going to be busy, and what he'd feared was coming to pass. That woman was working herself into the middle of this. He really needed to rack his brain for a way to get her what she needed without getting herself into trouble.

Although given her cop's instincts and impulses he figured he might be trying to stop a freight train. She'd been saying that she felt useless, that she wanted to help in some way.

Unfortunately, that could cause problems all the way down the line. She'd probably avoid most of them given her experience, but appearances mattered, too.

A former cop talking to a witness before the witness was formally interviewed. Oh, man, a defense attorney could make hay out of that, claiming that Kerri had enough experience to know how to lead a witness. Why the hell were the officers allowing it?

He jumped into his heavyweight winter uniform in record time, pulled on his gun belt and hurried to his car.

He arrived at the park just as the first gray light of dawn was filling the day. Clouds hung heavily overhead like a looming threat.

A large area had been cordoned off, the street was

full of cars with their light bars flashing garishly and officers appeared to be everywhere, both city and county.

Kerri sat on a bench with Edith Jasper, a woman who was well-known around town, partly because of her gigantic black-and-white dog, a dog who dwarfed Edith and must have seriously outweighed her. If anyone hadn't known her from encounters over the long years she'd lived here, they'd certainly know her from that dog.

Kerri sat beside her, Snowy at her feet. The dogs seemed to be getting along, as did the two women. He slipped under the cordon, greeting other uniforms as he went, trying not to disturb them as they worked and conferred. He'd get the story soon enough.

When he reached the bench, he looked down at Kerri and Edith. The Great Dane raised his head, sniffed at Stu's pant leg, then returned to rest.

"Not discussing the case, are you?" he asked. He tried to sound pleasant but was afraid his tone sounded official.

"Of course not," said Kerri. "I know better."

"There's nothing to discuss, anyway," Edith said. "I just saw her and called for you guys. Then they put me here to wait and I was shaking so bad. Kerri was kind enough to sit with me. Stu, I've never seen anything so terrifying in my life. And if I'm not allowed to say that to anyone I want to, too damn bad."

Well, Stu couldn't exactly argue with that. "It's just—"

"Appearances," Kerri interrupted. "I understand. But Edith was sitting here alone and so obviously distressed, what was I supposed to do? Just walk by? No one had any time for her just then."

"You were just walking by?" This was a long way from her apartment house.

"Well, it was still dark and I saw all the lights." She shrugged. "I'm as curious as any other person. Say, I wanted to get Edith some tea or coffee to warm her up, but I didn't want to leave her alone."

"I can take a hint," Stu answered, finally able to smile slightly. The uniforms around him seemed to have everything under control and no one was demanding his help. "Do you want to run over to Maude's?" Then he paused. "Stupid question. I've got a car, you haven't. What'll it be, ladies?"

He left with quite an order. A dozen or so coffees for the working officers, a latte for Kerri and a large green tea for Edith. He hoped Maude was ready to start.

It turned out Maude had opened early, expecting an influx. She'd apparently noticed the police activity, too. She already had several pots brewing and started the tea immediately when he placed the order.

"Might take a bit," she answered. "Or maybe if you want to go with medium coffees I can fill all those cups right up. I'll get Kerri's latte going, too."

How had she known it was for Kerri? he wondered vaguely. But that was far from the most important thing on his mind.

"Another rape?" Maude asked, and she started filling cups, then pulled some shots from her latte maker. Everything went into insulated cups.

"So I heard. I'm not involved yet."

"And you wouldn't tell me, anyway," Maude grumped. "I need a better source."

"If you find one, you'd better let us know. Talking out of school can ruin a case."

"So you people keep telling me. Everyone in this town knows I'm no gossip."

"You're right, but we still can't talk."

"Heard the ambulance scream its way toward the hospital. I hope she's not too injured." Then Maude stopped for a second. "Of course she's injured. This will follow her through life."

"Personal experience?" Stu asked as the cups began to go into cardboard trays and then into cardboard boxes to hold them steady. He didn't expect an answer, but he got one that shocked him to his very core.

"My father," Maude answered shortly. "And don't be telling no one."

That might explain a whole hell of a lot about Maude, Stu thought as he started carrying boxes of coffee to his vehicle. A whole hell of a lot. He felt sickened for her, sickened for the newest victim and ready to chew nails.

"What the hell is wrong with some men?" he asked himself as he backed out of the parking place.

Kerri really had been just sitting with Edith. The poor woman had been shivering like a leaf in the wind when Kerri saw her. Not one of the cops had tried to prevent her from crossing the cordon to sit with her.

She knew what Stu meant, though. She'd been very careful not to question Edith or talk about what she'd seen, but her mere presence here could be misinterpreted. Oh, well. She could explain her actions in court if it ever became necessary. Edith needed some support right now and Kerri was trained to provide it.

"How are you doing?" Kerri asked her.

"Better." Edith shook her head. "I know there's always been evil in the world but I don't think it was ever as bad as it's been getting around here the past few years. Maybe I was wearing blinders."

"This hardly seems to be a hotbed of criminal activity, and I've only been here for two months."

Edith gave her a wan smile. "The past always looks better somehow. Like we tend to remember good things, not awful things. Or maybe I'm just lucky."

Kerri couldn't answer that. She had enough bad memories that she was sure would never vanish. But she'd been more exposed to the ugly side of life than most people. Maybe it had warped her.

Stu returned with the coffee and tea and began handing it out, first the tea to Edith and the latte to Kerri. Then he passed around among the other officers where cups were gratefully received.

"Don't take those cups into the woods," said a crime scene tech who was covered head to toe in a white Tyvek suit and foot covers. He was carrying a bag with a strap over his shoulder. "Contamination."

"Like we need to be reminded," one of the cops answered, and the others laughed.

Then Stu handed him a cup. "Got plenty."

Well, that halted the man in his tracks. Then he shook his head. "Thanks, but I have to get back there while evidence is still fresh."

Stu put the empty boxes into his vehicle, figuring he'd take them back to Maude for reuse. Then he looked around, saw that things seemed to be settling and made his way over to the scene commander.

"Sexual assault?" he asked.

Jake Madison, the city's chief of police, nodded. "This time a jogger. She's not able to talk yet, but Ms. Jasper found her around five-thirty. We figure from the way it looks that the vic must have been out here for over two hours. At least the perp didn't cut any vital arteries."

"Near as we can tell she was out here jogging," Jake continued. "Weird time, but people have done more unusual things. Cut and beaten and currently unconscious."

"I hope she isn't concussed."

"Well, we asked Sarah Ironheart to follow her to the hospital. When she can talk, Sarah will question her. In the meantime…" Jake waved a hand toward the park. Near the far side, Stu could see that flood lamps were lighting the scene.

"I hope we get some good evidence."

"That would be nice." Jake put his hands on his hips. "It's only been five days since the last one. Just five freaking days."

"People aren't going to ignore this."

"Nope."

"We sure as hell can't go out there and pretend life is normal right now." Not that anyone would believe it after this. Stu shook his head, anticipating the public reaction. It could become a problem on so many different levels. For just one thing, everyone around here owned a firearm. What if they decided to start patrolling the streets like vigilantes? Or what if they got nervous and shot some innocent person? Women were going to be afraid to go out alone, and God knew what they'd do if they lived alone.

If every cop stayed on patrol all the time, the place would still leak like a sieve for the bad guy. He would find a way.

"Need me for anything?" he asked Jake.

"Not just now. Maybe after the techs wrap up. I'm gonna want to go over the scene with a fine-tooth comb. Again."

Stu understood. The light was still too dim for good vision. The techs would use every tool at their disposal but if they hadn't widened the search far enough, or hadn't looked up far enough, or...

"Hell," he muttered. "We *have* to find something. It's just going to get worse."

"That's what I'm afraid of."

With that, Stu walked over to Kerri and Edith.

Ivan knew he shouldn't go back to the scene. Too much interest on his part might draw attention to him. Still, curiosity plagued him. Eventually he decided that he could just walk by safely. Why shouldn't he get a glimpse of the excitement he had caused?

That appealed to him, as well. Not as much as taking the woman had, but he couldn't quite bring himself to stay home and miss all the people he'd affected. He loved to watch cops work. One of these days, he was going to be one, although not around here. Even so, he didn't go after the women because he wanted to watch police work.

No, the attacks were first and foremost to him. Watching the scene crawl with police was just an added way to enjoy what he'd done. Ripples spreading outward, he thought with satisfaction.

As he walked by, he saw the woman with the Great Dane seated on a bench within the cordon. Beside her sat that teacher from the community college, the one with the service dog. Kerri something-or-other. What was she doing there?

He walked a little slower, listening to people talk. Crime scenes always gathered a crowd of curiosity seekers, and this was no different. Everyone was hoping to learn something.

Before long he'd heard the Great Dane had found his victim. Okay. That old lady wasn't a threat of any kind. But the college instructor beside her? He quickened his pace again, trying to ease past the small throng as if he had somewhere to go.

Kerri. Hey, didn't she teach that criminal justice class? Didn't someone say she was an ex-cop? His stomach soured a bit, because it was unusual for anyone not involved to be allowed inside a police cordon. Special privileges? Or did they hope she knew something?

Well, she couldn't, Ivan assured himself. He'd left a clean scene behind, clean as always. He hadn't even forgotten to reclaim his jacket. He was sure the only thing they'd find was his boot prints, softened by leaves, and those work boots were of a kind worn by most men around here. Nothing identifiable.

He kept walking, and a block later had to restrain himself from whistling because he felt happy.

There'd be more, he assured himself, although he should wait a little while. Yes, there'd be more.

The memory of last night filled him with a surging sense of his own power. That was the thing. Those women had been utterly at his mercy.

And he was merciless.

When Stu reached Edith and Kerri, he patted the Great Dane, avoided touching Kerri's service dog as was necessary when the animal was on duty, then squatted in front of them.

"Are you going to be all right for a little while longer, Edith?" he asked. "It might be a while before we can take you to the station to get your statement." Never had he seen Edith look so frail.

"I'll be fine," Edith said stoutly. Her hand trembled a bit as it held the cup full of tea. "That poor woman. I've never seen such a sight and hope I never do again. I don't know how you police stand it."

"It's not easy," Kerri said.

"If it ever gets easy," Stu remarked, "it would be time to quit."

Edith nodded slowly. "I was just walking Bailey and…" She trailed off. "I'm not supposed to talk about it. But it was horrid, seeing them load her into the ambulance. The poor girl wasn't even moving. I can't imagine how long she was lying out there."

Kerri reached over and held Edith's hand gently. Stu was warmed by her instinctive caring. "Try not to think about it," Kerri said quietly. "I know it's all but impossible to put it from your mind but concentrate on the fact that you and Bailey found her and were able to help."

Edith nodded slightly. "It's all I can do." She shook her head a bit. "What is this world coming to? The granddaughter of a friend of mine was attacked only a short time ago by a man who had kidnapped her years ago when she was five. He was afraid she might identify him. Scared her to death and he *did* nearly kill her. But now this. This is even worse, and I can't really say why. Two women. Maybe that's why. What motivates them?"

"Power," Kerri answered. "A sick lust for power. It's not about sex, Edith."

"How could it be when they leave a woman bleeding and nearly dead?"

At that moment, Chief Madison approached. "Stu? You wanna take Miss Edith over to your office to get her statement? Gage says he's ready if she's willing."

Stu straightened. "Glad to do it." Then he eyed Kerri. "Time to get on with your walk?"

She stood and surprised him by blushing faintly. "I didn't go out of bounds. You should know that. I'm better aware of the bounds than most people."

"I'm sure, but appearances matter. I'd offer to drive you home but I need to go straight to the office. Edith would probably be delighted to be done with this."

"Of course."

"Like I'll ever be done with this," Edith said sharply. "There are times I wish I had a much poorer memory."

Kerri watched Stu guide Edith and her huge dog to his car, then sighed and rose, the ever-faithful Snowy moving with her. She felt very sorry for Edith Jasper. She'd rarely met someone who'd discovered a violent crime scene who hadn't been disturbed for a good long time. Some images simply couldn't be removed from the brain. She just hoped Edith hadn't seen very much detail. Maybe the darkness before dawn had protected her from the worst.

She decided it was time to head back to her place. She did indeed have a class to teach that afternoon, like it or not. She was willing to bet that most of today's class discussion would center around this morning's crime and the rape from last Friday night. It seemed impossible that the students would want to discuss much else.

She guessed she would have to wing it, then. She certainly couldn't use her planned discussion about how sentencing guidelines worked. It would be dry, unfortunately, much too dry for today. Although she had thought the subject would arouse at least some argument. Few were happy with the guidelines when they learned how they worked, and she'd expected plenty of people on both sides of the issue.

For example, should a man who stole a pack of cigarettes and thus became guilty for his third arrest and conviction have to face life in prison under the Three Strikes laws? That ramped up a lot people.

Habitual criminal, many would argue. But it was just a pack of cigarettes, others would say. Life for *that*?

Well, not today. She supposed she had better get ready for the difference between rape and consensual sex, and it didn't just involve beating the victim bloody.

* * *

At the station, Gage was waiting for them, directing them into a conference room where they'd have privacy. Stu eyed the elderly woman as her dog laid down beside her feet. "Want me to run down the street and get you some more tea? You look cold."

"That would be wonderful," Edith admitted. "And Maude knows just how I like it."

"Done. Gage?"

"Strong and black. If Velma complains, I'm ready to tell her to learn how to make coffee."

"Good luck with that. I hear she's been making it this way for a whole lotta years."

"Since the dinosaurs," Gage answered. He lowered himself carefully into a chair across from Edith and pulled out a micro recorder. "You don't mind?"

"Why should I? I just wish I had more to tell you."

"We'll start when Stu gets back, but in the meantime, the way it happens is this. You talk for the tape. Then I get it transcribed into the computer and print it out, so if we need you to sign it, you actually can."

Edith suddenly looked wry. "Imagine that."

Stu couldn't help smiling as he hurried out the door, then down to Maude's. She had the coffee ready in two shakes but the tea took a bit longer. "How's Edith doing?"

"Pretty well under the circumstances. I think she's getting past the shock."

Maude nodded. "Good. Imagine her finding that."

So, that much news had already made the rounds, Stu realized. "You hear anything else about it?"

"Just that. If anybody knows who she is, they ain't talking."

"Just as well. She probably would like privacy, at least for a while."

"Well, you just might mention to her that I can't deliver dinners unless I know *where* to send them."

He walked out with three big cups in a tray and wondered why he had never heard that Maude did that. Or maybe she had just started. Or maybe she didn't make a big deal out of it.

Back at the office, he carried the hot beverages into the conference room and handed them out. Gage was looking awfully tired, Stu suddenly noticed. Like a man who hadn't been sleeping well, possibly since the first rape. Gage really cared about the people of this county, like the previous sheriff, whom Stu had only been privileged to meet once. Nate Tate was still a legend in these parts, though.

Edith sipped her tea. "Maude knows exactly how to make it," she remarked again. "We have to talk about this?"

"I'm afraid so," Gage answered. Leaning forward he started the recorder, gave his name and Stu's name, then had Edith identify herself.

"What can you tell us about this morning and how you found the victim?"

"You ought to talk to Bailey, my dog," she said. "I'd never have seen her but for him. But Bailey started to get a wild hair almost the instant we entered the park. He kept tugging on me, which he never does, and pulled me down the path. Then he wanted to go into that little grove of trees and when I tried to stop him he nearly pulled my arm out of joint. No stopping him. I *had* to follow, although frankly, at my age, I worry about falling. Anyway, I saw what I thought was a pile of rags. Then I realized it wasn't. And I called you. That's it."

Stu noted that her hand had begun to tremble as she was talking. Afraid some liquid might slosh out through the drinking slot, he reached out and took it from her, placing it on the table. "Just till the tremor passes," he said. "I'm not surprised you're shaking."

She nodded. "I didn't notice. Thank you."

The rape victim wasn't the only victim in this crime, Stu thought. The unfortunate who discovered the crime was every bit as much a victim. The next victims would be family and friends as they were told or heard about it. But Edith had gotten the worst of it.

"Can you remember anything else at all?" Stu asked. "I know you were shocked, but maybe if you close your eyes for a minute and think back to the surroundings? Bailey was acting up, you said."

Edith nodded. "Not at all like him." Then she closed her eyes. Stu hated to ask this of her, especially when she probably wished she could just erase it all from her mind. She'd probably welcome a small amount of traumatic amnesia about now.

She drew a deep breath, but kept her eyes closed. "I wish I were Bailey. Or that he could talk. He probably noticed more than I ever would."

"That's the thing about dogs," Stu remarked. "They can lead you to the problem, but they can't tell you about it."

Edith relaxed enough to release a dainty snort.

"Great, isn't it? I'm more surprised that he didn't drag me *away* from the park."

Gage spoke. "I guess he didn't think you needed protecting."

"I don't," Edith said firmly. "I can take care of myself."

"Obviously," Stu said. "You certainly did this morning."

Edith sighed again. Her eyes opened. "All I can see is that poor woman lying like a pile of bloody, discarded rags. Now that I'm getting past the initial shock, I'd like to kill someone. Will you arrest me if I do?"

Gage half smiled. "Maybe not if you get the right guy."

Edith closed her eyes once more. "Men," she said disgustedly. "And you *know* it had to be a man. I didn't hear anything so it must have happened well before I reached the park. It's so quiet out there at that hour. Air is cold, too. Sound carries."

Gage scrawled something on the pad in front of him. "That's good information," he said encouragingly. "It helps with the time frame."

"It does?" Edith lowered her head as she kept her eyes closed, and the two men sat in silence. It was clear she was thinking about every detail, probably starting with the beginning of her walk this morning. "Well, I left the house a half hour before I reached the park." She lifted her head, her eyes open. "I know because it always takes us that long to get to the park. Bailey likes to read the mail."

"Read the mail?" Gage asked. Stu, who knew a lot about dogs, understood and nearly laughed.

"Does he dawdle a lot?" Stu asked her.

"Every bush and shrub, every post or fire hydrant. He keeps a close watch on the neighborhood and leaves a few of his own messages in return. He's got a route and he doesn't like to deviate. I guess he's attached to some of the dogs around here. Anyway, we left almost exactly a half hour before we got to the park. He usually lollygags his way through there, but not this morning. He was a dog on a mission."

"It would seem so," Gage answered.

"And I didn't hear a thing, except an early car or two in the distance. Oh, and some of the big trucks on the state highway, probably getting ready to pull in at the truck stop. Anyway, just normal sounds. And I didn't see anything out of place."

Gage reached forward to turn off the recorder. "Thank you, Edith."

She lifted her cup again, sipped some tea and studied her hand. "Steady as a rock." That appeared to please her.

Then, abruptly, she stiffened and her eyes widened a shade. "There *was* something wrong."

Both men leaned in and Stu felt his heart speed up a bit.

"The birds," she said. "There are always some that start singing before the sun comes up. Damn fools, if you ask me. What if an owl notices?" Then she shook her head. "I'm the damn fool. I wondered why they weren't making a racket this morning. This whole dang town was as quiet as a tomb."

Gage hadn't yet switched the recorder off. "What do you think, Edith?"

"That the disgusting man finished his fun just before I got there. The birds. The birds were silent. They know when something is wrong."

The birds, Stu thought as he walked Edith and Bailey to the door. He offered them a ride home but Edith refused.

"Need to walk this off," she told him. "Both of us. If you think Bailey was unaffected, you're wrong. Snoot full of blood smells, fear and suffering. Yeah, we both need to walk it off."

He stood for a minute, watching her walk away, utterly erect, her Great Dane beside her. Except Bailey was hanging his head. For the first time he considered how that mess this morning could have affected the animal. He'd heard about dogs getting depressed by things like that, but it had always been peripheral to his existence, certainly not the first thing to spring to his mind.

He turned to go back inside, thinking about birds. Edith might have just nailed the time frame during which the perp had left the scene. She might have come close to walking into it. Or perhaps she had saved the young woman's life, her and Bailey. Impossible to know now. The last rape had been violent but there was no evidence of intent to kill.

Until this time. Now they had something else to worry about.

Kerri had hung out at the crime scene. Not because she was a ghoul—God, no. She'd seen enough as a police officer to erase any possible ghoulishness she might ever have had.

Not that she thought the other onlookers were

ghouls. The victim had long since been removed; the cops were working mostly inside the park. *Nothing to see, move along.* But a lot of people weren't moving, but instead talking in low voices almost as if they were at a funeral. They were worried. Some, especially women, were scared. They sought comfort in numbers, and so many of them sounded like neighbors and friends.

She felt like an outsider, and hoped she wasn't bothering them by remaining, but she wanted to hear what they had to say. You could never know when someone might say something surprisingly relevant to a case.

So, she hung around, joining in the conversations when it seemed appropriate or she felt welcomed. Snowy helped a lot, drawing kindly attention her way, perhaps making her seem harmless.

However it was, while the morning was still early, and the gathered crowd had barely begun to disperse, a man approached her. He appeared to be in his late forties or early fifties, lean as a rail and friendly enough.

"Nice dog you got there," he remarked.

"Yes, he is. Thank you." She waited, wondering if he might be a threat. She'd left the streets a while ago and was no longer as confident of her ability to read people. Still, she was surrounded by a crowd.

"You know that deputy?" he asked. "Stu Canady?"

"Yes, I do."

"Thought so, the way he was talking to you. Can you step away with me a moment? I need to share something but I'm not sure I want the whole town knowing it, not when we got a creep like this running around."

She immediately walked about twenty feet away with him, asking, "Do you think you could be in danger?"

"I doubt it, but you never know." He faced her, then glanced around as if to be sure nobody else was nearby. "Here's the thing. I got me some awful insomnia. Hurt my back a few years back pitching hay. They keep wanting to cut, but no way am I letting a knife near my spine. Anyway, don't matter. Point being, I was up during the night, standing in my bedroom window, looking out and wishing I could be asleep like everyone else."

"I can sure understand that," Kerri answered.

"Reckon you can," he said with a glance at Snowy. "I'm not feeling sorry for myself, mind you. I could be that woman who got attacked this morning, or a few days ago. But anyway, I'm not sure this is useful, but you can tell Canady for me and see if it might be, okay?"

"Absolutely, Mr...."

"Webley, like the gun. Sheriff knows me, but if I go to the sheriff myself, the whole damn world will know. So just pass it to Canady."

"I can do that."

Mr. Webley nodded. "I live right across from the park. Just up there. Anyway, I'm standing there, wishing the sun would come up sooner than it will—you don't need to tell me how stupid that is."

Kerri smiled. "Trust me, I wouldn't."

He glanced at Snowy again, as if he took reassurance from the fact that she was another disabled person. "Anyhow, I see this lady jogger come down the street. Dang, I think, I used to be able to run like that. She wasn't going really fast or anything but running like she felt good in her own body. Know what I mean?"

"I do. I used to feel that way."

"Yeah." He issued a short laugh. "Some days get gone for good."

She wanted to corral him back to the point but got the feeling this man just needed to talk. Some people needed that connection, and what else would she be doing? Getting ready for a rape and law discussion with a class of young people, mostly men, some of whom probably still hadn't learned that no meant no. "She was a runner? That's helpful."

"She must have a lot of miles on those feet. Plus, she must have trouble sleeping, like me."

Instant connection, Kerri thought. This man probably had created a whole story about the victim. People tended to do that.

"Don't know who she was. Too dark, this part of the street needs a whole lot more streetlights. Anyway, she turns and runs into the park. She wasn't afraid. She wasn't expecting trouble. Why would she? Out for a quiet run in a quiet town. But you could tell she wasn't feeling at all scared. Not like she thought someone might be following her."

Kerri nodded. "I think that's an important bit of information."

"I thought it might be. Anyway, I'm standing there wishing I could run with her, then I notice a shadow. A man's shadow. All in dark he was. I think maybe he was wearing a ski mask. Yeah, it gets cold at night this time of year, but it caught my attention, anyway. Seemed over the top for someone who lives around here."

Kerri nodded encouragingly. "You'd know about that. I'm new here."

He reared his head back a little, then smiled. "Yeah, you're that new college teacher, right? I heard about you. But take it from me, *you* might want a ski mask at night right now, but a local wouldn't. Unless he was up to no good. And you wouldn't want it at this time of year if you're running. Too hot and you'd make it wet in no time between sweating and your breath. Probably itchy, too."

"He was *running*?"

"He was when he turned down that path behind her. Figured he was just another insomniac like her and me. I also figured he didn't know her because he wasn't running *with* her. Plus he was running a little faster. Anyway, I didn't think much about until…" He waved at the crowd and the cordon. "Then it hit me and I feel like a damn fool. I'd like to blame it on the pain meds, but I didn't take any. Hate the damn things. So I was just a plain damn fool."

"I don't think—"

"I do. Wish I'd called the police. Around here I don't think they'd ignore it if I told 'em some guy went running down the park path after a female jogger, especially at night."

He looked up as if watching the leaves fall in the fresh breeze as the day brightened. "Problem with living in a place like this is you don't look out for bad people. You usually know who they are before they grow up. You don't think about things like that man going down that path. You don't think it could be bad. Until it is."

He half turned. "Tell Canady. I'm going home to see if I can manage to lie down. If he or the sheriff wants to talk, that's where I'll be. Thanks for hearing me out."

He walked away, past the crowd, many of whom spoke to him, then vanished into a house just one door down from the park entrance. He'd unburdened himself, maybe felt less guilty for something he didn't need to feel guilty about at all.

Kerri looked up at the dormers on his second floor. He'd have had a very good view indeed. She needed to tell Stu.

But she hesitated. She'd heard the sheriff mention to him that they needed to come back to look around in better light. He might already be on his way here.

Or not. He'd taken Edith Jasper into the office with him. They might all still be there.

"Let's go, Snowy."

He didn't need any encouragement. Standing around doing nothing could hardly be his favorite thing. He did lift his head, though, and look back at the park. He must smell it.

"It's okay," she said, hoping to reassure him. She didn't believe it and doubted he did, either.

Stu had driven only two blocks from the office toward the park when he spied Kerri and Snowy. After seeing her with Edith Jasper this morning, he wondered if he should mention yet again the problems with her involvement. She might now be a civilian, but she *had* been a cop. Questions could be raised about whether she had subtly guided Edith's testimony. Not that Edith had seen enough to even fill out an affidavit.

He decided to let it ride. At this point, all she'd done was keep an elderly woman company after a shocking experience.

He pulled over and called to Kerri, offering her a ride. He could swing by her apartment if she wanted. He enjoyed his time with her, and it still wasn't quite light enough outside to help with another search of the scene. Give it another half hour and they'd be able to see things that might have been missed under the spotlights. Odd how artificial light never quite made up for the absence of natural light.

She smiled and waved, then crossed the street to climb in on the passenger side. Snowy took up residence on the back seat.

"How are you doing?" he asked her.

"I'm fine, of course. But I need to talk to you about something someone told me. He asked me to tell you."

At that point he stiffened a bit. "Kerri…"

"I know, I know. But I didn't ask. *He* asked, he told me, and all he wanted was that I should relay it to you. I'm not even sure how useful it might be."

He was still idling at the curb. "Why would he tell you?"

"According to him, it would be all over town if he came to talk to the sheriff."

"Damn! Why should he be afraid?"

He looked at her and saw her staring back. Her smile was gone.

She spoke. "Maybe because nobody knows how far this guy might go?"

Which was one of the primary reasons he didn't want Kerri to get involved in the investigation. Interesting twist, a witness coming to her. No way that could be prevented.

He checked the street, then pulled a U-turn, heading toward the apartments. "You've got a class, and the walk will be long enough when you're ready to go. In the meantime, want me to grab some coffee before we get to your place? Then you can tell me all about it."

He could feel it coming. She resented being cut out. Perfectly understandable, to his way of thinking. In her shoes he'd feel the same. It remained, however, that they had to walk a careful line mainly because she *was* a former cop, and he didn't want the perp to think she might be gathering evidence. Plus, she was almost exactly the kind of demographic this guy seemed to be looking for: a woman alone. In the isolated end of that damn apartment complex.

It was equally apparent, to judge by that man talking to her, that she drew something important out of people. Edith had welcomed her company even though she was a total stranger. Now this man felt comfortable telling her something he didn't want to bring openly to the sheriff.

If that kind of thing kept up, she was going to be nosing around on her own because she couldn't resist and people were willing to talk to her.

He ran into Maude's to get them coffee and Maude immediately asked, "One's a latte, right?"

Was he becoming that predictable? He almost laughed. He and Kerri were just friends but making that kind of impression on Maude, that they were an item, would probably start spreading. He wondered what Kerri would think of that.

She didn't say much on the way to her place, which gave him a new concern. Was she angry that he was taking her home? He sure as hell couldn't invite her across the cordon to join the investigation.

Once they got upstairs, however, she seemed like her usual self. Maybe she'd just been pondering what that man had told her. Concerned as he was about her getting involved, he wanted to hear her opinions about it.

This morning also gave him a good idea of why her department had selected her to be a mediator in domestics and a victim advocate when necessary. She had the magic touch, it seemed.

They sat at her bar with their coffee.

"What did he tell you?"

"Apart from letting me know it's not only women around here who are going to be scared? That really got my attention, Stu. It's not like the guy witnessed the crime but he seems edgy about the fact that he probably saw the perp."

Stu's interest rose a few notches. "He did?"

"So it seems. Nothing identifiable, unfortunately. But let me tell you his story. Insomniac. Lives across the street from the park entrance. Saw the vic enter, jogging, then saw a man all in black—keep in mind that it was night and dark colors of any kind could pass for black."

He nodded, swiveling so he could see her. Here he was, listening to her report, and thinking about how much he liked to look at her. From the living room right behind them came the sound of Snowy gnawing rawhide. Teeth scraping.

"Anyway," she continued, "he thought it was odd the guy was wearing a ski mask but didn't make much of it. Didn't make anything of the fact that the guy turned into the park after the jogger. Said he was running a little faster than she was and he didn't think they were together."

Stu nodded. "Which means the man was far enough behind not to seem connected."

"Anyway, the guy's name is Webley. The sheriff knows him, I gather. You might want to talk to him because he might have noticed more than he realizes. But I don't have to tell you that."

No, she didn't. Common enough in crime investigation. Like Edith with the birdsong this morning. Things didn't always seem relevant until they were. "Did he say what time?"

"No, I didn't press him. I figured you guys could do that."

"I'm impressed. I think you've got more self-control than I have."

Her expression turned wry. "I heard you this morning. I know you're right. But when people come up to me to tell me something, I won't shut them down."

There it was. Her personal declaration of war. She might be on the outside, but if people talked to her she'd soon be on the inside.

"You're going to bring up the assaults at every opportunity, aren't you?"

"Why wouldn't I? Everyone else is." Then she threw the gauntlet again. "I have a skill set, Stu. You can't just expect me to forget it because I left the force for disability. I get that I can't be a real law enforcement officer anymore, but I'll use my skills whenever it's appropriate. Trust me, I'm not going to interfere in your damn investigation."

Whoa, he thought. She was well and truly fired up now.

She rose and carried her latte with her, pacing the small living room. Snowy looked up from his rawhide bone, evidently decided everything was cool and went back to gnawing.

"Do you have any idea how maddening this is?" Kerri demanded. "I worked on cases like this in the victims unit. I was trained to question the victim, to support the victim and to question witnesses. I not only mediated domestics, but I helped solve rape cases. I get why I can't do it anymore, but I don't have to like it."

"Of course you don't." His chest tightened a bit as he again faced this woman's losses. Here she was trying to settle into an entirely different life, to rebuild on the ashes, and then the kind of case she knew inside and out was happening right under her nose. He had a pretty good idea how *he* would feel.

He added, "I hope you understand my position."

"Hell, yes. I said I won't interfere. But if stuff falls in my lap like it did this morning, I'm going to pass it on to you and run with it if I have to."

He tensed. "Run with it? What do you mean?" That sounded suspiciously like getting involved.

"Follow it," she said.

Dang, her eyes were practically shooting fire at him. Evidently, he'd uncorked the bottle.

Just then, Snowy rose and trotted over to her to nudge her thigh. Twice because she ignored the first one. Then she looked down at him. "Oh, damn." She quickly set the coffee on the end table and lowered herself in the recliner.

"You can leave," she said. "I'll be okay in a minute or two."

Then she was gone. He'd seen it once before, but it was startling how her face changed. A terrible coldness seemed to come over it, as if she were empty, but then there was the anger that seemed to join it.

He didn't leave. He waited. He didn't want her to imagine he was running from her seizures. Nor did he want to. A horrible sadness invaded him. For her. He'd have done just about anything to free her from this.

But all he could do was wait for her return.

Kerri hated the return from her seizures at least as much as she hated the seizures themselves. The momentary feeling of confusion, as if she'd landed on a strange planet. It was less troubling if nothing had changed, but it was still bothersome because uncertainty overtook her along with that inexplicable confusion.

She always needed to get her bearings again, as if she'd made an unexpected journey and then dropped back into space and time. It was easier and quicker when nothing had changed. Sometimes she barely noticed except for a brief confusion as if she'd lost her train of thought. Other times it was much more difficult.

Oh, it was hard to explain even to herself. She

looked around, gathering scattered thoughts, trying to remember exactly what she had been doing, making sure that her entire world, or even part of it, hadn't changed too much.

Well, something had changed. Snowy was resting his head on her thigh. Instinctively she reached for him and began to knead his neck. He grounded her. He made her return easier.

Then she saw Stu at the bar, his elbow resting on the counter, waiting.

"I'm sorry," she said automatically.

"No reason to be. Don't apologize."

She lowered her head, looking down at Snowy. Didn't Stu recognize how broken she was? That almost nothing was normal for her now, nor could it ever be again? She felt useless in so many ways that she had begun to apologize for her very existence.

Then she realized something. "Did you sit there and watch me?" Annoyance flared.

"I was waiting," he said levelly. "Did you really want me to disappear while you were out?"

"I hate anyone to see me like that. Dead to the world, glaring. Oh, God, I wish there was some way to stop it."

"You weren't glaring, and what are you going to do, dammit? Become a hermit?"

"I wish."

"Hardly. You were out in a crowd this morning, following your cop nose, and you got some potentially useful info by talking to a stranger. I can tell you don't want to live in a cave, and frankly, I've been admiring you."

"Me?" Surprise lurched through her. She didn't feel admirable at all.

"Admiring you. Starting a whole new life despite being sort of disabled."

"Sort of?" She gaped, wondering if the always-simmering anger in her was about to boil over. When she was honest with herself, she knew her underlying emotion was rage—not self-pity, but rage.

"Sort of," he repeated. "You're teaching. You're trying to stick your nose into an investigation. Maybe it's only for the dog's sake, but you go out for walks and run into people like you did this morning. You're not the hiding type, Kerri."

"How would you know?" She began to wonder if she was pouting like a kid. Damn, did she have any nice emotions left in her?

"I've spent enough time with you in the last couple of weeks to form an opinion, and what I think is that you're remarkable. And beautiful, too."

"Who cares what I look like?" Now she knew she *was* being childish. She also knew what she absolutely didn't want: a relationship that went beyond friendship. Beautiful? Was that a warning?

He abruptly changed tack, as if he felt he was heading in the wrong direction. Well, he was.

"They tried every possible medication on you, right?"

"Yes." She almost spat the word through her teeth. "I'm on two now, the only ones that helped at all. I used to do this eight or ten times a day. It's rarer now."

"That's good."

"Really," she said sarcastically. "I can't drive. You

had to rustle up a bunch of your fellow cops to make sure I didn't freeze on my way to campus when it gets colder. Do you think I like that?"

"You don't have to like it. There are a lot of things we don't like, but we have to deal, anyway."

He was frowning now and she was beginning to feel awful about the way she was behaving. This man had been nothing but kind to her. He didn't deserve to be the target for her anger. Her dissatisfaction.

He fell silent, drinking coffee that must be getting cold by now. Leaving her alone with her ugliness.

It worked. A couple of minutes later, she'd shaken off her mood and acknowledged that while she didn't want anyone to see her seize, mainly she didn't want Stu to see it. Not good. But she wasn't going to say she was sorry again. He'd probably tell her to quit apologizing.

She spoke. "You don't put up with my garbage, do you. Thanks."

He smiled faintly. "It's not garbage. But there isn't much I can do about that bag of rocks you're back-packing around."

"Nobody can do anything." Now gloom was trying to settle in. No way. She patted Snowy's head and he went back to his rawhide. Then she stood. "You must need to get back to work. I heard Gage say that he wanted to check things out with better light."

"Yup." He, too, rose, taking his cup with him. "Cold is better than Velma's coffee," he remarked. "Okay. See you later?"

"Class won't be over till five."

"I remember. I'll meet you at your office. Five, it is."

Then he astonished her by hugging her. "Adjustments are hard. You'll make it."

The hug left her feeling amazingly warm. His muscled body seemed to have imprinted itself on her. She'd have liked another one. But no. She had no business becoming involved when she'd just be a burden.

# Chapter 8

Stu drove back to the park to apply his eyes to the scene. Thinking about what had just happened with Kerri, he was sorry that she felt awkward about her anger and her responses to him. She had every right to whatever her changed circumstances made her feel.

After all, she'd been following the life of her choice until some jackass had threatened his family with violence, then had shot the one person who was trying to help. His family surely hadn't deserved that violence, and Kerri even less so.

Some guy who was either drunk or stoned had wiped away essential parts of a woman's life. Changed her irrevocably.

That was plenty to get mad about. And he'd doubtless overstepped by arranging a ride pool for her without consulting her.

She probably wanted to say, "How like a man."

Yup. He was a problem solver from way back, but that didn't mean he should tread on anyone's toes by acting without permission.

Well, he'd done it, and he'd bear whatever consequences came from it. No shirking. He just hoped the consequences weren't too severe because whether she wanted it or not, that woman was beginning to curl up in some important place deep inside him.

He'd meet her at five and maybe they could iron a few things out. Assuming she didn't find a way to vanish before he got to the college.

Ten minutes later, he joined Gage and a few other officers as they searched high and low for anything that might have been missed. It was extremely rare when a perp didn't leave something behind, and now that the sunlight was filtering through tree branches that had lost most of their leaves, it might reveal things. Then, of course, there was the possibility that the evidence they wanted was hidden under some of these fallen leaves.

He told Gage about Webley's conversation with Kerri.

Gage's response was thoughtful. "Guess I need to send someone who's not obvious to visit Webley. We sure didn't hear this during our neighborhood canvass this morning. Interesting that he told Kerri to tell you. Interesting that men are starting to get uneasy, too. Or at least one is."

"Well, everyone could be a target if the perp thinks they might know something."

"Yeah." Gage studied the sky overhead. "I used to like autumn."

Stu didn't ask. Gage's background in the DEA had been horrific, and he suspected the sheriff's comment had sprung from that. That was a place Stu didn't want to pry into.

The daylight search didn't prove to be helpful at first. They poked around, paying special attention to areas that might not be in a direct line with where the woman had been raped. The rapist had to have been concealed from her most of the time or she'd probably have started a speedy sprint. He probably wouldn't have been able to close in on her.

He suspected most of the women in this town, and possibly the entirety of Conard County, would be wary of men late at night while they were alone. He doubted it would even have to be a male stranger at this point.

He looked around this wooded part of the park, which wasn't exactly huge, and wondered what had led the victim to come through here. A sense of safety, maybe, given the hour when almost no one was about, or maybe she hadn't thought about it at all.

He knew how many people lived with the belief that bad things wouldn't happen to them. Truth was, people couldn't handle life if they worried all the time. He had seen enough of the ugliness in war to know that bad stuff really happened to people, and maybe that was part of the cause for PTSD. Facing mortality and the horrible messes that could happen ripped away any illusion of safety. Like survivors of tornadoes and other disasters. They suffered for years afterward.

He sighed. Then he saw it. He let out a piercing

whistle and activity stopped. The woods grew nearly silent.

"I got a footprint," he called.

Staring down at the scuffed leaves he saw the dirt had been bared and there was the unmistakable print of a work boot, maybe size ten or a little larger. He looked toward the street and saw some scuffing in the leaves.

Damn, the guy had circled around the vic like a shark.

"That explains why she wasn't alerted to the slap of running feet behind her," Stu said to Gage and Guy Redwing as techs made a cast of the print and other LEOs gently swept leaves aside looking for another. They'd be messed up by the leaves if they found any, but they could describe the perp's path. Any information at this point would be better than none.

"Apparently so," Gage replied.

"Do we know who she is yet?"

"Finally. She wasn't carrying ID. Why would she? But a coworker of hers heard about what happened, realized she was late to work and hadn't called in sick by about nine-thirty and went to the hospital when May didn't answer her phone."

Stu nodded, his mind running rapidly, trying to assemble pieces into something useful. Probably wasting his time trying to. This was like a thousand-piece jigsaw puzzle with only a half dozen pieces available. "Who?"

"May Broadwyn, a clerk of court. When her name made the rounds, one of the city guys said he'd seen her running last night as he patrolled. Headed the other way."

Stu wanted to swear violently. He'd dated May a

couple of times right after he moved here. They simply hadn't meshed, mainly because his demons had poked up more frequently back then.

"What's her condition?"

"As bad as it looked. Last word was she was slated for surgery. Might be able to question her late this afternoon."

Stu did swear out loud then.

"Yeah," Gage replied. "Most of us knew her from her job if not socially. A lifelong local."

"I knew her," Guy Redwing said heavily. "She was always helpful. Nice lady."

Gage caught Stu's eye, then jerked his head to the right. He said, "Guy, keep an eye on things for a moment."

"Sure, Sheriff."

Stu followed Gage to the far edge of the copse. If they kept their voices low, they couldn't be overheard. Stu was a little surprised but he wasn't going to demand reasons. Gage would tell him soon enough.

Gage turned to look back through the trees, apparently satisfying himself that there was no one nearby. "Okay."

"What's up?" He waited, never expecting what came next.

"You know this Kerri Addison pretty well, right?"

Stu hesitated. Crap. First Maude, now his boss. "We're friendly but I've only known her since that day you chose me to speak in her class. Coffee, a few dinners. Casual. That's all." Which wasn't the full truth, he guessed, because those dinners had been followed by evenings with her.

Gage appeared to roll his eyes. "I'm not asking for intimate information. What do you think of her so far?"

"Bright. Very bright. Former victims advocate, domestic disturbance mediator and investigator."

"Epileptic, I heard."

"Yeah. She got shot when answering a DD call. Killed her career in law enforcement but other than that I don't think it's as bad as *she* thinks it is." What the heck was this about? Her conversation with Webley? Stu began to tense, ready to defend her.

Gage nodded. Stu let him think. This was going somewhere and nerves began to niggle at the back of his neck, the way they had when he was on security detail in a combat zone. Or checking the perimeter of an operations base.

Something was coming.

"How bad is the epilepsy?"

Stu shrugged. "Enough that she can't drive or be a cop anymore. She checks out, is all. Anywhere from a half minute to two. A bit of confusion when she comes back. You wouldn't think something so minor could wreck someone's life. But I can see why she couldn't interview witnesses anymore. If she drops out, she might miss something. Same at a desk on the phone."

Stu figured he'd never have a better opportunity. "Maybe we can find some way to involve Kerri. I think she's getting frustrated. She said to me that this is the type of case she used to work on, and the restrictions on civilians during an ongoing investigation are chafing her, I believe."

Gage eyed him. "You reading my mind?"

"Just listening. Anyway, she's bright, determined and not real happy about having to sit on her hands." He kept to himself his own worry that if she became involved in any significant way, she might become a target for the rapist. Too many criminals attacked those they thought might have evidence against them, if they didn't flee. This guy was growing increasingly violent, a disturbing trend.

"Any concerns?"

He nodded, admitting it. "I don't want her to come to the rapist's notice."

"She would if she were in uniform."

Stu admitted it was true. "Do you want to make her a uniform?"

Gage gave a little shake of his head. "I could deputize her, but not make her a full-time cop. I was thinking she might be able to talk to the victims and they might be more comfortable with her. You talk to her. See how she feels about that. I don't have a trained victims advocate on staff. Never really needed one before, certainly not enough to justify the training and a full-time position. But if she's willing to help out, I can sure as hell use her. At least now."

"Okay." But Stu had mixed feelings. He wanted to protect her from danger, but on the other hand, he had the strongest feeling that she was going to find a way to get involved somehow. In fact, he believed she was already working on it. She could have cut Webley off and told him to speak with a deputy. She hadn't.

God, he didn't have the right to deprive her of what she so obviously needed and wanted. That didn't mean he had to like it.

Then he and Gage returned to the hunt for the perp's trail.

* * *

Kerri was surprised to find Stu waiting for her when she emerged from the campus building that contained her office. She hadn't exactly been pleasant to him this morning. In fact, she'd been angry and argumentative, and had even criticized him for staying with her during her seizure. She couldn't have blamed him if he wanted to distance himself from the unpredictable bomb she apparently had become.

But she was glad to see him. She liked him. Unfortunately, she was also drawn to him in ways that made her squirm given her disability. Why would any man want to be saddled with a woman who depended on a service dog and couldn't even drive in a place that had no buses or taxis?

In some respects, coming here hadn't been a well-thought-out choice. She'd never even looked into the question of public transport. Maybe she'd lost some of her basic intelligence in the shooting. The things she hadn't thought about, like getting groceries and dog food. Duh.

Snowy apparently recognized the SUV, because his tail started wagging the instant he saw it. He never left her side, a good dog as always, but he was clearly glad to see Stu.

The cold air nipped at her cheeks a bit, but since night was falling rapidly, she supposed the temperature might be dropping.

Stu hopped out of the vehicle and opened the passenger door for her and Snowy. He was back in civilian clothes, and his gray-green eyes crinkled at the corners. "Hi. And you're starting to look cold already."

His smile made her smile in response. "I'm a thin-blooded Southern girl."

"That won't last. At least not for long."

"I hope not."

He climbed in behind the wheel, turned over the engine and started them toward town. She assumed to her apartment and wondered if she should offer to make dinner for him. Her mind began to click over the possibilities. She hadn't really shopped for two.

He answered the question before she mentioned it. "Do you like sub sandwiches?"

"Yes." Where was this going? She was sure that wasn't on Maude's menu.

"With all the trimmings, like lettuce and tomato?"

"That's part of what makes it a good meal."

He nodded. "Then we'll swing by the grocery. At this time of day the deli there, while probably not what you're used to, makes a great turkey or roast beef sub."

"Sounds good." It did. Her mouth watered at the very idea.

He made a turn. "I know all the places to feed my face that don't involve cooking. I think I need to grow up and learn how to do more than heat up a can of soup or a frozen meal."

She turned her head, daring to look at him, almost relieved that he seemed to be putting this morning into the past. Still, she'd have to give him an apology. "I bet you can do more than that."

He flashed her a grin. "Don't try me. You'll regret it."

She bit her lip, wondering if she should bring up what happened this morning, then decided to let it rest until a better opportunity arose. Right now they were heading out to pick up dinner.

She was used to larger selections at most of the supermarket delis back home, but this one wasn't bad at all. She was able to order a half turkey sub with all the good stuff, like cheese, tomato, green pepper, lettuce, onion...oh, yeah. She could hardly wait to eat it.

Stu went for a whole loaded roast beef that must have used nearly every topping available.

"Wanna eat at my place or yours?" he asked as they climbed into the car.

"Mine, please." Because she felt secure there, and as much as she wanted to see where he lived, from the internal lurch she experienced at the question, it was going to have to wait.

"No problem. I can promise, though, that you don't have to worry about a bachelor mess. The Army taught me to keep everything squared away."

"It's not that," she admitted. Oh, hell, she'd showed this man enough this morning that she shouldn't be embarrassed by a little truth. "I just feel more comfortable in my apartment. In case."

"Well, sure. That's natural. Another time, then. I wanted to ask, how did your class go today?"

"About like I expected. Lively discussion about rape, penalties for rape, how women are treated during investigations. If it was even remotely connected to the subject, we tossed it around. Which sounds as if it was lighthearted, but it wasn't. There was a lot of intensity, probably because so many of them knew Sandra Carney. This is striking close to home for most of them."

"It should be. Did you get any defenders of date rape?"

"I expected more, but there was only one guy, and he kind of settled down after I suggested that he take a no as a no until advised in so many words that she hadn't meant it."

"Ah, man." He sighed. "It was a problem in the Army, too. Entirely too much of it, if you ask me. It's like some guys think women were put in their lives as their personal playthings."

"Isn't that what we are?" she asked. "I get that impression all too often."

He pulled into a parking place in front of the building, then switched the car off. "But it was mostly a good discussion?"

"Better than I expected. There was only that one sour note, and I had anticipated running into a lot worse. When I was cop I ran into more of it than I could believe. But this class was pretty good. Maybe knowing the victim made it more real. They all seemed to know Sandra Carney."

"They mostly would. She grew up here."

Upstairs, she broke out some plates and napkins to eat with and asked him if he wanted a beer.

"Sounds good. Thanks."

They settled at the bar while a happy Snowy started enjoying his tennis ball. Kerri often threw it for him, but he seemed to enjoy tossing it himself and chasing it. The clatter behind her made her feel good. She loved that dog.

The conversation rambled around. He mentioned the county's dog trainer, Cadell Marcus, once more, suggesting they could take a drive out to meet him, maybe next weekend.

That sounded hopeful, she thought. Like there wouldn't be another attack. She suspected he didn't believe that. She sure didn't. While two instances didn't prove they had a serial rapist on their hands, statistics said otherwise. Heck, given the violence of the first rape, it should have been a suspicion from the start unless they found someone who had a grudge against the first woman. Now the count was two, and they'd probably be looking at a third before long.

She hated to think about it, longed to try to bring down the hammer on this guy before he could act again.

As they just about finished eating, Stu changed the tack of the conversation again.

"Gage wanted me to ask you something."

She tensed. Her heart speeded a bit. Was he angry that she had talked to that Webley guy? Or involved herself with the witness, Edith Jasper?

"What?" she asked, dreading to hear she'd stepped on the sheriff's toes. Not a good person to irritate in such a small town. Given her former career, she didn't want to get on the wrong side of law enforcement. Not that Gage would do anything to her. It would just make her uncomfortable in a new way to learn she had crossed a line Gage believed to be important.

She had to get over this need to get involved. She was no longer a cop. Period. All she could try to do now was teach in a way that would make better cops.

She braced herself. "Did I do something wrong?"

"No. Seriously. Gage had an idea."

She turned her head to look at him, remains of her sandwich forgotten. She felt Snowy come closer without nudging her, and thought, *Oh, my God, no. Not another seizure today.*

"Gage was impressed by the fact that Webley came up to talk to you today when he didn't want to talk to a uniform. And that Edith Jasper was willing to turn to you when she was so upset."

She let out a puff of air, relieved. "So I'm not in the doghouse."

"Nope." Stu swiveled his seat on the stool to look at her. "He wants to deputize you. At least for now."

She gasped. Her heart skipped beats and she wondered if it actually stopped. "What?" she asked hoarsely. "You're joking."

"Serious as a heart attack as they say. He can't afford the training and expense of hiring a victims advocate because this kind of thing is far from routine. Small town," he added by way of explanation, as if she needed to hear that.

She stared at Stu, almost falling into his unusual gray-green eyes. He wasn't joking. He really wasn't joking.

"Question is, would you be willing? And keep in mind that you might attract the attention of the perp because you'll be spending a lot of time with the women. He might see you as a threat."

She nodded slowly, trying to read his expression. "You're unhappy."

"I'm worried. Whole different thing. You aren't even armed, Kerri. And you won't get a weapon just because you get deputized. You'd have to pass firearms qualification first."

"I can't do that," she said bluntly. "In fact, I don't want to have a pistol. It wouldn't be safe."

"That's why I'm worried."

She frowned, wanting to leap at this chance, but acknowledging that he might have legitimate concerns.

"I'm not unarmed," she said slowly. "I have my collapsible baton. I know how to use it."

"I can see about getting you some pepper spray."

"No. Snowy." Nothing would make her risk getting that dog into a cloud of pepper spray.

"Okay. I take it you're saying yes. Want some time to think about it? I mean, this could get you so involved you won't have much time for yourself for a while. We've already got two victims who need you, and I believe Gage is hoping they might feel freer to give you details. We *do* have other women on the force who—"

But her mind was made up. She interrupted him. Joy nearly swamped her despite the gravity of the task facing her now. She leaped off her chair and wrapped her arms tightly around Stu. "It was you, wasn't it? Oh, man, I'm so happy!"

She tilted her head back to look at him, and saw the flaring heat on his face, in his gaze. He wanted her.

A problem. A big problem because she wanted him, too. Quickly she pulled back, forestalling any hope of feeling those strong arms around her, that powerful body naked under her hands, the thought of how a kiss would feel.

She slid back onto her stool. "I'll do it for as long as

I'm needed, Stu. And don't worry about me. I know a lot of ways to look after myself."

She also knew that a minute of inattention because of a seizure could cost her a lot. Maybe her life. Because the perp *could* focus on her, and she was pretty much alone out here.

She didn't care. Life as she was living it now left her feeling unfulfilled. Now she had something important to do.

Stu watched the joy being born in her and wished he could be as happy for her as she was for herself. He *was* worried, though. Concerned. Because, yeah, she might attract the attention of the rapist, but also because of her seizures. During one of them she would be totally unprotected unless Snowy went on the attack, and he figured the dog had been chosen for service in part because he wasn't aggressive.

But he'd also seen how totally disconnected she became, and he'd seen the confusion when she returned. It hadn't lasted long, but it had been there. It was enough time for someone to take a knife to her.

The way the rapist had taken his knife to the others. But he also couldn't stop Kerri. He had no doubt she'd find a way to initiate casual conversations about these brutal assaults. What if she initiated one with the rapist? At least with a badge she'd become one of the cops. Maybe that alone would protect her.

Hell, there was no good solution to this one.

Nothing except to watch the change in her as she absorbed the news. She sat straighter now as she finished her sandwich. Her head came up. Her face relaxed.

This was what she wanted. He just hoped neither of them would come to regret it.

Ivan took another walk by the park that evening. It was getting dark again. The darkness always gave him a secret thrill. The police cordon remained, and he saw a few officers milling about. He doubted they'd found anything as he was exceptionally careful. He did notice, however, that the women cops who'd been there earlier in the day were absent now. Might not mean anything, or it could be a precaution. He'd have liked to take credit for that.

He'd really like an inside look at the investigation. No such chance existed that he was aware of. He'd learned a while back that cops, at least the ones around here, never discussed an ongoing investigation. Even with their wives or husbands from what he'd heard.

He sure would have liked a leak. He wondered what his victims were saying. They shouldn't have much to offer, though. They'd never seen his face, hardly heard his voice. He suspected the only thing they'd fixated on had been his knife. Glistening, gleaming, even with little light. They wouldn't have missed that.

One of them, the first, was still supposedly comatose, anyway. That news had flashed around. The other was coming out of surgery today and should be too woozy to be interviewed yet.

Not that it would matter, he assured himself. He was smart and had paid attention in the evidence course he'd taken last year. Close attention.

The pressure was building again, however. Too soon, he warned himself. Not that that made much difference to the urge. He'd try to quiet it by scouting another woman. Last night had been low-hanging fruit, unexpectedly offered to him. Next time would likely be different.

He still needed to know who was alone at night and when. Who was the type of woman he preferred: young, dark-haired if possible. Reasonably good figure. Plenty of women around here fit that description. Well, at least enough of them did.

He paused a moment to watch the cops, making sure he didn't stay too long, then moved on. He didn't want to be noticed. A casual pause could have been made by anyone. The belief that the perp always came back to the scene to watch the cops...well, that one worried him enough to keep him moving.

He needed to find out more about the woman who'd been talking with Edith Jasper. She'd been sitting there with a service dog, which meant she couldn't be a physical risk. Disabled people seldom were. But how had she gotten so close to that Edith woman? Why? Why had she been allowed to remain inside the cordon?

He knew she taught at the college, so maybe he ought to see if he could find her on the web page. He didn't remember seeing her on campus while he'd still been a student. That meant she was new.

Yeah, he had to find her on the faculty pages. New could be a threat. Someone who didn't see this place like everyone else. Someone who might spy something that no one else would notice because of familiarity.

Like him. He'd lived here for a couple of years after his divorced mother had brought him back when he was four. He'd always hated losing his father but that didn't matter much anymore. What mattered is that nearly everyone had thought they knew him. That poor little Raspin boy. He'd been so glad when his mother had moved them to Idaho.

But there was nothing "poor" about him anymore. He held immense power now.

That was one of the things he took from women. Sure, he loved their fear, the way it seemed to tingle all the way through him. But they gave him power with their terrified eyes and cries.

The next morning, Kerri walked to the sheriff's office. Stu had apologized for not being free because he'd been called to a theft case and had offered to ask another deputy to pick her up. She preferred to walk with Snowy. They both needed it and it probably wouldn't be too long before they had to take shorter walks because of weather.

A smile danced around her mouth as she wondered how many hours she was going to be tossing a ball around her apartment to get the dog some good exercise. A good reason not to have someone living in the apartments around her. They'd have gotten really irritated by the thump of that ball and Snowy's running feet.

The sheriff's office was in the center of town, not too far from the diner, but still a bit of a distance from her apartment. She enjoyed the brightening day and didn't give a thought to the open space around her when she first departed. She wondered if the field had been left undeveloped because the college owned it and was thinking of expansion, or if it was just an accident of geography for some reason.

Regardless, it wasn't too long before she reached the outskirts of Conard City and began to pass widely spaced houses that looked newer than the ones closer to the town's center. One of these days she was going to have to learn something about this place's history. The longer she was here, the more her curiosity began to grow.

Or maybe it was the idea of being deputized that made her want to look forward again. Really look forward, not make haphazard stabs at it, going only as far as wondering if she would teach an additional class next semester.

Gage's offer had lifted her sense of gloom. She hoped it would last.

She stopped at the diner to get a coffee from Maude. She hadn't missed all Stu's remarks about the coffee in the office. "What does the sheriff like?" she asked Maude.

"Strong, black and big," Maude answered. "You want a latte for yourself?"

Scarcely five minutes later she was headed up the street, a half block and one intersection to the office. She was still getting used to the fact that this town, seriously, had only one traffic light. And that at night it blinked.

That was an element of charm she had never dreamed about.

Gage was just about to enter the office when he saw her. He smiled, at least as much as he could with one side of his face scarred by a burn. Someday she wanted to hear the story about that, but she wasn't going to ask *him*.

"Good morning, Sheriff. Coffee?" She handed him the large cup.

"You're a lifesaver, Kerri. Can I call you Kerri?"

"Of course." She smiled. She had no idea whether it was Stu or Gage behind this unexpected opportunity, but she felt lighter on her feet than she had in a while.

"Then call me Gage. Let's go into the conference room."

She felt eyes on her, all of them friendly enough, as she and Snowy walked with Gage across the squad room, for lack of a better word, to the conference room. Apparently, this place was so small they didn't have their main office divvied up by groups. All in it together. She actually liked that idea and believed it would cut down on the inevitable politics.

Once they were inside, he closed the door, giving them privacy. They sat across the long table from each other and Gage sipped his coffee. Kerri unzipped her jacket.

"Bless Maude," he said. "She's saved my stomach countless times. So Stu told you what I'm thinking?"

"Yes."

"I took the liberty of checking your file from your last organization. A lot of commendations."

She felt herself blush faintly. "They handed them out freely."

He shook his head. "I read the letters of commendation. You were on your way to a great career. I'm sorry you got diverted."

Diverted was a nice way to put it, she thought.

"Anyway, I saw your interaction with Edith and found it interesting that she was willing to sit and talk with you. At first, I thought it was just a woman thing when she needed some steadying. But then I heard about Mr. Webley approaching you. It looks like people instinctively trust you."

She hesitated, unsure how to respond to that. Her heart kept tap-tapping as she waited hopefully for the offer she'd never dreamed she might get. Aware, painfully, once again of her limitations.

"I talked to Stu about you. He explained your situation and why you're no longer an officer, but other than that he's impressed with you. I understand why you could no longer work full-time in law enforcement, but you're a qualified victims advocate. I need someone like you, at least periodically, but I wonder how hampered you might feel between your job and your epilepsy."

She folded her hands tightly. She had to be absolutely honest with this man while keeping in mind that this was a job interview. It wasn't in the can, however encouraging Stu had been. Well, except for his worry about her, which she thought was probably overblown.

But as usual, the honesty was going to be painful.

"Hampered," she repeated, not as a question. "I'll let you decide that. I have absence seizures. I'm sure there's a technical name of some kind but I forgot it somewhere in the road through recovery and rehab. Anyway, I just freeze. The problem is that I might as well be unconscious. Anywhere from half a minute to two minutes. As far as I know, none have been longer than that. When I come out of it, I feel confused for a bit. How much confusion depends on how much has changed, but there's always some."

She wondered how many times in her life she was going to have to explain this. But the details seemed important, especially right now, especially given what Gage was contemplating.

He nodded. "And your job?"

"Right now I teach three hours a week. I usually don't need much prep time because I did the work for so long. An hour, maybe two, depending on the subject. That leaves a lot of time."

A whole lot, she thought. She was getting tired of trying to keep herself occupied with long walks and reading. She had a TV and sometimes watched true-crime documentaries, but she feared that abyss. She might wind up lost in it and turn into a virtual couch potato. She needed to screw up her nerve and build some kind of social life.

"If you were dealing with one of these rape victims, how would you handle your seizures?"

"Be honest about them. I'm not happy about constantly having to explain. If there was any way I could just forget them, I would. But if I'm with a victim, she'd have to know."

"Why?" He drank more coffee and waited.

"Because I guess I don't look very friendly when it happens. Because I could miss something. So I'd tell them how my dog alerts me so they could recognize the warning, and explain that they might have to repeat themselves sometimes. But I can't guarantee that nothing would get lost along the way."

She leaned forward, expressing a pain she rarely

shared. "I can't trust myself," she told him. "You want the bare bones of what I feel? I'm scared I might miss something important."

She settled back in the chair, aware that her clasped hands were beginning to cramp. She tried to ease them. After what she had just said, she figured he was going to let her go. Who wanted a cop who could miss important things? Who couldn't drive herself to where she needed to be? It didn't sound good, but these were the very reasons she'd had to take disability.

At last he put his cup down. "Pretty much what Stu told me but with less passion." He winked. "Can't imagine why."

Her stiff lips tried hard to frame a smile.

"Okay, then. If you want the job, it's yours. I don't have to tell you it won't be pleasant, but I want you. These victims need someone like you. Still interested?"

The tension left her like a popping balloon. "Absolutely." She could have jumped for joy.

"I'll expect a daily report of anything they say that you consider significant. Or sooner if you think it can't wait."

"Of course."

"Then consider yourself deputized. You promise to uphold the laws of city, county, state and federal government. And to serve and protect. We take that last part very seriously around here. Do you so swear?"

"I do."

He swiveled his chair and pulled open a drawer in a console against the wall, then pushed her a seven-pointed brass star badge in a leather folding case. "There you go, Deputy."

She looked down at it, drawing a deep breath, reading the magical words across the top of the center circle: *Deputy Sheriff.*

"I'll get your ID card sorted out, but you don't need a uniform. Not for this job. Oh, and I'll need your mug shot for your ID." He gave her his crooked smile.

"Thank you," she said. The words came from deep in her heart.

"Think about that," he said jokingly. "You may change your mind. Anyway, we've got one woman who needs your visit this morning, and the other is starting to show signs of coming out of her coma, so you might have a long day at the hospital today. I advise you to get breakfast or lunch before you see them. There's no predicting how much they may need you."

She rose, feeling that he was dismissing her, but paused to ask, "What about the night?"

"Night?"

"That's when they were raped. It might be the worst time for them."

"Yeah. I know. I was hoping you'd bring that up. They'll have an officer out front for at least a while, but in the meantime, you decide when it's most important for you to be there. Dammit, Deputy, you have to sleep some time."

At last she laughed. It had been trying to bubble up since she'd realized she had the job.

"One more thing," he said as she was about to open the door to leave. "The pay is lousy."

She felt as if she were floating as she left the conference room with Snowy. As if sensing her mood, the dog pranced alongside.

She also knew better than to believe the euphoria would last much longer than it took her to get to the hospital.

She tucked her new badge onto her waistband, its weight familiar and good. When one of the deputies offered to drive her, it struck her. He was her colleague now.

Once again, her life had abruptly changed course. Despite the ugliness that awaited her, she couldn't have asked for a better change.


Stu found Kerri at the hospital. "I heard," he said. "Feel good?"

"Wonderful," she answered with a brilliant smile.

"I'm glad." He was very happy for her. As for him, he could keep his worries to himself. He had years of practice at that.

"May Broadwyn, the second victim, is still in recovery. She's waking up slowly."

He nodded and took the chair beside her. No one else was in the room, so he felt free to talk quietly. "She's going to be okay, though."

"Depends on what you mean by okay."

He couldn't argue with that. All kinds of things could be meant by words like *okay* and *fine*. Once the physical trauma healed, the emotional trauma would remain.

His mind suddenly slipped backward in time. "Field hospital," he said.

"Huh?"

He knew she was looking at him but he couldn't look at her. Not just then as he tried to take control of a memory that wanted to take control of him. "Back in the war. Too many times I had to sit on a folding chair waiting for word on some of my men. The smells here are more antiseptic, though."

He closed his eyes, wishing he couldn't still see it. Hear it. It was quieter here, too. He'd left all that behind. At least physically. He had some idea of what May Broadwyn was going to face.

"Stu?"

Kerri's soft voice drew him back.

"Should you leave? I mean…"

He finally looked at her and saw she was biting her lower lip. "I don't have to tell you that we just need to get through some things. Including memories."

She nodded and looked down at her hands. Her jacket lay on the chair on the other side of her, and Snowy, ever alert, rested at her feet.

He needed to redirect. "That badge looks good on you."

She offered him a smile. "Thanks for helping with this. I don't know how it looks, but I know how it feels. It feels right."

"I bet." He was glad for her and dragged himself away from the mire that bubbled in one corner of his mind. He tried never to slip into it, but this was an exceptionally bad time to let it take over.

"Stu?"

"Yeah." God, her green eyes were beautiful. Giving up, he allowed himself to notice her loveliness. Rusty red hair, cut in a businesslike manner he suspected she'd worn in uniform, small soft curls just beginning to show. A smattering of light freckles over her cheekbones, and a mouth perfectly sized for the rest of her oval face.

He glanced away, reining himself in. "You were saying?"

"I wasn't in the war, but I saw…things."

"I know you did. They come back to haunt us sometimes, don't they."

"Yes."

His hand rested palm down on his thigh, and he felt zapped when she reached out hers to rest on top of it. He'd been aware of how much she generally avoided contact with him, and this surprised him as well as causing his internal temperature to rise. Was this a sea change of some kind?

"Anyway," she continued, pressing gently on his hand, "I've been too self-absorbed lately to think much about it. I just want you to know that I have a small idea of things you must be dealing with."

"Probably more than a small idea."

He watched her shake her head. "War is a whole different thing. A bigger thing. I'm glad I never had to see it."

Then she withdrew her hand, as if trying to break the connection she had started to make.

At that moment, a scrub-clad woman entered the small waiting room. "Deputy Addison? They're bringing her back from recovery. I doubt she'll be very awake for a while, though."

Kerri rose to her feet. "Did you reach her family?"

"They called. I guess your office told them? Anyway, they're on their way from Missoula. It's a long enough trip as is, but Mr. Broadwyn said they'd run into some heavy snow in the mountains and might not be able to make it."

Kerri nodded. "She'll need someone there when she wakes up. Will I do?"

The woman smiled. "You can be with her longer than I can."

Then she looked at Stu. "Hi, Stu."

"Hi, Mary. How's it going?"

"Not bad." She started to turn away. "Oh." She looked at Kerri. "Are you involved with Sandra Carney's case, as well?"

"I am," Kerri said.

"There's some evidence that she might be returning to us, but she's still a long way from communicating. That creep gave her a really serious concussion."

Stu saw Kerri's hand rise to the side of her head, then drop.

"Any family on the way?"

Mary shook her head. "Sandra Carney has been here all her life, but I don't know what happened to her parents. Even in a small town, people come and go. But I'm sure we'd have heard if they'd died here. That much I can say with certainty."

Stu spoke. "I'm sure we're on it."

Mary nodded. "I'm sure you are."

She walked out and Kerri turned to Stu. "Doesn't she have friends who would know?"

Stu shrugged. "I can sometimes be the last to know."

"What were you doing this morning?"

"Chasing escaped cattle out of a road before someone had a serious accident."

He watched her laugh. "What can I say? Law enforcement in a county full of ranches. Cows are easier than sheep, though. Let me know when you're done for the day. I can once again be the bringer of dinner."

"Oh, Stu, you don't have to."

"Unless you just don't want me around, I *want* to. Eating alone is seldom a great experience."

"I'd like to see you but don't wait. I don't know how long I'll need to be here."

"You got it."

Kerri watched him leave, shrugging into his jacket, and wondered if he'd just said something important. Eating alone was seldom a great experience? Well, that was true enough, but they both must be used to it. It was especially difficult for people who often worked different shifts from their friends.

So you ate alone. She gave an internal shrug. He'd probably meant nothing at all, but she made a mental note for her next shopping trip. Buy enough to cook for two.

Then she picked up her jacket and Snowy's leash and headed for the room where they'd earlier told her would be May Broadwyn's. She definitely didn't want the woman to awake alone.

It was around seven that evening when May woke enough to do more than groan. At last she saw Kerri sitting nearby. "Thirsty."

"I'll bet. Let me get a nurse to find out if you should have water or ice chips."

Before stepping into the hallway, Kerri pressed the

call button into her hand. "If you need anything before I get back, press the button under your thumb."

The woman gave the slightest nod.

A nurse happened to be coming out of the room next
door. "May's thirsty. Water or ice chips?"

"I'll get her something. Given she's on a morphine
drip, I need to check her status first."

The nurse entered May's room and Kerri and Snowy
waited outside. She didn't want to intrude unnecessar-
ily on the woman's privacy, although at the moment
May probably didn't much care.

When the nurse emerged, Kerri started back inside.
"I'll bring more ice chips," the nurse said.

"Thank you."

She'd seen male nurses wandering around and was
glad they weren't sending any to May. She might not
be ready to deal with men.

Back inside the room, she settled on the visitor's
chair and watched May suck on some ice.

"Mmm. Needed that."

"I remember feeling the same way after I had surgery."

May's gaze drifted to her. "Who are you? Did I
see a dog?"

"My service dog. Snowy. I'm Kerri Addison, with
the sheriff's office."

"Oh, God, it wasn't a nightmare."

Kerri remained silent, watching tears seep from beneath May's closed eyelids. When the tears kept coming, she grabbed a tissue from the box on the bedside
table and dabbed May's face gently.

"I was hoping," May said, her voice still rough from

the breathing tube during the operation, "that it was a car accident."

"I'm sorry."

But May drifted off again, for a brief while escaping her memory.

Around seven, Gage sent another deputy to relieve her, Sarah Ironheart. Sarah was a tall woman with a kindly face and raven black hair streaked with gray.

"Gage said to tell you to get out of here, eat something and cadge some rest. I'll do for now." Sarah glanced at the sleeping woman. "I bet she doesn't come all the way back until morning."

Kerri, stiff from sitting, rose, taking Snowy's leash and her jacket. "Call me if she wakes up more? I need to grow some rapport here. Oh, and if she asks, her parents hope to be here by tomorrow. Something about a snowstorm in the mountains between here and Missoula."

Sarah nodded. "Up there they get snow in the middle of summer sometimes. I'll call. Give me your number."

They exchanged phone numbers. Kerri tugged on her jacket, picked up Snowy's leash yet again, then paused to look wryly at Sarah. "I'm from a pretty warm climate. This jacket thing is still defeating me."

Sarah laughed quietly. "You'd have remembered as soon as you got outside."

"I hope so."

"Oh, and Stu is waiting for you out front."

Kerri paused. "How'd that happen?"

Sarah grinned. "We thought he'd want to be notified if you were relieved."

Oh, man, Kerri thought. This was getting ridiculous. It was true she couldn't drive. Everyone in the department knew that, thanks to Stu's car-pool idea, but still. Any one of them could have come to give her a lift home.

Yet they had called Stu. If the man didn't get sick of her seizures first, he was going to get sick of feeling like her personal valet.

The day had already fled, leaving darkness in its wake. The moon was just rising, adding its silvery sheen to the lights in the parking lot. And there was Stu, near the front door, engine idling.

"They didn't have to call you," she said as Snowy leaped in and she followed, closing the car door behind her.

"You were supposed to call me, anyway. I asked, remember." The grin he gave her said he was enjoying this.

"I don't want to be an item," she said querulously. It struck her that she hadn't eaten as Gage had told her to. Hunger was affecting her mood.

"Too late," he answered as he put the car in gear and began to drive from the lot.

"Apparently. Sorry. I forgot to eat lunch."

"That'll put anyone in a sour mood. Don't worry about it." At the end of the lot, he turned on the road leading to the downtown. "You've got your usual choices. Preference for eating in or out?"

"What I'd really like is a huge breakfast."

"Well, there's actually a place you can get one."

Which is how she came to be introduced to the truck stop café. Trucks growled in the parking lot, waiting for drivers who were probably going to be on the road all night. Inside was fairly busy, but not so busy they couldn't choose seating.

"Counter, booth or table?" Stu asked her.

It had been a long time since she'd eaten at a counter. It had been common enough to grab a bite at one when she'd been on duty before. Quick, easy and out in a flash if necessary. The badge at her waist made her feel braver, she realized as she considered a stool. Then she looked down at Snowy. Things were not the same.

"Snowy," she said. "A booth or a table so he won't be underfoot. And no danger of tripping anyone."

The waitress who came over to take care of them was a student from Kerri's class. "Karen, how nice to see you."

Karen smiled. "Nice to see you, too, Ms. Addison. I wondered if you were ever going to find this place."

"I finally did. How's breakfast tonight?"

"Hasty—he's the owner and grill man—he'll make you one you won't forget. Try the onion omelet, if you like onions. It's my favorite."

"Then I will."

"Hash browns, home fries? Side of ham or bacon?"

Kerri looked at Stu. "I wasn't kidding about being famished. Home fries, Karen, please. With a side of ham."

"Toast or muffin?"

"Wow. You've got everything."

Karen laughed. "We get a lot of big appetites in here. Hasty will take care of you." She turned to Stu, whose order differed from Kerri's only in that he wanted biscuits and gravy instead of home fries.

The breakfast was delicious, everything perfectly cooked. Kerri glanced over at Hasty, working the grill, and wished she'd been able to sit at the counter. A good grill man practically performed a flawless ballet, well worth viewing.

She and Stu talked casually, both of them avoiding anything heavy. She talked about teaching; he talked about rounding up cattle and sheep.

Then as they were ready to leave, he said, "Now that I can talk to you, I'll share our few developments in the case. When we get out of here."

She nodded, understanding that this was something that must not be overheard. They drove back toward town until he took the turn to the apartment complex.

"You don't mind?" he asked.

"Why would I?" She was eager to hear every word. "Snowy must be desperate to eat by now."

Stu gave a quiet laugh. "Yeah, he didn't get offered a burger."

"Maude's being really nice about that."

"Maude has a very familiar and old clientele. Not one of them would risk shutting her down over giving a service dog a burger on a paper plate. Hasty, on the other hand, is dealing with truckers, some familiar, some not."

Made sense to her. "Just so you know, I wasn't expecting him to."

"Didn't think you were."

Once again they wheeled into a parking space. The lot was mostly empty, except for some cars at the other end. And it was not as well lighted as the hospital.

Snowy knew he was home and was looking forward

to his evening check of the grassy area in front of the building. "Got a plastic shopping bag?" she asked Stu. "I need to clean up after Snowy."

"I think I do." He twisted to look into the back seat where Snowy was alert and sitting up, his tail sweeping the seat.

"Yup," Stu said, pulling out a shopping bag. "I usually take them to recycle, when I forget my reusable bags."

"Good man," she answered, hiding her eagerness to get inside and get more details about the investigation.

Once there, Stu started a pot of coffee without asking. Obviously, he felt familiar enough to do that now. She liked it. She was also certain that he had something to do with the badge on her belt even though he wouldn't say so. She pulled it off reluctantly and placed it on the counter, admiring it. Then she fed Snowy, who ate as if he were ravenous. Which he probably was.

"You sure do like your coffee," she remarked.

"You're a cop. You should know."

"Hah," she answered, smiling. "A bottle of antacids in every car. But not just for coffee."

"Nope. Some parts of this job just kill the stomach."

"But not chasing cows?"

"Don't make fun of it. Best time I had all day."

At last he led the way into the living room. She declined the coffee, acknowledging that Sarah Ironheart had been right to tell her to get some sleep. Tomorrow might turn out to be awfully long and terribly stressful as she wended her way through the fear to gain the trust of May Broadwyn.

Instead of taking her favorite battered recliner, she sat on the opposite edge of the couch from him.

"Okay, the only real news I have is that apparently the rapist circled around May through the trees to come at her from the side."

"How do you know?"

"He scuffed the leaves and I found one big, beautiful boot print. We made a cast of it and the state crime lab is in the process of trying to identify the type of boot and which marks might distinguish it from others."

She nodded, considering. "So Mr. Webley saw him enter the park through the entrance, but the circling indicates clear intent. Nobody else would have done that."

"A kid, maybe, but the impression was too big, and probably too recent."

She frowned, her mind already buzzing. "Weren't the leaves dry? Wouldn't she have been able to hear him?"

"They were damp. As good as silent. The park has an automatic sprinkler system."

"Ah."

"The SAVE kits are out for analysis. We can hope there's some DNA, but you know how that goes. If he's a nonsecreter, no DNA. If he isn't and leaves some behind, it's no good until we get a match. We can hope he's in a database somewhere, but I'm not holding my breath."

She understood that frustration. DNA, once a questionable bit of proof, had advanced so greatly that now it was highly accurate.

She spoke. "Isn't it interesting how they're solving

cases from decades ago because of public DNA testing for people who want to know who their forebears are?"

"It makes me want to laugh, on one level." He smiled over his coffee cup. "As long as someone properly preserved the evidence, that is."

Another big problem. A lot of evidence disappeared after years. "Do you have a cold case rule here?" she wondered.

"Oh, yeah. If it isn't solved, the evidence stays in a warehouse. If someone is in prison, the same until he or she finishes the appeals process. You probably haven't seen it, but there's a big public records storage facility south of town."

"I haven't seen it. I guess I haven't been getting around enough."

"It's not worth going out of your way." He drained his cup and rose. "Want me to turn off the coffee or leave it on?"

"Leave it on," she decided. So much had happened that day that she felt a need to sort through it. And maybe take another look at the badge until she could believe it was real.

"You stay," he said when she rose. "I'll let myself out. Just be sure to lock up." He shook his head. "I'm not used to saying that around here. You have a good night."

Then he was gone and she was alone with Snowy and the otherwise empty apartment. That was okay. She needed to get some sleep if she was going to be any use to May tomorrow.

Unable to help herself, she went back over to the counter to look again at her new badge. It was real, and she found it almost indescribable to explain how it was affecting her.

Secure? She had certainly felt braver walking into that truck stop than she would have before. She'd felt taller, straighter, not as apologetic.

Ridiculous. Her seizures weren't a failure. But deep inside she couldn't help but *believe* they made her one. Now she had a badge again. A real purpose. Teaching criminal justice had only been second best for her, the only replacement for losing her career. If she could no longer do it, maybe she could teach it. Make better cops.

At least that was her stated objective, but it hadn't left her feeling fulfilled. Slinking around, almost. Not wanting to meet people for fear they'd see her seize. Might be a ridiculous attitude, but there it was.

She'd felt a shift when Gage had deputized her and handed her a badge. But how much of a shift she hadn't realized until she walked into that truck stop. An empty hole had been filled, but more importantly, some of her confidence had returned.

She could still do part of the job and she was being given a chance. She couldn't ask for more than that.

# Chapter 9

Ivan was getting nervous. The cops hadn't seemed like much of a threat after his first rape, but now he was hearing things, things like they'd found something.

No details, just the gossip floating around. He wondered if it was true.

Nerves wouldn't leave him alone, so he dragged out an old bicycle to ride past the park. He didn't want anyone to notice his interest, and he thought the bicycle would be good cover. Anyone who'd noticed him earlier might think they were mistaken. Besides, it was a good way to ride past as if he had no special interest.

Maybe he should have stayed with coeds. None of them had even considered filing a complaint. Although he had to admit, he hadn't cut or seriously beaten either of them. He'd maybe gone too far with these two.

But the power! It wasn't just a rape. He'd been holding the lives of the last two in his hands. Now *that* was true power.

He seldom wondered why he had such a thirst for power over women. He just knew it was a rush greater than any other. His drug, he thought, and laughed inwardly. He was no addict.

Which completely missed the point that he was.

He saw nothing to alarm him as he rode past the park. The operation seemed to be winding down. Fewer cops. Maybe later he'd be able to ride down the paths and get another look at where he'd done it.

But he mustn't slow down, he reminded himself. A glance or two, no more.

He looked toward the street and saw a sheriff's SUV drive by. What the hell was that teacher doing inside it, that new one from the college?

Crap. He'd wondered when he'd seen her hanging with that old crone, Edith Jasper. Did she have something to do with this? Some role?

He needed to find out. He needed to know where all the pieces were in case he had to do something.

Like playing chess, he told himself. Move pieces on the board, find a way to neutralize threats.

He was a decent chess player. He'd keep outsmarting them all.

Sarah was still sitting in May's hospital room, looking weary.

"You stayed all night? You should have called me, Sarah."

"I've pulled all-nighters before," Sarah answered.

"May is starting to wake some, for longer periods. She hasn't said anything except to ask about her parents. I told her they were caught in a snowstorm. She fell asleep again so fast I'm not even sure that registered."

"Thanks so much for everything."

Sarah smiled wanly. "At least you look better. Anyway, it got me out of patrol, so I'm not complaining. We might have to work out some shifts, somehow. Gage said you were worried about the nights."

"Yeah, I am. The dark may be too much for her to handle for a while."

"Well, if someone's there, she'll probably be able to sleep. After a few days, at any rate. We'll find a way."

Then Kerri was alone with May again. At least Deputy Beauregard had been in favor of stopping at Maude's for her to get a large latte. She imagined she'd be wanting them all day long, and no way to get one.

She resumed her post near the bed, waiting for May to wake enough to talk. Nurses came and went, checking on her, but none of that disturbed her.

She was hiding, Kerri thought. She'd done a bit of that herself, making use of the post-op morphine to stay drowsy and slip away. There were times when a person just needed to escape reality and was reluctant to return to it again.

Around noon, however, a staff member appeared carrying a tray of what appeared to be soft foods for May. She was shortly followed by a nurse who gently woke her.

"Ms. Broadwyn. Ms. Broadwyn, you need to wake up and eat. If you can't, the doctor will reduce your pain medication. Would you like me to raise the head of your bed for you?"

A groan answered her, but May's eyes opened. "I don't know," she said, her words slurring a bit.

"I know you'd like to sleep," the nurse continued. "I know it hurts to move, but it's not good for you to hold still for so long. Like it or not, you have to at least sit up."

May winced as the woman raised the head of her bed and Kerri winced right along with her. She had no idea of the extent of May's injuries, but she remembered how badly her own head had ached and burned, and how a change of position could cause her brain to pound.

The woman smiled and put the tray table in front of May so she could easily reach it. "Your friend here will help, I'm sure."

"Friend?"

For the first time May seemed to see Kerri. Kerri had discarded her jacket so her badge was plainly visible. Snowy was visible, too, because he sat up giving the dog version of a smile.

"A dog? Isn't this a hospital?"

"He's my service dog. Does he bother you?" What she would do if May had an aversion to dogs, she couldn't imagine. Clearly she'd be unable to stay and someone else would have to take the job. The thought made her heart sink. She *wanted* to do this.

"No. He doesn't bother me." She looked at the tray in front of her. "I don't want to eat."

"The morphine they have you on can depress the

appetite. Are you sure there's nothing there that you couldn't even take a bite of?"

After a minute or so of staring at the food, May raised an arm, wincing, and took the bowl of red gelatin. "I hope it's not cherry," she said. Then she lifted a spoon, wincing again.

"God, what did that freak do to me?"

"You'll have to ask your doctor that. Because I don't have the details."

May sighed and managed to get a spoonful into her mouth. "Raspberry, thank goodness." Her eyes were growing clearer and her gaze settled on Kerri. "Why are you here? You think he might come after me again?"

"No, we don't expect that. I'm here to give you whatever support you need, and to be someone you can talk to."

"I can talk to my mother when she gets here."

"Sure. All the details?"

At that May stopped moving for a few seconds. "Maybe not," she said finally. The gelatin seemed to have wakened her appetite because she next dived into a fruit-and-syrup-covered cake. "The calories," she muttered.

"You need them right now, so enjoy them."

After a few more mouthfuls, May reached for the carton of milk. "Can you help?"

"Sure." Kerri turned the glass upright, opened the container and poured half of it into the glass. Then she opened the bendy straw, put it in the glass and passed it to May.

"Okay," May said when she finished the milk. "You're not here to protect me so are you my watchdog?"

"I doubt you need one right now," Kerri said drily. "No, I'm here to keep you company among other things. I've worked with quite a few women who had experiences similar to yours. Guess what, I can be sympathetic, insofar as possible. And I'm also here in case you remember something that would be useful to catching this monster."

May nodded slightly. "But I don't want to remember."

"I'm sure, but it's been my experience that details will pop up, anyway, at any time. You can tell me. Honestly, you can tell me anything about this."

May's attention drifted to Snowy. "Why do you have a service dog?"

Kerri went through the explanation once again. Oddly, repetition didn't seem to be making it easier.

"You were shot?" May's eyes grew wider. "Oh, man."

Kerri couldn't shrug it off, so she simply nodded.

"And now you're disabled."

"Yes."

"Man, that stinks." Then May pushed weakly at the table. Kerri obligingly moved it to one side.

"Better?"

"Thanks." But May's eyelids were growing heavy again, and soon she fell back to sleep. Kerri wondered if she should lower the head of the bed, then decided against it. She didn't want to disturb the sleeping woman.

Her stomach growled. While May was sleeping she

ought to go to the hospital cafeteria and take Snowy outside to do his business. Poor dog. Maybe she'd buy him a burger.

She paused just long enough to let staff know where she was going. Snowy pranced with delight to be moving again. He also wolfed down the burger once they were outside.

*My kingdom for a latte*, she thought when at last they headed back to May's room.

May was awake, and the instant she saw Kerri, she said, "I thought you'd left me alone."

"I just had to get something to eat for me and Snowy."

May sighed. "Okay. I'm not being rational. There are lots of people here. *But I don't want to be alone.*"

And thus, thought Kerri, began the real fallout. Not the physical wounds, which were bad enough, but the emotional ones.

May would never again be the same.

Late afternoon, May's family arrived carrying flowers and apologizing for the snowstorm, as if they could have prevented it. The visit quickly dissolved into tears and gentle hugs between parents and daughter. When at last they calmed down a bit, May's mother, on hearing why Kerri was here, thanked her.

Then she said, "You must need some time for yourself. We'll sit here with May."

Kerri paused long enough to look May in the eye. "Anything you remember," she reminded her. "Day or night. The sheriff's switchboard will connect you to me."

"I'll let you know."

Kerri hoped she would keep that promise in the coming days. Information was best fresh, but there was no way she could interfere with the family visit. It was too important to May.

She stopped in to see how the other victim was doing. She couldn't be given a lot of detail, and besides, she was sure the techs had already learned what they could about the condition of Sandra Carney.

The nurse shook her head. "She's still working her way out of the coma, and she's pretty much incoherent. Try again tomorrow but she's had a severe concussion."

And probably didn't remember much, if anything, that led up to that blow to her head. Kerri still wasn't sure how much she didn't remember about the events leading up to her shooting.

Stu had been avoiding Kerri for the last three days, primarily because he had the sense that she wasn't happy with the idea of being *an item* in the public mind. He didn't care one way or the other because he'd learned how gossip worked around here, and how fast it could just die down as something new came up. What's more, being an item was hardly a malicious thing.

But he *did* notice something important, and soon other deputies were talking about it. Women were staying off the streets as much as possible. The vibrancy of this town had died down. He wondered how many shotguns were ready in those houses. A dangerous number, he was sure, especially if it was a woman alone, however temporarily.

So far Sandra Carney was hardly talking. May's

family was getting ready to return to Missoula. He wondered how that was making May feel. Maybe they'd offered to take her with them, and she'd refused. At this point he had no idea.

He thought of Kerri again and realized he was missing her. Given the distance she had tried to maintain between them, he told himself to forget it.

Only forgetting wasn't working very well, not with anything. There was a rapist prowling these streets, looking for his next victim. The feeling of a threat just beyond the edge of his knowledge was one he was too familiar with from war. Now here it was again.

And Kerri was hanging out at the empty end of an apartment building. He didn't trust the dog to protect her. Snowy was a service animal, probably chosen in part because he wasn't aggressive. What she needed was a Doberman or rottweiler. Trained by Cadell Marcus.

Yeah, she needed Snowy, but not for protection. Not against physical threats.

"Ah, hell," he said out loud.

Then the dispatcher called. "Four ninety-two needs a ride home from the hospital."

He answered immediately. "Seven sixty-five. I've got it, Velma."

"Should have known it would be you, Stu."

"I just happen to be nearby."

"Yeah. Sure."

Dang that woman. She acted as if she were everyone's mother and had a right to comment on nonpolice matters. Nobody objected, however. Velma had been part of the scenery in all their lives.

He pulled up in front of the main entrance and Kerri and her dog emerged almost immediately, bundled up against the increasing chill in the weather. He turned up the heater a notch for her benefit. Adjusting would take some time.

"Hey," he said as she allowed Snowy to climb in first, then slipped into the passenger seat. "How's it going?"

"Nowhere," she answered bluntly. "Can I stop to pick up something for dinner? The hospital cafeteria isn't bad, but the selection is limited and I'm tired of it."

"Sure," he said as he put the car in Drive. "What are you in the mood for? If you're really desperate there's a pizza chain at the outskirts. If you like soda cracker crust, that is. I swear yeast has never come close to it."

She laughed. "No thanks."

She looked tired, he thought. Very. "What are you hungry for? Given the limitations of the local menus, that is. I hope that Tex-Mex place opens soon." He glanced at his dashboard computer and communications console. An upgrade through state funding a few years back, he'd heard. Maybe overkill for this area, but useful.

"I'm afraid the bakery is closed for the day. I need to get you there for lunch sometime. Sandwiches and a soup of the day that you can die for."

"Sounds good and you're making me even more hungry." She shook her head a little. "I'm feeling useless again. May has her family right now, so I'm kind of superfluous. She agreed to call if she remembers anything. Oh, well, the family is leaving in the morning and I guess she's going to stay here. Gutsy woman."

"I'd have guessed," he remarked.

"And Sandra Carney is nowhere near ready to talk."

Stu glanced over in time to see her bite her lip. "The concussion?"

"Really bad. I'd be surprised if she remembers much at all, when and if she recovers."

"Yeah. That may wind up being a blessing for her."

"I doubt it. She'll always wonder, and the fears will sprout from what others say. But at least forgetting the violence would be good."

They were almost into town and she evidently made up her mind. "Maude's," she said.

He smiled. "Just what I'm in the mood for."

He felt her look at him.

"You don't have to eat just because I want to pick up something."

"I'm famished, too. Collision out on the state highway at five this morning. This is my first break. I was headed back in when I got the call that you needed a ride."

"You shouldn't have stopped, Stu. I could have waited."

"I was practically here." And she was expressing her wish for distance between them. At least that's what he read. He could always be wrong, but this time he doubted it. The feeling caused an unusual ache in him, one that went beyond the increasing desire for her that kept settling in his groin. It was getting so that at night when he closed his eyes he imagined her naked in his arms, felt her satiny skin close and warm to him. A fire waiting to turn into a conflagration.

Dangerous. He forced his mind away.

Instead, he wondered why she was so skittish. He knew she considered her epilepsy to be a big problem, understandably so, but it shouldn't prevent her from forming relationships, should it?

He pulled up to Maude's and his stomach started growling so loudly he felt the need to apologize.

Kerri surprised him by laughing. "Mine feels about the same. Let's go clean out the diner."

"I'm all in favor."

Inside the only patrons were older men, and there weren't very many of them.

"This town is beginning to shut down," Stu remarked quietly. "Nerves. Fear."

She nodded as they made their way to a table near the back, away from nearly everyone. "You can never guess how far a guy like this might go."

"That's always the problem."

Maude arrived and slapped the menus in front of them. "Coffee, same as always?"

"Please," they answered in unison.

"You catch that creep. He's killing my business."

She stomped away and Kerri looked at Stu with wide eyes. "Her *business*?"

"That's Maude. Easier to talk about for her."

"If you say so."

He watched Kerri begin to study her menu, then damning anyone who might see, he reached across the table to touch her hand. Her head snapped up.

He squeezed her fingers gently, feeling the soft skin, feeling the warmth. When he slid his hand a bit higher, he stroked the inside of her wrist lightly, watching her eyes widen, hearing her intake of breath.

He chose a safe topic while the touch between them worked its magic. He wished he knew some damn romantic thing to say.

She spoke, her voice a bit husky. "It must be hard for you to spend so much time at the hospital. After your own experience."

When she didn't answer immediately, he risked it. "Kerri, I'd have come from the far end of the county just to pick you up."

She drew another deep breath, looking down at his hand but didn't pull away from his light touch.

She spoke again, referencing what he'd told her about being in the war. Clearly searching for safer ground. "I thought *you* were the one having a hard time with being in a hospital waiting. I didn't have to wait, just survive."

"True."

Then she astonished him by turning her hand over and clasping his fingers to give him a gentle squeeze. "I hope you're not hoping."

"Hoping?"

"For a relationship between us. It has nothing to do with you, Stu. It's all me. I'd just be a great big burden. I don't want to be a burden to any one person. I even hate it that I need someone to drive me to the store. Why would any man want to be saddled with that?"

Well, he didn't think it was a saddle, but he wasn't sure how she was reading so much into a single touch.

Except she wasn't wrong. He was dodging his attraction to her because he believed she didn't want it. Now he knew why.

And his face must have betrayed more than he ever would have guessed.

"You wouldn't be a problem," he said firmly, then withdrew his hand and changed the subject, for his own comfort as much as anything. "I hope the state lab comes back with something useful soon."

She nodded. "What did you think of that boot print?"

"It's probably going to turn out to be like a million other work boots."

That brought a smile to her face. "So, no great Night Stalker reveal?"

"I wish. That was pretty much one in a million." He had read about the case, where they'd finally found a serial rapist because he was wearing a rare athletic shoe, one that had been sold to only a handful of people in the area. The cops looked at the handful and found a shoe with a distinctive cut mark across the sole. Nailed him.

"Yeah, too much to hope for. Still, it was a great find. So much of what we find is only useful later, but I wouldn't want to question a witness or go to trial without it."

Maude brought their coffee, two lattes not just one, eyeing Stu and saying, "You okay with that?"

"Oh, yeah, I'm famished. The milk will be good."

"I thought so. Decided yet? I'm assuming the hound wants another burger, but what about you two?"

After dinner, Stu drove her back to her apartment, then asked before they went inside, "Game for a walk? I need to stretch."

She hesitated, then said, "Yeah, that would be nice

for both Snowy and me. I'm not getting nearly enough activity these days."

"Because of the new job?"

"It's not just that. I seem to be suffering from reluctance."

Reluctance about a lot of things, Stu thought as they climbed out of his vehicle. If he wanted anything more with this lady, he had his work cut out for him. She'd made her reasons clear, but he needed to convince her they didn't matter to him, not if they involved her physical problems. If she didn't like him in any way except as a friend…well, that was her right.

But he felt an increasing need to know for sure. Her protest about not wanting a relationship didn't quite ring true. And maybe he was just being a pigheaded fool.

Damn, he hadn't felt this way in a long time. He had his own problems that had made him reluctant to get involved. Sandra Carney had ditched him when she couldn't handle his PTSD. If anyone should understand Kerri's position, it should be him.

But the attraction he had begun to feel for her was overriding logic. If she could stand his problems, he could definitely stand hers, which actually seemed minor to him.

She had plenty of reason not to see them that way. They'd changed her entire life. But maybe he could encourage her to see herself differently. After all, everyone had some problems. Nobody was perfect.

All that mattered was that you meshed, and he liked the way they were beginning to mesh.

They'd only gone halfway around the block when she unzipped her jacket. "Stu?"

"Yo?"

"Is it getting warmer or am I adapting?"

He nearly laughed. "I wish I could tell you you're already getting used to the cold, but at this time of year we often get a few warm spells. Enjoy them to the fullest because once winter really sets in, it might be after New Year's before we get what we call a January thaw. How much of a thaw depends on the temp and duration. Makes nice icicles, though."

Ivan noticed the warming weather, too. It was midnight again, as he made his rounds seeking his next victim, and he felt the air changing. The chill became less biting, and the air seemed a little softer. Better for his purposes, especially if it lasted for a few days.

He knew from experience that these bursts of warmer weather caused many locals to open their windows, even at night. Everyone was braced for the months ahead when opening one of those windows could invite frost in the bedroom.

But for now a respite, one that many would be eager to take advantage of. What harm could come from cracking a window an inch or two, and it would freshen the indoor air.

The streets were even quieter than usual tonight, and he took full credit for that. He enjoyed knowing he'd frightened most of the town. More power.

He loosened his coat a bit and considered taking off his watch cap, then decided against it. He didn't want to be too identifiable if someone remembered seeing him out here at this late hour. His ski mask would have been too much, though. It would definitely have made him stand out as the air warmed.

He'd been listening closely to casual conversations at the grocery, and at Freitag's where he pretended to be hunting up a new sweater. While the town had quieted during the daylight hours, it was still clear that people felt safe enough in retail stores. They seemed to him to be staying longer and talking more, as if they didn't want to go home.

It pleased him that while nearly everyone mentioned the rapes, they apparently hadn't realized his method, except that he found women alone late at night. The opportunity in the park had given him an additional level of cover. No reason for most people to suspect that he was seeking women in their own beds.

But that's where he really wanted them. In their safe space. It made the violation so much stronger. He liked to think about his first target here in town. The second one might not ever feel safe about jogging in the middle of the night but the first one... The first one would never feel safe in her own bed again.

Sometimes he liked to sit back and envision his deeds like ripples spreading forward in time, making his mark on those women permanent. He was permanently stamping his mark on the future.

Too bad he couldn't sign his work, but not even his compulsion would drive him that far.

Because of snatches he'd overheard today, he had four addresses to check. Women who lived alone or would be alone for a few days while a roommate or husband was traveling.

One of the four. He needed to check the environs around the addresses so he could plan his escape and see if entry was feasible from any angle. If he found a good one or two, he'd start watching.

Because as sure as the weather was warming a bit, one of them might dare to crack a window.

Not that he was limited to that. He *could* pick a lock. But the more he had to do to gain entry, the longer it took and the greater the possibility he might leave evidence behind. Simple was best and safest.

And *so* many people preferred to sleep with a little fresh air. All he needed was one.

In the meantime, he'd continue to spend a little time listening and waiting during the day.

For right now he was glad to see the streets so quiet. Easier for him. Powerful for him. Damn, he'd found a new rush.

# Chapter 10

Eventually, May's family had to return home. Kerri assured them the sheriff and police intended to keep an eye on the house, but that it was rare for a rapist to return.

The family left because they had jobs to return to. May sent them on their way as if she were fine and said she would keep in touch so they didn't have to worry.

Kerri went to the hospital to check on Sandra, but when she spoke to her it was inescapable. The woman had been so severely injured by blows to her head, and perhaps loss of blood, that she wasn't even coherent. She not only acted dazed, but she couldn't even manage the words to ask for water. Would she recover? No one knew yet.

Then back to May's house. Her mother had refreshed the place and done the laundry, trying to be useful. But May looked at Kerri and said honestly, "I can't sleep in my bedroom anymore. I'm afraid of looking out at the backyard. It's so dark. There are so many shadows…"

Kerri nodded. "Do you have another room? I can make it up for you and move anything you want."

May managed a wan smile. "Thank you. I didn't tell my family I was afraid. They're worried enough. But you understand, don't you?"

"Yes, I do." Carefully, Kerri reached out to touch her hand. "I'm here for you."

"I know. Thank you."

They were sitting at May's kitchen table, and Kerri asked if she wanted coffee or tea.

"Coffee, please. If you don't mind."

It was while Kerri was putting the grounds in the filter that May gave her a slight jolt.

"I like your service dog."

"He's great, isn't he?"

"You know what the trauma feels like. You were shot."

Kerri closed her eyes momentarily, then resumed making coffee. A carafe of water went into the drip machine. "Yes, I was," she said, hoping she wouldn't need to say any more. "But it was different. It felt less personal."

"Were you afraid, too?"

Kerri knew that only a truthful answer would suffice, so she crawled back into that dark den of her memory. "It's hard to recall now. I was severely concussed. Confused for a while. But since I'd been shot on the job, I wasn't worried about myself when I was home. Especially since the guy was already in jail."

"That would help," May admitted, then burst into tears. "Oh, God, I couldn't even cry when my family was here. I didn't want to upset them more. Do you know what it's like to keep holding back tears? If they lived next door it would be different, but both of them have to work, and they had to get home."

Kerri came to the table and sat while the coffee brewed. "So that's why you told them you'd be fine and to just go?"

May nodded. "Why should that monster ruin their lives, too?"

Good question. Unfortunately, crimes had a way of rippling out, affecting friends, family and even entire communities. This one and Sandra's seemed to have the whole community on edge. How many friends and colleagues did she have who were shaken to their cores by this? All of them, whoever they were.

"It's rare when a crime only affects the victim."

"I suppose." May reached for a tissue from the box at one end of the table, wiping her eyes with no thought of how sore that was going to make her skin. As if she didn't care.

Kerri rose and poured May some coffee. "How do you like it?"

"There's some cream in the fridge. Just a little. No more than a teaspoon or so."

Kerri brought it back to the table and resumed her seat.

May spoke as she stared into her cup. "You're hoping I'll remember something."

"I think we all do, but that's not the only reason I'm here."

May raised her eyes. "No?"

"I'm here to support you in whatever way you need. Friends care, of course, but some of this may be awfully hard for them."

"And you're used to it?" May's tone sharpened a bit.

"I'll never get used to it. I just have more experience. Trust me, that's a very different thing."

"Maybe. But if you've never been assaulted like I was, you can't possibly know."

"In that sense," Kerri said quietly, "no one will ever know. Your experience is unique to you. Even if you shouted every detail from the rooftops, nobody would fully understand where you've been and what you're dealing with now. All I can say is that I've sat with an awful lot of rape victims. I try to understand. I certainly care. But I'm here for *you*."

"I don't want to remember," May burst out, then began to cry again.

"Then don't." As if May would ever be able to forget it. Memory might ease its stranglehold with time, but it would never go away.

May fell silent for a long time. She was drinking her second cup of coffee before she said, "I couldn't sleep. It happens sometimes. So I went out for a jog. It's usually safe out there. Usually. I wasn't even paying attention."

Kerri leaned across the table, feeling everything inside her tense. She knew where this would lead. "May, listen to me."

Those sad eyes rose and met hers.

"This was not your fault. Not even in the smallest way. You should have been able to jog anywhere in this town, including the park pathway, without having to be afraid or concerned. You are *not* responsible for what happened. Don't even let that seed take root."

"But I should have been more alert!"

"No. Alert for what? A random madman bursting out of the trees to assault you? That was all on him. Every bit of it. People sometimes don't get it, but you are entitled to be safe. *Entitled.* We can't all go creeping around in fear. We can't. You didn't do a damn thing wrong."

"But what about you?"

"This isn't about me," Kerri argued. But from May's pinched eyes, she realized she wasn't going to get off that easily. "What about me? I'll tell you. First of all, I was a police officer and I knew every time I put on a uniform I was taking a risk. Usually a small risk, but still a risk. You never know. So in my case, I had to be cautious. That's different. You weren't on a job, you were taking a run in your own town, which, from what I can tell, is usually a pretty peaceful place."

May nodded slowly. "Yeah."

"So it's different. But here's the thing. I was trained in victim support, and I was also trained to handle DDs. That's domestic disturbances. Funny how people live together when they can't get along. Do you think that's because they like the adrenaline high? Or are they just too afraid to leave? I'll never know in every case, and it doesn't matter. My job was to cool off the situation, trying to keep anyone from getting hurt."

May was focused on her, temporarily forgetting at least some of her trauma. "Must have been scary."

"A bit. But in all the disturbances I went to, I was eventually able to cajole some sense into the situation. The few times I couldn't, SWAT moved in. I hated when that happened, because sometimes the wrong people got hurt. So I worked very hard at trying to calm the problem."

May nodded again, listening intently.

"Anyway, what had never happened before was a guy shooting at me the instant he opened the door. No way to be ready for that. Usually I got inside, started talking and listening, and at the very least the people who were being threatened got away. One way or another. That last time, I wasn't expecting that guy to pull the trigger before the door opened all the way. In fact, I wasn't ready for him to shoot that soon. Couldn't be ready for that. No way. And the idiot didn't shoot for center mass, where my vest would have protected me. Maybe he was too stoned to aim. I don't know. Grazed my head good."

May looked over at Snowy. "And now you need him."

"Yes, I do. If there's one thing I can identify with for sure, it's having my life permanently changed in a single second."

"Oh, God. Now I know, too."

"Unfortunately."

But May wasn't done with her yet. "You weren't wearing a helmet?"

Kerri shook her head. "Too intimidating. I never wore a helmet to those things. Usually went bare-headed, trying to look as unthreatening as possible. It's so important not to make people feel more threatened than they already do when we arrive."

"I can see that," May said. Then she burst into fresh tears. "How long does it take?"

"For what?"

"For me to feel safe again."

There was no answer to that. None at all. "With time it'll get easier." As if. "You need to consider therapy as soon as possible. Yes, I'm here to support you, but I'm not a therapist. They can help you a lot more than I can."

"But you need me to remember!"

"Don't force it. Please."

"I want him caught."

"We all do."

May's sobs eased a bit. "What does the dog do for you?"

Here we go, thought Kerri. "He lets me know when I'm about to have a seizure."

May wanted to know something about that, too. Anything to distract her. Once again, Kerri told her all about the seizures.

"Maybe in some way I was lucky," May said, her voice shaky.

Kerri didn't think so, but she also didn't want to say that to May. She'd watched how the woman winced every time she moved. Those pains would eventually heal, but the scars were permanent, the ones on her body and in her mind.

Then May surprised her. "Can I get a dog like yours?"

"A service dog?"

"A police dog. To protect me."

Well, that wasn't such a bad idea if it would make this woman feel safe in her own home, or even on the streets of this town. "I got a buddy I'll ask. He knows the man who trains the K9s for the department."

"Thank you." Then May dissolved again.

Kerri reached out and squeezed her hand. May clung so tightly it hurt. It was so little to offer.

After Kerri helped May move into a much smaller room closer to the front of the house, Connie Parish arrived. A great-looking woman just reaching middle age, Kerri had heard that her husband, Ethan, had been a deputy for a while before resigning to help his father at his ranch. Micah Parish, Ethan's father, still worked part-time for the department, but he was getting up in years and was probably grateful for his son's help. Connie, on the other hand, had replaced Ethan in the department.

Seemed like an odd exchange, Kerri thought. Nice but unusual. And that was one of the things she was coming to very much like about this town. Nearly every time someone's name came up, if she expressed interest she got a whole lot of background. It was also nothing that was either too personal or potentially embarrassing.

Connie and Kerri cleared the exchange with May. May already knew Connie pretty well, so she didn't have an apparent problem with it. "You need to sleep sometime," she told Kerri.

For the first time it occurred to Kerri that her presence might be problematic. *She* was the stranger around here. May might find it much easier to talk to Connie, someone she had known for years.

On the other hand, the sheriff had wanted her because of her training. All she could do was hope it helped.

The day had grown perceptibly warmer, the afternoon breeze welcome for the first time in days. A great break from the chillier temperatures that had made her wonder how long it would take for her to adapt.

She found Stu without any trouble at the office. He sat at a computer, filling out reports. The other deputies greeted her pleasantly. Unfortunately, she thought she caught a couple of smirks as she walked over to Stu's desk. Oh, well, that would go away eventually.

"Hey," he said, glancing her way. "Couple of minutes."

"Sure." It gave her an opportunity to stare at him, just a bit because she didn't want it to be obvious to everyone in the room.

Hunk, she decided, admitting it to herself at last. The way his heavyweight uniform shirt stretched across his shoulders when he twisted to reach for something was almost enough to make her drool. She found herself wishing she could have a taste of that without any involvement.

Hey, men got away with that, didn't they? She'd heard otherwise about women, but at this point she might have liked to find out. One-night stand sounded so good.

Except... Except what? She was working here now.

That might make things even more uncomfortable than her epilepsy.

She sighed, not realizing the sound was audible.

Stu looked up. "Sorry. Just another minute."

"I wasn't sighing out of impatience. It's been a tough day. Go ahead."

Bending over in her chair, she gave Snowy a neck rub. If he'd been a cat, she was sure he would have purred.

At last Stu hit one of the keys emphatically and swiveled his chair to look at her. "What's up? Coffee? Dinner?"

"May," she answered. "She wants a dog for protection. I said I'd ask."

He smiled. "I guess it's time to introduce you to Cadell Marcus. But coffee first. It's been one of those days. Too busy to pull over and finish my reports."

"Escaped sheep?" she asked.

He cracked a laugh. "Nah. Disagreements between neighbors, brandishing a firearm. Drunk and disorderly. Yes, at this time of day. People are already acting as if they'd been snowed in for a couple of months."

She laughed with him. Even though the moon had just passed its first quarter, she asked, "Full moon?"

He grinned. "You never know. I never bought the idea, but I'm open to being proved wrong. Ready to go?"

The day had grown even warmer, possibly pushing into the low seventies. Cool for her, maybe not so much around here. Regardless, she enjoyed it a whole lot.

They decided to walk to Maude's, allowing Snowy

to stretch his legs a bit and check the new smells. He seemed to find quite a few of them.

"I wish," Kerri said, "that I could sense what he senses. How he sees the world. But only sometimes."

Stu wrinkled his nose. "Not unless I could change my preferences in odors."

That made her laugh again, such a welcome distraction after a day spent with a woman who was very depressed and frightened. May had every right to feel that way, and she was holding up well, but Kerri couldn't help feeling for her. Plus, it was bringing up some of her own memories of how she had felt when she woke in the hospital and learned her life was coming apart at the seams.

The drive to Cadell's training school and ranch was a nice one. It was the first time Kerri had driven out of town in this direction and she was amazed. "It looks so flat, but then the mountains just leap up to the west, like they spring out of nowhere."

"We're actually in the foothills at the moment, but it's difficult to tell as deep as the grasses are. The ground is rolling, and if you catch it in the right light, you can see it. But, I understand, glaciers pretty much leveled this place. If you see large rocks, you can blame it on them. Just try to imagine a river of ice filling this valley."

Her mind boggled. Oh, she'd seen pictures, of course, but looking along the huge valley and trying to imagine it filled with ice was overwhelming.

"Okay, my mind's blown."

"It's hard to conceive," he agreed.

The air smelled sweet out here, she thought, glad

he'd cracked the windows an inch or so. Snowy was leaning right over her shoulder, his nose pressed to the narrow opening, and she could hear him drawing in long sniffs, then huffing out air to make room for another lungful.

"Somebody's sure in heaven," she remarked.

"He's about to meet another kind." Stu turned them off the paved county road onto a dirt road, then again onto a slightly rutted drive with a farmhouse at the end.

"Cadell and his wife, Dory, live here. You probably won't meet her, though, because she keeps a place in town. She's a graphic artist and needs the better internet connection. It can be spotty out here."

"I'm not surprised."

Cadell must have heard them coming because a tall man came around the side of the house and waited for them, giving a brief wave.

After introductions were made, Stu explained the situation.

"Kerri is keeping an eye on May Broadwyn for us."

"The rape victim?" Cadell's face settled into stern lines. He looked at Kerri. "How's she doing?"

"Scared, of course, and she still has a lot of physical pain. Anyway, today she expressed a wish for a police dog. I know she can't have one, but a dog. A support-type dog like Snowy here, but one that will make her feel safe. Especially at night."

Cadell nodded. "I might have one or two." He glanced at Snowy. "Beautiful service dog you have. What's his name?"

Snowy's ears pricked, and his nostrils rapidly flared repeatedly as his nose tested his environment.

"Well, when I got him, his name was Snowball but I just call him Snowy."

Cadell laughed. "Dogs get a lot of nicknames. He's beautiful. He's working out well?"

"Very. He's certainly more patient than I deserve."

"Well, come around back to the kennels. These days I'm training more service dogs than K9s for the police, because they have a limited need. But me and dogs... My wife often claims I love them more than her." He winked and Kerri laughed.

"Anyway," he continued as they walked around the house, "I hear you've been deputized. You may see me at the office from time to time. I'm still a part-timer, and often get called when they need extra hands."

"Everyone in this county seems to know everything," Kerri remarked.

"Not quite or we'd have the damned rapist in a cell already."

Kerri couldn't argue that.

There were eight dogs in kennels, but not in cages. All had an indoor area with bed and bowls that opened onto grassy areas surrounded by chain-link fences. Long enough areas to let them run.

"Those two down there are in training to become K9s for another PD. Sometimes I have to let them go." He shook his head. "Anyway, I've got four here that I can guarantee will be protective. I realize service dogs need to be incredibly patient and intelligent and totally obedient, but... It's always seemed to me that a disabled person could need protection at any time, so I don't work to get rid of *all* their aggression. These are larger breeds, though. I don't work with the little ones that are better suited to be comfort animals."

Kerri spoke. "I think she'd feel safer with a larger dog. But gentle, too."

"Of course, gentle," he said. "First requirement." He pointed out two to the left. "Both mutts, which usually promises great health and great smarts. This one over here, the one that's black and white? I call him my gentle giant. He even likes kittens. The other one is a bit smaller, but practically built out of patience. How about I bring those ones over to meet May tomorrow and see what she thinks?"

Kerri thought about it. "Let me make sure it's okay with her? We've been pretty much keeping men away for now. But the idea of a dog for protection may do the trick."

"Sure, just give me a call. I'll keep working with these two until she's ready."

"I liked Cadell a lot," Kerri remarked. "So ready to help out."

"I think everyone would like to find a way if we could."

"Probably." She leaned against the car door with her shoulder and let the breeze wash over her. It was cooling again, but maybe it wouldn't drop as low as yesterday. She could hope.

Snowy had happily taken care of his business at Cadell's place but had remained obediently beside her even though he must have wanted to check out the dogs. For her part, she kept looking at Stu, wondering. Wondering what it would be like if he touched her.

Feeling a nearly forgotten warmth between her legs. The bug had bitten. Maybe she could try to be a little less standoffish.

"Do you ever think about what dogs would do if we let them choose?"

Stu laughed. "I'm sure they'd like to spend their time playing with other dogs."

"Yeah, that's likely." He reached out, touching her thigh almost absently. She hoped it wasn't as casual as it seemed.

"On the other hand, they seem to choose us an awful lot."

She couldn't deny that.

Then Snowy nudged her cheek. Hard. "Oh, hell," she said, and then she was gone.

Confusion filled her. How had she gone from the countryside to being in front of Maude's diner? How had it happened so fast? Gradually, she settled into the moment, accepting that it had happened again. Then she had a godawful thought and terror began to creep through her.

She turned her head and saw that she was alone in the car with Snowy, who was whining. He never whined. Then he started licking her cheek as if in welcome.

My God, how long had she been out? Too long. Longer than she ever had.

How was that possible? Another wave of confusion ran through her. How did she get here in two minutes? Not possible. No way. Had she had repeated seizures? If so, she was in more trouble than she thought.

Movement caught her eye and she saw Stu emerge from the diner with two very large brown bags. He put them in the back, then came around to the driver's side to hand her a large coffee.

"You ready for a latte?"

She accepted it with a trembling hand as Snowy settled into the back seat. "Stu..."

"We'll talk about it all when we get to your place, okay?"

Talk about what? That she'd been out of it for a creepy amount of time? A terrifying amount of time? She struggled to remember her last moment of awareness, and to try and figure out how long it had taken them to get here.

"Stu," she said again.

"Take it easy, Kerri. Just take it easy. I want to see you get some food in you. Have you eaten at all today?"

"Uh... Breakfast."

He just shook his head and backed out before turning them toward the apartment.

He insisted on carrying everything upstairs, said he would feed Snowy, then when they were inside began pulling out food containers. "Do me a favor and eat something, dammit. Or just drink the coffee. I put sugar in it, and no complaining."

She didn't feel like eating so she sipped the coffee. A new terror wrapped her and she hardly paid attention as he poured kibble and fresh water into bowls for the dog.

"He'll probably want his walk after he fills his belly," Stu remarked. As he passed behind her, where she sat on the stool, he squeezed her shoulder, followed by a hug that she wanted to melt into. She ached when he let go and sat beside her. No. Not when she had this problem.

"I'm serious about eating. If you had low blood sugar, that may have made things worse."

"How long?" she asked, looking at him, seeking his reassurance.

"I can't say for sure," he answered. "Does Snowy often lick you when you're seizing? Or just after?"

"Not that I've ever known."

"Well, then, you need to take better care of yourself, get regular meals and so on. Because after about a minute and a half, that dog started getting seriously upset. He barked. He whined. Then he started licking you. He was trying to wake you up. And if he doesn't do that when you're seizing, best bet is you had low blood sugar."

She felt the first twitch of hope. "Maybe."

He began to open containers. "Help yourself. The thing is, just to be safe, you need to see a doc soon. But considering the stress, and that you've been so focused on May, and tense, probably, about a bazillion things, this may be a one-off."

"God, I hope so."

"Anyway, no point worrying needlessly. You weren't out all that long. We were almost to town when it hit, it didn't take me long in Maude's so relax until you know something different."

But she couldn't relax. What was going on with her? Her former trust in her innate health was long gone. She wasn't invulnerable. Bad things happened.

All that crap she had dealt with as a cop could happen to her, too. Some of it *had* happened.

And it put her out of running for a romantic relationship. God, what if it happened during sex?

Desperate, she drained the coffee. Stu pushed a burger in front of her. "Calories," he said.

"You can't know…"

"Eat. What I know is you didn't eat all day and you've been dealing with a mountain of stress—"

"May's the one stressed." She hardly cared that she interrupted him. She still didn't want to eat, but the first interest in the burger eventually poked through. She lifted it, telling herself she needed to eat it regardless.

"She's stressed, all right, but do you honestly believe she's the only one?"

"What do you mean? She's in an awful situation."

"Bite. Chew. I'll keep talking."

"Don't order me around."

"I will until I get your attention. Your body knows what you need even if your brain doesn't."

She took a bite, then realized her hunger had reawakened. It was a good burger, too. "I'm listening," she said when she had swallowed. Her stomach suggested she eat another mouthful.

"How long has it been since you wore a badge?"

Her head swung around to look at him. He had opened a burger for himself.

"Over a year," she said. "There was the neurologist trying to find a med for my seizures, and I had to train with Snowy. Then it took a while to find this teaching gig."

He nodded, pushing his burger back a little as he rose and went to her fridge. "Orange juice?" Then he grimaced. "Not good with a burger, huh?"

Despite everything, she almost laughed. "There's bottled water in there."

"But no calories in it." He made an exaggerated sigh, but brought her a bottle, unscrewing the top before he put it in front of her. He settled in beside her and lifted his own burger to his mouth. He was apparently hungry, too, because he ate half of it before putting it down, sipping coffee and wiping his mouth with a paper napkin. Then he turned to look at her again.

"Okay, more than a year of dealing with the loss of a job you loved, a new health problem that complicated everything and was probably a huge blow to your self-esteem. Add job hunting to that list, moving to a strange place, starting all over again."

She opened her mouth to respond, but he held up a hand. "Let me finish, okay? Then you can argue with me."

She nodded. The lingering taste of food in her mouth made her reach for more.

"So, on the subject of stress. You're in a new environment. You've had to deal with all these changes and I would hardly say that you're fully settled in. You've still got a long way to go before you feel fully comfortable here."

She nodded. She couldn't disagree with that.

"So, out of the blue, you get your badge back. You're handed a tough first assignment. Here you are, wanting to be perfect, to do everything right, because you want to hang on to that badge and the purpose that goes with it. You're worried about messing up somehow. You're worried about May. You're hoping against hope that you can find some helpful tidbit of information, all the while hoping you can help May get through at least the first part of her shock and wounding."

When he put it like that, she didn't know how to argue. He might be exaggerating her stress a bit, but the stress remained real. She hadn't been looking at the wider picture, but instead had been relying on what was right under her nose at any moment.

"Then," he added after finishing the rest of his burger, "you're probably not taking the best care of yourself. Sleep, food, all those essential things are going by the wayside at this moment. So if you want to know why you passed out in the car briefly, my guess is you're freaking worn out and need to cut yourself a little slack. *And* take care of yourself. Gage isn't going to snatch that badge back because you can't solve this crime. For Pete's sake, Kerri, he's got a bunch of investigators. They're not exactly solving it, either."

She had to agree with that, too. Except for one thing. "You make me sound stupid."

"You're not at all stupid. You're a bulldog. Believe me, I recognize the trait. I suffer from a bit of it myself. Hence arresting damn near thirty of my troops for drug violations. I suspect my predecessor in the unit took the easy way out. Not me. No. So I get it. But…to stay healthy and on top of all this, at least look after yourself."

Well, she had started to argue with him before he said a word, then had listened and she no longer really wanted to fight with him. He was right. She'd been applying thumbscrews to herself for some time now and regaining a badge and the law enforcement responsibilities she was allowed to hold... Yeah, they'd added new stressors. She'd lost her job once. She couldn't bear to do it again.

Now the home fries caught her attention, and she ate one. Then another. They were still good, although not quite as good as fresh from the fryer.

"I'm a mess," she said presently.

He shook his head. "Nope. Not gonna say yes to that."

"Are you going to agree with me at all?" she demanded, feeling a few sparks of irritation ignite.

"You're just dealing with some heavy stuff. Frankly, you're dealing with it well, as far as I can see. Nothing to apologize for, Kerri. Quit kicking your own butt. Other people will supply the kicks for you."

A fugitive grin tugged at the corners of her mouth despite all her other worries. Why did she want to be mad at him, anyway? Because he'd lectured her? But he'd been right in most of what he said, if not all.

"Just don't make a habit of lecturing me," she said.

"I don't intend to. But I figured since I was watching you start to crumble, a little shoring up might be needed. You've got an awful lot to be proud of, and you sure don't lack determination. There, now go figure out your own problems."

He gave her an amused look and she laughed reluctantly.

She ate quite a bit, more than usual. It seemed he might have been right about her blood sugar, and she promised herself that when this case was in the bag she'd visit a doctor about it. Well, if it happened again.

Another matter soon distracted her, though. That matter was Stu. He was so close, and the stirrings of desire she'd been trying to ignore were bubbling up, grabbing her attention whether she wanted it or not.

Despite the few times she'd read desire in his gaze, he'd been perfectly proper with her. Maybe that was because of her. She envisioned signs and stickers all over herself saying Do Not Approach.

Because that's how she'd been feeling for some time. While she didn't like to think of herself as a coward, in some ways she'd become one. She kept to herself most of the time because she feared someone would see her have a seizure. That badge Gage had given her had overcome some of her reluctance because it said she was still useful in one of the ways that mattered most to her.

But her cowardice went further. She was afraid of relationships because someone might turn on her. Most especially she was afraid of involvement with a man because he might quickly tire of her limitations. Who wanted a wife who couldn't be trusted in a kitchen, who couldn't drive herself anywhere? Who might turn into a public embarrassment by freezing at the wrong time, like during a conversation with friends, or even ordering from a menu?

Stu had been infinitely patient, as if it didn't matter to him, but how long would that last when the reality hit home? When it became frequent?

Then there was today. He made a good case for a little problem with low blood sugar, but there was no way to be sure her seizures weren't getting worse or enduring longer.

Ivan stood outside the apartment building, seriously troubled. He didn't know what to make of what was going on. At first when he'd wondered if Kerri Addison was somehow gathering information, he'd mostly shrugged it off, even though he'd heard someone remark that she'd learned something that had been reported. She was nobody but a college instructor and she had no right to actually question anyone. She was limited to casual conversation.

But today when she'd come out of his second victim's home, her jacket had been unzipped and he'd seen the sheriff's badge. Glinting and unmistakable on her belt. No gun or anything, but that badge loomed large in his mind.

So he'd hit the college library and looked her up in detail on the computer. Damn, the woman had awards for her work with victims, for helping to solve cases, especially rape cases. She was a trained rape counselor and investigator.

And now she wore a badge. Whatever she did had become official, not casual, and she'd be looking carefully for information because it was her *job*.

Uneasiness crept along his spine. He was unsure what she might have learned already. There were a few people around town he'd overheard once again talking about how she was helping and gathering information.

And while he was convinced that he'd left no evidence behind, he had no way of knowing if he'd betrayed himself in some way to the victims. Especially the second one who was conscious and able to talk. That Addison woman was spending a whole lot of time with her.

He looked up at the lit windows on her second-floor apartment, thought about the cop cars he hadn't paid much attention to previously because they just kept coming and going, but had to face the fact they were transporting her to and from the hospital, and now to one victim's home.

She was on the case, and given her background, she might be the biggest threat he faced.

He'd been thinking about his next victim, and as he stared up at those lit windows, he decided he needed this one. And he needed to do more than before. He needed to remove her permanently.

She was at the isolated end of the building. Her nearest neighbors were at the other end. He'd have time to take her out, and even enjoy it while he was doing it.

But there was the dog. He had to think about the dog, but his fear of the animal was decreasing in direct proportion to the growth of his fear of what Addison might learn.

He could feel himself zeroing in on her at various levels. She'd make a good victim. She was clearly disabled in some way, given her service dog, and might be even easier to take than the others.

He did want to kick himself, though, for repeatedly turning his attention elsewhere even when he started to have niggling concerns about that woman.

Teacher. Disabled. None of that, he now feared, outweighed "former cop." Certainly the sheriff didn't seem to think so.

Ivan agonized over what his second victim might remember. His voice? His eyes? He couldn't conceal them behind that damn mask. Something else that hadn't even occurred to him? If she recalled anything that could link him to the crimes, that Addison woman wouldn't miss it. Hell, no. She was *trained* not to miss it.

He was certain that's why the sheriff had taken her on. Nobody on the force had the kind of experience with this type of crime that Addison did. Matters that might fly by others as insignificant could set off her alarms. And be reported. Oh, yes, reported, and given her new status the cops would listen.

He stood there, staring up at those windows, and nearly ducked when he saw a man's figure appear in one of them. But Ivan was sure he'd picked a puddle of darkness that would effectively conceal him from anyone looking out of a lighted room.

Canady. Another problem. Ivan would have to wait for a night when Canady didn't hang around. Although he did leave early enough usually. Ten or eleven. Which left Kerri Addison on her own for long enough.

He needed to scope out the building to make sure there'd be no one close enough to cause a problem. He could do that tomorrow in the daylight, and if anyone asked him what he was doing, he'd just say he was considering renting.

Easy enough. He had some idea of the layout, but he wanted to be sure where all the players were located. That the building was indeed as empty as he thought.

Then the dog question. Would it be best to throw

a steak? Or just kick the mutt in the side hard enough to break something?

A kick would be so much more satisfying.

He settled in to wait. If Canady left soon, he could check out the building tonight. He scanned it from one end to the other, looking for lights. One after another they winked on.

People were home. And they were all at the far end.

Yeah, he could do it. Satisfy himself and take care of the threat all at once.

He felt for the knife holster in his pant leg. The knife could take care of the dog, too. He nodded to himself. Just wear thick sleeves. He could handle the dog.

Then he could handle *her*.

"I'm so grateful Cadell is willing to give May a dog," Kerri said. "She'll feel so much safer."

"Who wouldn't?"

They'd moved into the living room after cleaning up from dinner. Kerri had told him he'd better come over for dinner tomorrow since she had enough food for an army now.

"Not really," he laughed. "But the leftovers might make you a good lunch tomorrow. I can't come over, anyway. I'm on duty until eleven or twelve."

Her stomach sank. "Really?" Only then did she realize how very much she enjoyed his visits. She didn't want to spend an evening without him, although in fairness this wouldn't be the first time he hadn't dropped over.

But it was the first time she faced how attached she was becoming. Warning bells wanted to ring but they were muffled now. She didn't want to hear them. Wisdom was escaping her, replaced by a syrupy sensation that filled her. Every cell in her body was growing soft. And heavy.

Oh, man, she had it bad. Ignoring it wasn't going to be enough.

She looked at him again and saw the heat in his gaze. A slight change in his expression that seemed to call to her.

As if drawn by a spell, she rose from her recliner and went to sit beside him on the couch. He watched her, never taking his eyes from her, making her feel warm all over.

"Stu?" she said, her voice little more than a whisper.

"Mmm?"

"You know my problems. I seem to have more of them than I even realized. But…" She bit her lower lip.

He didn't help her or press her, simply waited for her to speak. For once in her life she wanted to be interrupted, to hear her words come out of a man's mouth. It was not to be.

She drew a deep breath. She was *not* a coward, and despite her self-doubts, she needed to prove it. "I'm so attracted to you," she blurted. "Do you think we could…would you… Just once?"

"Just once?" His brow knit. "I don't know about that. I got this crazy feeling that once might not be enough."

Elation filled her, pushing her common sense far into the background. "Maybe a couple of times?"

"How about we play it by ear. But I can promise you, once will not be enough."

Then he wrapped her in the tightest of hugs. "You're an adorable, beautiful, brave bunch of contradictions," he said, his voice growing husky. "I've never been so fascinated in my life."

Then his mouth found hers in a kiss at first tentative, then deeper, more possessive and demanding. When his tongue traced her lips, a tingle ran through her that was almost like an electric shock, and her head fell back as she surrendered to the amazing moment.

She had missed this so much. But *this* was even better than she remembered. There had been a couple of boyfriends; dating cops she worked with had proved a problem, but there had been others. Others she had invited into her life who hadn't been able to endure her hours or the perceived dangers of her job.

Short term had described her romantic life. She'd survived the breakups before. But somehow, deep within, she knew she didn't want this to be short term. A niggle of fear almost pulled her back, but Stu circumvented it.

In an easy movement, he swept her up in his arms. Part of her wanted to resist his strength, his making her feel small and light by comparison, but another part reveled in it. She clung to his shoulders and simply gave in. It was a beautiful feeling to be so wanted.

When he slowly lowered her to her feet, she was already wrapped in the magic that was Stu. Like a sorcerer he had elevated her to the heights and he'd hardly really touched her or she him.

Her heart raced. She couldn't find enough air. She heard his breath speed up as he pulled her polo over her head to reveal her breasts cased in their plain white bra. For the first time ever she wished for lingerie, but he didn't appear to miss it.

Cradling her shoulders with one arm, he smiled faintly and found her breast with his hand, squeezing. The squeeze caused her entire body to clench in response.

"Let me know if you don't like something," he murmured.

She believed she was going to like every bit of this. But it was also a first time, and an unusual shyness tried to overtake her. To conceal it, while he massaged her breast to engorged excitement, she reached for the buttons of his shirt and worked them. She wanted to see the chest she'd only been able to admire through clothing. To touch it, to learn the textures of his skin. She wanted to discover his strength and vitality with all boundaries erased.

As she pushed his shirt aside, she discovered his chest was all she had imagined. Well-muscled, but not overly so, smooth, inviting. Her palms couldn't resist reaching out to touch him, a sensation so powerful to her that she never noticed when he released her bra and her breasts spilled free. She was absorbed in him, hardly aware of the places he was transporting her to, feeling only that she touched perfection.

But her own sensations began to poke through her preoccupation. Her nipples, now almost painfully sensitive, felt the brush of his thumbs, then the lightest of pinches that struck her to her very center with a huge jolt of pleasure. A brief cry of delight escaped her.

Revelations continued to come as he managed to bend and shove down her jeans. The brief break in contact pushed her to make a protesting sound, but he dropped kisses on her breasts, tonguing her nipples until she believed she had reached perfection in a new way.

Desire pounded inside her, filling every inch of her with ravening need.

Then he stepped back again, letting her see through heavily lidded eyes as he stripped away his own jeans, revealing all his glory. Revealing that he was ready for her in every way. She wanted to grasp him, but again he evaded her touch, kicking off his work boots.

Then he lifted her again, placing her on the bed, causing her to squeal. A husky laugh escaped him, but his purpose was soon clear as he pulled away her boots, her jeans, her undies.

There was an instant when fear almost yanked her back. "What if I seize?"

"Then I'll wait for you." He pulled the last of her clothing away.

She lay naked beneath his devouring gaze as the throb of desire grew and grew until she felt she could barely contain it.

Then, with a half smile, he muttered, "Beautiful," and lowered himself to the bed beside her.

Together they began a journey of exploration. Hands traveled everywhere, learning each curve and contour as need began its inevitable crescendo. Before long she was almost panting with excitement.

At some point Stu slipped inside her, stretching her and filling her in an achingly good way. A sense of rightness permeated her as the real climb began.

He moved slowly, her head cradled between his

hands as he dipped to kiss her lips, her throat, her neck, making her feel safe even as the climb up the mountain grew steeper and seemed to draw her completely out of herself.

She was lost in a haze of stars as she reached the peak, surrounded by velvet inkiness that embraced her even as it showered her with prismatic pinpricks of light behind her eyes.

Then she tumbled into freefall, an endless fall that nevertheless ended too soon, filling her with aching, joyous completion. A moment later she felt him jerk and knew he had fallen with her.

Into spiraling galaxies of light and heat that she wanted never to end.

It was hard to do, but Stu lifted himself off her, rolling to her side. They were both damp so he found a blanket from the foot of the bed and drew it up over them. Then he wrapped her in his arms and held her as close as he could as he let reality reluctantly creep back.

Reality? This had been reality in the best sense, he thought as he held her. He wished they could remain like this, in peace and beauty forever.

Because it had been beautiful. He'd reached a pinnacle with her he was sure he'd never reached before. Something about this woman…

Sighing, he closed his eyes and enjoyed the way she snuggled into him. He had almost no doubt that things between them would get rocky soon. He sensed all the hesitation in her because of her disability, because of repeated blows to her self-confidence.

It would all come up again, he was sure. Especially since she'd virtually asked him for a one-night stand. That had never been his thing, which was probably why he had so many ex-girlfriends in his past. He went for the long term, and they weren't interested anymore when he flew away on duty. Or, as in the most intense of his relationships, when they discovered he had issues to deal with after the war.

Even so, he felt bad for Kerri. Had she felt that she was only entitled to one night? She devalued herself, and he wondered in what other ways she diminished herself that she hadn't yet revealed to him.

"You know," he murmured into the darkness, "you talk about your epilepsy as if it disqualifies you from so much. I get it."

"Get what?" she asked hazily.

"I still have to deal with my past, with repeated tours in a war zone. I've been dumped because I don't always deal well. You need to be aware of that."

If it were possible, she snuggled closer, then wrapped her arm over his chest. "Everyone has problems," she answered quietly.

"Perhaps that's my point. We all have problems. How will you react if I get into a rage one day? Or withdraw completely into memories of terrible things? I think it's better now, but I'm still doing it."

"I'm so sorry, Stu. I truly am."

"I don't need pity, Kerri."

"It's not pity. I could never pity you."

He lifted his head, wishing there was more light in the room than just the pale stream coming down the hallway. "Did you hear yourself? Why in the world would you think I pity you if you can't pity me?"

"It's not pity I'm worried about."

She sat up, and instead of the revelatory sharing he'd been hoping for, he knew that the clash was coming. Well, better clear the air before they carried this relationship to a point that might cause more pain. He hoped their friendship was secure at least.

She pulled a thick robe off a hook on the back of the door. "Oddly," she said, "I'm hungry again."

It was as good an excuse as any for her flight. Maybe now she'd just come out and tell him. She'd mentioned being a burden, but he wasn't sure that was all of it.

And as burdens went, he knew damn well he could be one himself at times. Shaking his head a little, bracing himself, he rose and pulled on his jeans, leaving them unbuttoned. She might as well get used to that, he thought. He *liked* to go shirtless unless it was cold.

Even though it was getting late, she was brewing coffee. In for the long haul, he thought with amusement. He'd never turned down a cup of fresh brew, though. It didn't interfere with his sleep at all. Sometimes he wished it would actually keep him awake. Hah!

"What do you want to eat?" she asked.

"There was dessert we never got to. Peach cobbler, some cherry pie. Whichever."

She pulled out two of the plastic containers and placed them on the counter. "Warmed up?"

Oh, this was getting businesslike. "Sure, if you don't mind."

He sat on the stool, watching her buzz around, and reminded himself she wasn't angry, even though she was doing a good imitation. No, he'd brought up a sensitive topic and she was trying to deal with the required honesty. She really didn't want to go there. His fault, but he knew they were going to have to address it all. Their own fears. Each other's fears.

He had just wanted her to understand that she wasn't alone in those very things she'd mentioned before. Now this. He should have kept his mouth shut until a better time, not when they were enjoying the afterglow.

On the other hand, what better time? They were as open to each other as they could be at this point in their friendship.

Soon she had two plates in front of them, and the warmed desserts ready for serving. There was more than enough of each for two, so he helped himself to some cherry pie. She chose a small piece of cobbler.

With hot coffee, the combination was like ambrosia.

"Thank you," he said.

"You're welcome."

Then she didn't say any more. Oh, this wasn't going to be fun. He wanted her to lead the way. She struck him as a very strong and independent woman and he sure as hell didn't want to step on her toes over something so important. She'd already accused him of lecturing her.

"You know," she said at long last as she reached for a second piece of the cobbler, "I want you to know that you just gave me one of the best experiences of my life."

"Then I blew it."

She gave a small shake of her head but didn't look at him. "No. No, you didn't ruin it. Reality had to return sooner or later."

That so closely echoed his earlier thought that he gave her his reaction to it. "That *was* reality. The best kind. But go on."

He thought he saw a wisp of a smile touch the corner of her mouth. He craved another round with that mouth. Hell, they'd hardly explored all the avenues available to them.

He took another bite of pie and restrained his natural impulse to take charge. This one was for her.

"I don't even know how to explain this," she said slowly. "I've told you my problems, but I'm not sure I've conveyed what they've done to me. I not only feel like I could become a serious burden but…"

She trailed off and finally looked at him. "Stu, I'm scared all the time."

Wow. That was an important moment, deserving of full attention. He nodded to let her know he'd heard her, but he wasn't sure how to respond. Or even if he should respond. His desire to reassure her might be exactly the wrong reaction when she'd admitted something that must be perilously difficult for her to say.

"I never used to be this scared," she said after a few beats.

His heart was thundering now, and he felt as if he were on the edge of something that could be dangerous or could be wonderful.

"It's been like one shock after another," she said quietly. "Being deputized by the sheriff had me walking on air. Then I remembered all the ways I could mess up. Not just by missing something because I have a seizure, but a million other little things, from not realizing when something was significant, to failing to gain May's trust, to just being generally rusty."

He nodded again, keeping his gaze on her, pie and coffee forgotten. He wanted her to realize that she was the only thing on this planet that had his attention right now. As if he could think of anything else.

"I keep telling myself to put one foot in front of the other, to keep moving, to deal with one thing at a time. Well, that's a form of hiding from myself. It's not coming at me one thing at a time. It's been coming like a tsunami since I was shot."

"I bet," he answered, and said no more.

She looked down, passing her hands over her face as if wiping something away. "I can't even begin to explain, because once I start, everything has to be linear. This then that. Only it hasn't been linear, and it sure hasn't felt like it's one thing at a time. How many do I have to list, anyway?"

"However many you need to."

She sighed, rubbed her eyes again. "Yeah. The laundry list. First there was waking up. Big hole in my memory for a while. By the time most of that came back, they'd done enough tests to know I had brain damage. Brain damage! That was worse than realizing I'd been shot. Gut shot would have been emotionally easier to deal with. Dammit, Stu, they told me my brain was permanently altered. I wasn't *me* anymore."

"That would be scary," he agreed. Very scary. "How could you tell how much of you had changed?"

Her gaze searched him out. "That was it. That was

exactly *it*. When the brain changes, you can't know how or how much. Not really. What had I lost? How different was I? No way to know. Not unless it was something obvious to people who knew me, and I doubt any of them would have told me, anyway. I get that we all change with time, but it's not the same when you don't even have a touchstone anymore. It's gone. Part of me was gone. Maybe. How was I to know?"

He nodded, then reached for his coffee. Cold. "Want a warm-up?"

"Please."

He rounded the counter, emptied their cups in the sink and poured fresh. Then he sat beside her again. "Okay, the terror of losing part of yourself. No way to know how much. I can't imagine, but I've seen it happen to others. And then?"

"And then. Then. An MRI doesn't tell you when you have seizures. At least not unless it catches them happening. I had my first observed seizure about the time they put me in physical therapy."

He looked sharply at her. "Physical therapy? You had physical problems from the shooting?"

"It was mostly to regain my strength. Bed rest is a killer to muscles. During one of my sessions, the therapist caught it. Then off to an EEG to see if my brain waves were dancing around the wrong way. The side I'd been shot on?"

Stu nodded encouragingly.

"They said it was working slower than the other side of my brain. Whatever. Out of sync sometimes, I guess. As it happened, I was diagnosed with a seizure disorder. I don't know if it had a particular name. Just that it meant I lost touch sometimes. Then off to neuro again to try to find a medication that could at least smooth out the jumble. You see how well that worked. They reduced the number but couldn't erase them."

"That sucks," he said frankly.

"You bet." She sighed, sipped the hot coffee and lifted a crumb of the cobbler to eat. "Okay, that was all pretty much a straight line. Not the way it felt, but a straight line, anyway."

He was aching for her, even though he'd only heard a part of what was coming. She was opening up like a person who desperately needed to talk to someone besides herself, and he knew they were at the tip of the iceberg. If he hurt for her now, he was going to hurt more very soon.

"Then I went back to work, but I was already worried about whether I could do my job. *Part of me was missing.* I couldn't escape that. It kept beating on me."

"I guess I can understand that part," he said, keeping his voice calm. He didn't want to interrupt her in even a small way.

"They sent me to a psychologist, routine after a shooting like that, for evaluation. I assumed it was about how well I was dealing with being shot. No, it was a necessary step toward retiring me on disability. For the next several months I sat at a desk stacked with folders and papers, all stuff I couldn't screw up, while the disability was processed."

She paused. "Stu, I felt betrayed. I couldn't help it even though I know it wasn't justified. They couldn't keep me around as a glorified clerk forever. They needed an active officer to replace me. Hell, I couldn't even work in the evidence room because I could slip up. No more badge, no more law enforcement work, no more job. I crashed."

"I bet." He could understand the sense of betrayal despite her own admitted understanding of why it happened. Police were a brotherhood, and her brotherhood was deserting her. Not because they wanted to, but because they had to. Awful.

"Everyone was so nice. Even after I packed out and went home to try to figure out if it was worthwhile to carry on, my buddies stopped by often. But even that became too much. It was a constant reminder, crazy as that sounds."

"Not crazy." Then he shut up again.

"It was sometimes like having salt rubbed in a wound. But other times... Stu, this *is* going to sound crazy. I started to get worried about the way I was leaning on them."

"Leaning?" He sipped coffee and pushed the cobbler closer to her. As stressed as she was right now, talking about all of this, he believed she needed some naked calories.

Seeing his gesture, she reached for a fork and took a piece into her mouth, swallowing it with coffee.

"Leaning," she repeated. "I realized I was waiting for them to come over and talk about the job. I'd begun to live vicariously. Well, how far was that going to get me?"

He gave her high marks for realizing what she was doing. A lot of people would have clung to those visits, never realizing how dependent they were becoming. This woman had. She was amazingly self-aware.

"Anyway." She shoved the cake around with her fork, drank more coffee and sighed. "I realized it was time to accept that my whole damn life had changed permanently and I'd better get going on building a new one before I turned ninety and realized I hadn't left my apartment in nearly sixty years, y'know?"

He nodded. "Almost got there a few times myself."

She cocked an eye at him. "Really?"

"This isn't about me. You can ask me later. This is about you."

A spark of life had reentered her pretty eyes. "Promise?"

"Promise. You can have my core dump later if you want it. Go on."

She nodded. "None of this was any kind of sequence," she went on. "Like I said, it wasn't linear. Things would bubble up, then dissipate for a while. So while I was leaning I was also beginning to consider other possibilities. Flip-flop time. And all the while I felt as if I was staring into a huge, black hole of uncertainty. Afraid. Where could I go? What could I do? Then, even before I'd answered that question, it slammed me hard. I had to get away from everyone and everything or I'd never have any clarity again."

"Heavy."

Her face quirked a little. "Shocking, maybe. I wasn't just thinking I needed a new job. I was thinking I needed a whole new life. A friend suggested that I could probably teach criminal law and I seized on that, maybe because I'd still be close to my first love. But I wanted a small place, not one where there'd be too many people."

"Why?"

"Because by that time I'd become terrified of my seizures. A charity got Snowy for me, and we trained together, but I was still terrified. I knew he'd protect me from freezing in traffic or something, but he couldn't deal with people and the way they'd react. I wanted to keep contact to a minimum."

"Okay." Now his chest was really aching. "I guess you came to the ends of the earth."

She shook her head. "Not quite. This is a nice town. Small, comfortable. My classes aren't big enough to be intimidating. The only thing I didn't consider was public transport, probably because it was so easy where I used to live. So here I am, building that much-vaunted new life, and I'm still scared all the time. What if I do something stupid when I'm seizing? What if the seizures get worse? Like today. What if that was a seizure?"

"Snowy acted differently."

She shook her head. "Nobody knows how Snowy will react if I drop out for ten or fifteen minutes. It's never happened. So the question remains, what if it's getting worse? What if it becomes more frequent? What if I screw up this amazing chance Gage has given me? What if I blow every damn thing, including any possible friendship?"

"Kerri..."

She waved a hand. "It's possible, Stu. Nobody's infinitely patient. But the bottom line is, I'm scared all the time. *All* the time. I don't trust life anymore. I'm sure you know all about that."

He did indeed but talking about the lessons of war

didn't seem appropriate right then. She'd had her entire life upended. Of course she didn't trust life. Most people lived blithely with the belief that tomorrow would come, that horrible things wouldn't happen out of the blue, that they'd eventually dandle grandkids on their knees. Soldiers lost that faith, and he could sure see why she had.

Surviving was no guarantee, and once that trust was lost, it didn't return easily.

He'd have liked to offer comfort and reassurance, but those would just be words. She needed to wrestle with herself on this one, just as he wrestled with himself. Even group therapy and talking to others in the same boat couldn't change that.

She'd fallen silent and he decided to speak. "Have you considered that you're grieving?"

She turned her head slowly to look at him. "Grieving?"

"There doesn't have to be a death to cause it. The loss of your old life is enough. A part of you died. That's why it comes in waves. Maybe. Just a guess. I don't see a psychology degree on my wall."

But she was thinking about it. "Grieving," she repeated as if trying it on.

"From what I've seen and heard, it's not a level ride emotionally. You can go through different parts of it over and over again. Anger to despair and so on. Bouncing around. Which, I would think, makes it harder to deal with."

She nodded slowly.

"But the brain can only take so much," he said. "You've heard of the thousand-yard stare."

"Yes."

"That's a sign that someone has checked out from overload. The brain can't handle it, and just shuts down to an elemental level. Anyway, I suspect grief is much like that. Just so much a person can handle at one time. God knows you've had enough to handle."

"I feel weak. Like a fraidy-cat."

"Good heavens! That's the last way I'd think of you."

At last a wan smile dawned. "Thanks. But that's how I feel. I'm a mess, but I don't want to admit I'm a mess. I'm trying to soldier on, if you'll pardon the expression."

"It's a good one."

"I don't know how well I'm succeeding. But there you have it, at least as much as I know how to explain. My biggest fear right now is that I'll blow everything up, from my teaching gig to this job Gage has given me. To our friendship."

That last almost wounded him, but he reminded himself that she probably didn't feel she knew him well enough to trust him completely. Unfortunately, he couldn't create that trust. Time and experience had to do that.

Snowy whined and her head whipped around. "He must need a walk."

At once Stu stood. "I'll take him, if that's allowed. All I need to do is pull my shirt on."

"And button your pants," she said drily.

He flashed a grin. "I'm showing off."

"Doing a good job of it, too. Yes, you can take him. He likes you."

"Will you be okay?"

"Without his support? I think I can manage that. I'll just sit someplace where I couldn't possibly fall. As in not this bar stool."

A minute later he was out the door with the eager dog. A glance back told him Kerri had settled on the recliner.

She thought she'd be a pain to other people, but when he considered the adjustments she was making, he figured she was the one with all the pain.

Outside the night had grown crisper, though not cold. He wondered if they'd even have another warm day. As Snowy did his thing, Stu turned slowly around.

They needed more streetlights here. He didn't understand why they hadn't been put up when these apartments were built for all the people who'd come to work at the semiconductor plant.

The now vacant plant. As near as he could tell, boom and bust was a frequent cycle in this small town, at least since the heyday of ranching. Sad. It really *was* a nice place.

For an instant he thought he caught sight of a shadow among the shadows, but then he couldn't be sure. His eyes weren't fully dark-adapted yet and could easily play tricks during the adjustment period.

He turned his head to look away, then quickly looked back again. No shadow. His imagination.

But uneasiness suddenly clung to him like cold, wet leaves. The rapist. Could he be hanging out around here?

He looked up at Kerri's windows and saw the lights.

Not very inviting to a guy who depended on the darkness to conceal him.

Snowy didn't seem disturbed, so he took that as a good sign. In fact, the dog evinced a desire to head back inside. Apparently, he wanted to be close to Kerri again.

Now that was something Stu could fully understand.

Ivan had withdrawn to the deepest shadows beneath the trees that shaded one end of the parking lot. Not that they had many leaves left, but he'd hardly stand out among the trunks.

Except for that one instant he'd feared the cop had seen him. Maybe he'd moved. He froze himself into a statue and waited. At last Canady and the dog headed back inside.

He was safe from discovery, at least for now.

But damn, was the guy settling in for the night? Was this going to become a regular thing?

The more he thought about it, the more worried he got about that Addison woman. Of course, she'd make a tasty morsel for his needs. Subduing her would be a triumph, since she was a cop, had been a cop.

Even if she was disabled somehow. That didn't necessarily make her weak. Far from it, he figured.

But not only would she sate his need, her silence would be to his advantage.

For now, though, he had to wait and be patient. In the morning, he'd come back to check the layout of the place. He counted the lit windows on the far side of the building and figured out which apartments were occupied.

Except for the lighted stairwell, there was a yawning darkness between Addison and her nearest neighbors. Those dim hall lights wouldn't count at all, unless someone was there to catch sight of him.

Dang, he felt like his head was buzzing with bees as he tried to deal with his urges and his needs both, and right then they seemed to conflict.

Maybe he'd get her tomorrow night. For right now, though, he needed to find a treat for himself somewhere in this town. A woman who wasn't afraid enough to zip herself tightly inside her home.

There'd be someone, he was sure of that. He'd met enough fools to know.

He had to admit, though, he was surprised how quickly this town seemed to have buttoned down. He wouldn't have thought two rapes would have done that. Only one had been inside a house. The other in the park. He'd have better understood if people had just stayed indoors at night.

But no. Doors were being locked, windows latched. As he wandered around in the daytime, hitting the grocery, stopping at the bakery, he heard things.

And what he heard was fear. He had to admit that gave him a huge thrill. But it also made it harder for him to fulfill his needs.

Shaking his head, he mounted his bike to head back into town. Maybe on the side farther away from his earlier rape he'd have more luck. A better chance of finding a woman who wasn't afraid.

Then he'd check out the situation in Kerri Addison's building in the morning. And if he was lucky, he could take her tomorrow night.

He already knew the door locks in that place weren't the best. Some time ago, he'd checked that just in case and had been pleasantly surprised to find that the dead bolts didn't go deeply enough into the doorframes. Someone had cut a corner, and just like a movie he could use a shim to open them.

Unless the Addison woman had lucked out, her apartment might as well be wide open to him.

As for the dog. It didn't seem very frightening, especially since it had walked out here with Canady and hadn't so much as looked in his direction. No threat from that animal. It probably couldn't do anything except its job looking after the woman.

Yeah, he could deal with the dog. Jumping on his bike, he headed toward the subdivision on the other side of town. He needed a backup plan to keep himself content if he couldn't go after Addison tomorrow night.

Her turn would come.

# Chapter 11

Kerri felt badly in the morning, primarily because she figured she had ruined last night with her meltdown. She and Stu hadn't made love again, probably because he was either upset by her timing, or because he was disgusted with her bout of self-pity. She couldn't blame him.

Yeah, he'd held her most of the night, but that was small consolation. She'd screwed it up, and not with her seizures.

Before leaving he *had* said he'd come back when he was finished for the night, between one and two in the morning, he thought, and he'd bring breakfast from the truck stop if she liked.

Well, being a cop, she'd learned to love breakfast at any hour, and the wee hours were no exception. She'd smiled and agreed and wondered if he was going to ease himself out of her life now.

She assured herself it would be for the best if he did, but mostly she didn't believe it. Stu's company had become terribly important to her. Which meant she needed to face another truth: much as she had tried to avoid it, she'd formed a deep relationship. An attachment. That man had slipped past all her fears.

When she arrived at May's house, shortly after six, she found Connie was gone, no one had replaced her and the patrol car sitting out front had vanished. What the heck?

Inside she found May curled up on her sofa, dressed in jogging clothes, a blanket across her knees. Her face still bore the bruises of the attack, a reminder that would take weeks to completely vanish.

"Morning," she said. "Where is everyone?" Because it disturbed her to think May had been sitting here alone, probably in fear.

"I sent them away. I've gotta get used to being in this house by myself or I might as well sell it and move away."

Kerri totally understood that. It sounded like what she'd done but this seemed rather soon for May to reach this point. "Are you okay with me being here?"

"It's different. You don't feel like a guard."

That felt good. Kerri smiled. "Want me to make you some breakfast or something?"

"Sure. I'll come with you."

May unfolded from the couch and together they went into her small kitchen. "It wasn't so bad," she said. "Once we got past the witching hour, I was fine."

"Witching hour?"

"He came after me around two. Same as Sandra, I heard. I relaxed some then and Connie has kids who must miss her. Anyway, I'm mostly fine."

Kerri wished she believed that would last.

"Good news," she told May as they set to work together with coffee, eggs and toast. "Cadell Marcus, the dog trainer?"

"I know him."

"He's bringing you your very own dog today."

May's eyes widened. "Really?" Then a smile spread across her face. "Oh, wow! Then I won't be afraid at all!"

Kerri grinned. "Probably not."

"Well, you have Snowy."

The dog's ears pricked at the sound of his name, but he didn't move.

"He's for other things," Kerri answered. "I don't think of him as protection. But Cadell is bringing you a dog that *will* protect you."

When breakfast was ready, they sat together at her small kitchen table.

"How's Sandy doing?" May asked.

"Still struggling to come out of the coma. I called this morning to find out. I may go visit her later."

May frowned. "I feel so bad for her. Everybody loves her. She's just a fantastic person. I so hope she recovers."

"And what about you?"

May smiled as best she could despite the bruises. "There are good things about a small town, but I'm not sure where I'm going to put any more casseroles, cookies or pies. Or flowers. My spare room is full of them. The scent would probably knock you over."

Kerri laughed lightly. "It's good they care so much."

"Yeah, it is. I'm not complaining. Not really. But so much food. And the problem is, I can't donate it. It might offend someone if they see their casserole on a table at the soup kitchen. But maybe I could get someone to take most of the flowers to the hospital."

May sighed. "They're all so nice, but I could use a bit of a break, too. While Connie was here yesterday evening, I thought I was throwing a party. How can I explain that I'm worn out?"

"I don't know. I kind of went through the same thing. People want to do the nice thing right away. Some of it would still be nice a month later, and maybe more welcome."

"Exactly."

Kerri insisted on cleaning up after the meal. "You're still moving like you hurt."

Afterward, they settled in the living room.

"I'm afraid to open any windows," May said abruptly.

Kerri nodded. "How would you feel if I opened one while I'm here? You wouldn't be alone."

"That would be so good. This place needs an airing."

When Kerri resumed her seat, she noticed that May was staring into space. "May? Are you all right?"

The woman answered hoarsely. "I remember."

Kerri leaned forward intently. She'd been carrying a small recorder in her jacket just in case, because she might miss something. She pulled it out, turned it on and set it on the coffee table. "What do you re-member?"

"Him. I remember him."

"His face?"

"Just his eyes. He had this ski mask on. It was so dark…" May trailed off.

Kerri waited, not wanting to disturb the stream of recollection.

Eventually May continued. "I couldn't see the color. Too dark. I guess that means he had dark irises, be-cause I could see the whites of his eyes. Even as dark as it was out there, I caught them glistening. God, he looked like a monster."

"He is a monster," Kerri answered gently. "Any-thing else?"

"The knife. It glistened, too." She almost whis-pered. "It was like something out of hell. It seemed to glow brighter and brighter." At last she looked at Kerri. "That's impossible."

"Maybe your brain fixated on it and made it seem that way. It was the threat. When I looked down the barrel of a gun once, it seemed to grow huge."

May nodded slowly. "Yeah. Maybe. Anyway, I saw his eyes. Not much help. Then when he stood up—"

Again Kerri waited, knowing patience was essen-tial here. Her heart was beating faster, though. Maybe there was more. An essential bit to finding this creep.

"I don't want to remember this!" May's voice broke. "But after—afterward I saw him standing over me, zipping his pants and— Oh, everything seemed so hazy. I hurt all over and felt paralyzed and there he was zipping up. It's just a snapshot, but he seemed to have

trouble with the button on his jeans, and his shirt…
there was something embroidered on the pocket. Like
he worked for someone…"

May buried her face in her hands. This could be
useful information, but she needed to give May some
time before pressing her further. She rose and went to
sit beside the woman, gently patting her knee. "That's
helpful, May. Just take it easy. It's horrible to remember, I know. Just horrible."

May lifted a tearstained face. "Will I ever forget?"

Kerri couldn't honestly say she would. "It'll get easier. That much I know."

"Okay." May snatched a tissue from the box on the
end table beside her. "Who do I tell this to?"

"That's what I'm here for. I just recorded it. I have
only one question."

May nodded slightly.

"Can you describe that much to a sketch artist?"

"It's so little!"

Kerri reached for her hand and squeezed it. "If you
can do it, you'll be surprised at the detail you remember when you start seeing the artist draw it. Maybe
nothing important. Maybe something big. But you
don't have to do it right away."

"Will you stay with me?"

"Absolutely."

Ivan saw the cop car missing from the second victim's house. He guessed the cops must have lost interest in her, which was a good thing. Meant he was
in the clear.

Then, when he rode past a while later, he saw another cop car pull up. Well, well, well. It was the K9 trainer with a dog. Were they giving a dog to the woman?

He almost laughed. A little like closing the barn door after the horse escaped.

Then the Addison woman stepped out with her big, shiny new badge and talked to the man before taking him into the house.

Hell, Ivan wanted to see what happened next, but decided for the sake of his own safety, he couldn't hang out here. He rode off again, then stashed his bike behind a small store before walking back.

Now the man was leaving, without the dog. It was almost impossible for him not to laugh this time. He wasn't interested in that woman any longer. But he *was* interested in Kerri Addison.

Because the whispers were growing that she was learning things about him.

Ivan was past the point of knowing how much he was overhearing and how much was being generated inside his own head.

He just knew the Addison woman had to go. And if that Canady guy didn't show up tonight, then tonight it would be.

Kerri spent a couple of hours with May and the sketch artist. May was hesitant at first, and more often than not said, "That doesn't look right."

But the artist, a middle-aged woman with a limp, was patient. Evidently she had plenty of experience with a victim gradually finding the way to what looked right.

That "looking right" was a hard thing to explain. It

was seldom conscious, but people had quite a memory for other people, and when they knew something wasn't right, it was usually for a good reason.

So the artist erased with a big rubber eraser the parts May didn't like. Occasionally she just tossed a sheet of drawing paper aside and started fresh, including many of the details from the earlier drawing that May hadn't dismissed, and waiting for May to correct or add.

And add she did. By the time May was satisfied, they had the guy's posture, the way he looked down at her, his size, including a slight beer belly, and a hint of the shape of his nose. Then there were the eyes.

The eyes were the most arresting part. The shape May described was probably enough to use facial recognition software, but only if they had enough comparison photos. And this was no photo.

Kerri looked at the artist. "Any way this could be plugged into facial recognition? Especially the eyes?"

The woman shook her head. "The shape is good enough, but another detail is how far apart they're set, and there's no way we can tell that from a drawing. A photo, yes. But not from a sketch."

Well, there went that, Kerri thought. "It's a great drawing, May."

May leaned back against the couch, reaching for a bottle of pain reliever. "It's more than I thought I could remember."

The artist began packing up, saying, "If you think of anything else, let Kerri or the department know. I can come back and we can add any detail you want."

The dog had been an immediate hit with May. By

the time the artist left, Hoss was curled up on the couch beside May, seeming to love it every time she dug her fingers into his ruff. He also seemed to sense she was sore and injured, because he avoided the usual doggy stuff of kisses and his head on her lap.

He liked Snowy; they exchanged tail wags, and then both settled down after a good sniff.

"You don't have to stay here," May told Kerri. "I'm so grateful for Hoss."

Cadell had made it clear the dog would protect her. "He's been trained to do that," he'd said.

"Strange name for a dog," Kerri remarked.

May gave a small laugh. "But I like it. He's big."

After reassuring herself that May would call her, and understanding May's need to regain her own space, Kerri phoned for a lift and Deputy Redwing showed up to drive her and Snowy home. Fear would still trouble May, she knew. Despite the dog, the fear would creep back, and fear didn't answer to logic. It just *was*. She ought to know.

The warm spell still endured, but by the time Kerri and Snowy climbed the steps to her apartment, night had begun to send its first dark tendrils of cooling temperatures. Once inside, she fed Snowy and relieved him of his working vest.

Then she studied the leftovers in the fridge and decided on the salad they'd ignored last night.

Then she had nothing to do except feel the emptiness of the apartment around her and miss Stu's comforting and steadying presence. And his strength, and the massive attraction she felt for him.

And the fear that he would start withdrawing. God,

what had possessed her last night? Of all the bad timing in the world, she had chosen the worst. Her fears and hang-ups had risen like a wall between her and everything she wanted, and she'd spewed them.

Worse, she wasn't sure she'd torn down any of that wall. Maybe she'd just added bricks. She sure as hell couldn't blame Stu if he pulled back and decided they should just be friends without any of the so-called "benefits."

She kept glancing at the clock, counting the hours. He'd said he'd come between one and two with breakfast. She had no doubt that he would. He was a man of his word.

The test would be if he remained afterward. She prepared herself for disappointment.

The silence and emptiness surrounded her more and more strongly as the evening passed. She ought to turn on the TV, but she knew it wouldn't distract her.

Instead, she sat there growing uneasy and she couldn't explain why. Something didn't feel right. Silly. How many nights had she already spent alone in this apartment? A lot. It was familiar. Did she think she had a ghost or something? Ridiculous.

But ridiculous or not, she pulled her collapsible baton out of her bedroom closet, extended it and placed it beside the door, on the hinge side. That made her feel a bit better.

Nor did it feel as absurd as sitting here with a pistol on her lap would have felt, even had she been able to possess one.

There. Satisfied, she tossed the tennis ball for

Snowy, watching him race around the apartment until he decided to amuse himself with a knuckle of rawhide.

She told herself to take a nap so she'd be rested when Stu arrived. She wouldn't miss him because she'd hear his knock. But she couldn't settle down, which meant that Snowy followed as she paced, and then she grew annoyed with herself because she wasn't allowing him time to relax and pursue his own amusements.

At last she plastered herself to the sofa and picked up a book. She didn't read a word. She felt as if doom were marching her way. She'd blown it with Stu. Conviction filled her.

Just before one, everything changed. Snowy went on alert. She didn't often see him that way. Was Stu here early?

The dog fixated on the door, and his hackles rose. Now Kerri became alert. Snowy had never raised his hackles. Was someone outside her door?

Rising, she walked quietly to the hinge side of the door and picked up her baton. Holding it firmly, she waited. If some thug tried to enter, he was in for a hell of a surprise. The baton's weight reassured her.

Then two things happened almost simultaneously. Snowy growled, a deep, deep sound as the doorknob rattled. And then he poked her leg hard.

God, no!

Then she was gone.

When she returned, everything was different. Snowy lay on his side whimpering. A man wearing a ski mask was in her apartment and walking toward her. What was going on?

When she saw the knife, she responded instinctively. Confusion vanished. The threat was clear despite everything being changed. It pierced her usual fog.

She felt the weight of the baton in her hand.

Snowy rose, limping and snarling, and charged for the man. That caused him to back away. Kerri wasn't backing away. She didn't care if she killed the man with that baton.

Snowy didn't feel much differently apparently. Hurt though he was, he dove for the man and latched on to the back of his calf.

The man howled and Kerri saw him raise his knife as if he were going to stab the dog.

She leaped into immediate action, raising her baton, every inch of police training rising to the fore.

"Drop it. Freeze!"

He did neither. Whatever he'd meant to do when he broke in here, he was in agony and wanted that dog off him.

She moved in, baton at ready, gripping it so hard her knuckles hurt.

"Freeze!" she ordered again, then without another warning, she swung hard at the arm holding the knife.

Stu had gotten off duty a little early and had run by the truck stop to get Kerri her midnight breakfast. After last night, he was feeling bad that he'd had to work all evening, and worried that she might be feeling abandoned by him. She understood his need to go to work, but emotions were different.

Bags in his hands, he was walking down her hall when he heard her shout.

*Freeze?* Was she really shouting that?

He dropped the bags in the hall and ran to her door. He didn't waste time testing the lock. Without hesitation he lifted his foot and broke it open.

The scene horrified him but didn't stop him. He saw the masked guy, saw Snowy latched on to his calf, saw Kerri raise her baton and strike. All of that in an instant.

Adrenaline must have been running strong in the man because despite the blow to his arm he still held the knife, a big ugly hunting blade.

Stu needed no more. As the man pointed the knife at the dog, he jumped in, warning Kerri.

"Don't hit me."

The baton paused before a second blow and Stu rushed a diving tackle, grabbing the guy around the waist and knocking him to the floor. This time he lost the knife.

Snowy got out of the way in the nick of time and the intruder crumbled.

"I want to hit him again," Kerri snarled. "He hurt my dog."

The freaking creep was howling his fool head off. "The dog bit me! She broke my arm!"

"And you broke into her apartment," Stu growled as he forced the man to roll over and quickly cuffed him. "If you want, she can break your other arm. I'll swear I never saw it. Now shut up."

The howling died to a whiny snivel. Stu put his knee on the man's back. He spoke to Kerri, whose eyes glowed with fury like flares. "You want to call the shop or do you want me to do it?"

The next night Kerri and Snowy were home together. Snowy had evidently taken a couple of kicks. His ribs were bruised and his foreleg had been broken, but he got around on the cast well enough. Simple fracture, Dr. Windwalker had said. He'd heal just fine, although the rib bruising might be painful for a few weeks.

Snowy, however, seemed to have little problem dealing with what had happened. He showed little interest in his tennis ball, but he still enjoyed his rawhide and his walks outside. Kerri kept them short because of his injuries, but watching him she decided little could keep him down.

"He's a tough guy," Stu said. He'd gone out to get her the breakfast he'd promised for last night and was laying it out on her china. "But then, you're tough, too. As long as I live I'm going to remember you swinging that baton."

"I'm glad I had it handy." She bit her lower lip. "Stu, I spaced again. I couldn't even protect Snowy. When I came out of it, he was already injured."

He took her hand and drew her to the bar, setting a hot regular coffee in front of her and a plate full of eggs, home fries and toast. "It's not like you stood there frozen because you wanted to. You sure as hell kicked into action the instant you saw what was happening. Ya done good."

"Doesn't feel like it."

"Dammit, Kerri, stop telling yourself you're not

good enough. You did a spectacular job of catching an armed man, and you acted *before* he could kill Snowy. You saved him."

She shook her head a little.

"Listen, that guy breaks in. You're not ready for what he's going to do. How could you be? Before you could even react, even if you hadn't had a seizure, the first thing he would have done would have been to kick that dog. There is no way on earth you could have guessed he would go for Snowy first. You simply didn't have time to prevent it. That's the long and the short of it."

She ate for a few minutes, then sighed. "You're probably right. I never imagined Snowy would guard me. That's not what he's supposed to do. I wouldn't have been surprised if he'd taken off to another room when that guy walked in. Or huddled against me."

"Instead, he fought for you. Did a damn good job of it. Anyway, *Snowy* made the guy deal with him first."

She hadn't thought of it that way, but realized it was true. Her mood began to leaven. "Thanks."

"It's true. And now you know you have your own personal K9."

That drew a laugh from her. Stu always made her feel better. She turned to look at him and started to drown in his eyes. "Stu…"

"We have some unfinished business," he said. "From the night before last. You can't imagine the things I want to do to you."

Her heart skipped and heat began to drizzle through her. As simply as that, he woke the strongest desires in her.

"First," she said, "I want to apologize for my melt-down. Bad timing, if nothing else."

He shook his head. "I don't want your apology. We got close, you got scared, and you dumped your fears. You've got every right and I didn't mind at all. No apologies, ever. Not for anything like that."

She smiled. "You were going to tell me your story."

"Not tonight. I've got other things in mind." His smile was crooked, as if he was holding something in. "Say, are you through eating? Can we just leave the dishes? I mean, we can warm most of this up in a little while if you want, or trash it, I don't care."

Startled, her eyes widened. "What's going on, Stu?"

"I think we need a little celebration. You caught the rapist. Sandra is showing some signs of recovery. May can rest easy now. That's worth a celebration."

"I didn't catch him," she protested. "He kind of caught himself."

Stu made a sound of disgust. "Stop it, Kerri. You broke the thug's arm. Made it easy for me to cuff him. You get the arrest."

Her heart skipped. "I do?"

"That's the official decision. Your arrest. Great way to start, huh?"

It was, it was indeed. A happy glow began to fill her. Yeah, that was worth a celebration.

"But there's more."

She blinked. "More of what?"

"As much of me as you can handle. When I saw what was happening, you could say I had a major epiphany." He reached for her hands and drew her from her stool until she stood between his legs.

"What kind of epiphany?" All of a sudden she was having trouble catching her breath. Something about the way he was looking at her, drawing her closer.

"I realized it would be awfully hard to live without you, Kerri Lynn Addison. I realized I want to spend the rest of my life with you. If you can stand the idea."

Her mouth fell open. Joy filled her heart. "But... But..."

"I know. All your problems. Well, stuff them in a trash bag and throw it in the nearest dumpster. I've seen them all, I've heard them all, and I can tell you they don't change my mind one bit. I'll give you time to learn my problems first so you know what you're getting into, but, darlin', I need to know. Will you just *consider* marrying me?"

Her heart lifted on wings. The one thing she had been sure could never be part of her life was holding her right now and telling her he wanted her, mess and all.

She really didn't need to wait, but she understood he'd feel better if he was sure she wanted him warts and all. Finally she found her voice. "You bet, Stu."

"Good. Because I love you, heart and soul."

And that seemed like the only thing that really mattered. "I love you, too, Stuart Canady."

A smile spread across his face, the warmest happiest smile she'd ever seen from him.

Gloom about the future was gone. In its place had come sunlight and joy.

The impossible had just become possible.

\* \* \* \* \*

## #2127 COLTON 911: UNDERCOVER HEAT

*Colton 911: Chicago*

### by Anna J. Stewart

To get the evidence he needs for his narcotics case, Detective Cruz Medina has one solution: going undercover in chef Tatum Colton's trendy restaurant. But he doesn't expect the spitfire chef to become his new partner—or for the sparks to fly from the moment they meet.

## #2128 COLTON NURSERY HIDEOUT

*The Coltons of Grave Gulch*

### by Dana Nussio

After a pregnancy results from their one-night stand, family maverick Travis Colton must shield Tatiana Davison, his co-CEO and the daughter of an alleged serial killer, from the media, his law-enforcement relatives, and the copycat killer threatening her and their unborn child.

## #2129 THE COWBOY'S DEADLY REUNION

*Runaway Ranch*

### by Cindy Dees

When Marine officer Wes Morgan is drummed out of the military to prevent a scandal, he has no idea what comes next. But then Jessica Blankenship, the general's daughter whom he sacrificed his career to protect, shows up on his porch. Will he send her away or let her save him?

## #2130 STALKED BY SECRETS

*To Serve and Seduce*

### by Deborah Fletcher Mello

Simone Black has loved only one man her whole life, but he smashed her heart to pieces. Now he's back. Dr. Paul Reilly knows Lender Pharmaceuticals is killing people, but he needs Simone's help. Now they're both caught in the line of fire as they battle a conglomerate who believes they're untouchable.

Neema suddenly sat upright, pulling a closed fist to her mouth. "I'm sorry. There's something we need to talk about first…" she started. "There's something important I need to tell you."

Davis straightened, dropping his palm to his crotch to hide his very visible erection. "I'm sorry. I was moving too fast. I didn't mean—"

"No, that's not—"

Titus suddenly barked near the front door, the fur around his neck standing on end. He growled, a low, deep, brusque snarl that vibrated loudly through the room. Davis stood abruptly and moved to peer out the front window. Titus barked again and Davis went to the front door, stopping first to grab his gun.

Neema paused the sound system, the room going quiet save Titus's barking. She backed her way into the corner, her eyes wide. She stood perfectly still, listening to see if she could hear what Titus heard as she watched Davis move from one window to another, looking out to the street.

"Go sit," Davis said to the dog, finally breaking through the quiet. "It's just a raccoon." He heaved a sigh of relief as he turned back to Neema. "Sorry about that. I'm a little on edge. Since that drive-by, every strange noise makes me nervous."

"Better safe than sorry," she muttered.

Davis moved to her side and kissed her, wrapping his arms tightly around her torso. "If I made you uncomfortable before, I apologize. I would never—"

"You didn't," Neema said, interrupting him. "It was fine. It was…good…and I was enjoying myself. I just… well…" She was suddenly stammering, trying to find the words to explain herself. Because she needed to come clean about everything before they took things any further. Davis needed to know the truth.

*Don't miss*
Stalked by Secrets *by Deborah Fletcher Mello,*
*available March 2021 wherever*
*Harlequin Romantic Suspense*
*books and ebooks are sold.*

Harlequin.com

HRSEXP0221

# Get 4 FREE REWARDS!

## We'll send you 2 FREE Books plus 2 FREE Mystery Gifts.

**Harlequin Romantic Suspense** books are heart-racing page-turners with unexpected plot twists and irresistible chemistry that will keep you guessing to the very end.

**FREE** Value Over $20